THE MAN IN MY ATTIC

THE
MAN
IN MY
ATTIC

ROBIN MAHLE

Joffe Books, London
www.joffebooks.com

First published in Great Britain in 2024

Cover art by Nick Castle

ISBN: 978-1-83526-709-7

PROLOGUE

Family was the ultimate gift, worth more than any material possession. It was something I'd desired for as long as I could remember, never having one of my own. A relentless search for a flicker of humanity that had always been just out of reach.

I'd obeyed the rules of society, attempting to work within its confines. Morphing into what others had expected. Jobs, friends, girlfriends. I'd achieved two out of three, though none of it came easy. Each endeavor always ended in heartache and disappointment. Could I really be blamed? I'd had no examples from which to learn. I simply observed from afar what others had, learning from their mistakes. It hadn't helped. Nothing had. The harder I tried, the greater pushback I received, until finally, I'd become an outcast.

Now, I skirted the fringes, living among the ignored and discarded. Taking odd jobs that offered only enough to survive in the loosest sense of the word. I still coveted what others had — their families, their happiness. But I'd found a way to fill the gaping hole. I'd blended seamlessly into their lives, hiding among them in plain sight. If only it could last forever. It hadn't yet, but my hunt was far from over.

Great pains had been taken to observe the Tomlins' routine. When the kids left for school. Their sports practices. I'd known when the husband put up the Christmas lights. Even down to Eleanor's two-drink luncheons with her girlfriends every Wednesday at twelve, sharp.

They'd become my newest family. Their home, a grand old Victorian that had proven ideal. Its intricate details and sinuous layout offered many options. Not to mention years of poorly thought-out additions, creating hiding places to conceal all manner of sin.

One such forgotten place, I now called home. I could almost smell the fermented yeast, believing this cellar in which I'd taken shelter had once been used during Prohibition as a distillery. Easily accessed through a rotting wood storm door, the Tomlins had neglected this perfect refuge. Though on this cold winter evening, the stone walls provided no warmth. My physical discomfort, however, was secondary to my emotional contentment, simply knowing that I was near them.

Too far away to hear the echoes of their chatter and laughter. No hint of the aroma of home-cooked meals. I had to be satisfied to observe their happy home from a distance. But as always, the fleeting moments of happiness were quickly overshadowed by the return of reality, leaving me once again alone in the darkness.

As I sat in my unlit corner, a blanket over my shoulders, I thought about how I would do it. Best to do it tonight while they slept.

Shame, though. I'd become fond of the young kids. Claire and Robby. Both still in middle school, neither having yet developed a distaste for parental authority I'd come to hear was common in teenagers. What a life to lead. A wife, kids, a warm and loving home. I longed for that connection.

Yet just when I begin to feel comfortable, I take it a step too far, as I had today. Eleanor. I was certain she'd heard me. I'd made a hurried escape, back to my hidden alcove, while

Eleanor had been in her living room, enjoying the quiet time before the kids returned from school.

Now, I waited. Hours had gone by with no sign that a search for me had begun. The father would be home soon. Would Eleanor tell him of her suspicions?

It was when the heavy wooden door of the shelter raised that I'd received my answer. Gray light spilled in from a half-moon above, reaching me in my tucked-away corner. A gust of cool air chilled my skin. Someone was coming. I'd waited too long.

Christmas was still a week away, and I'd hoped to be here with my family. To watch from afar. Claire and Robby opening their presents. To feel the warmth of their smiling faces as they shared in each other's joy. But yet again, it was not to be. Nevertheless, I wasn't unprepared. I'd been here before.

I threw off the blanket and grabbed my knife. The Tomlins didn't come down here, so whoever it was had come with the intention of searching for me now. As I crouched in the shadow, my veins turned to ice, knowing what must be done. They would not understand why I was here. They would see me as a threat, which was exactly what I would have to become to ensure my survival.

While I couldn't yet see her, the soft steps atop the cellar stairs must've belonged to beautiful Eleanor. I loved her, just as I loved all of my family. How I adored the way she swayed to the music while making dinner. The way she embraced her children whenever they appeared. I could've been part of their lives. But that dream would now be their nightmare.

I moved closer with cautious steps, navigating the corridor of the cellar. Despite the cold, my adrenaline-fueled body formed beads of sweat along my forehead. My thinning hair allowed it to fall into my eyes. I wasn't a young man, after all. Nearing middle age, my thin frame and short stature aided my efforts at concealment. Apparently, not enough.

A brief reflection appeared in the knife that glinted in my hand. It was her, suggesting that the husband was preoccupied, or had dismissed her concerns while she'd come out to inspect. This would create a problem, but not an insurmountable one.

My presence remained undetected as I closed in on her, but our fate was sealed. The darkest recesses of my mind had been awakened, erasing any trace of humanity.

"Is someone here?" Eleanor called out.

I rounded the corner, readying my knife. She stepped toward me with apparent unease. She sensed me. I could smell her fear. And when I saw her shoe step beyond the corner where I stood, I lunged toward her, grabbing her, muzzling her voice with my hand.

"I'm so sorry, Eleanor, but I knew you wouldn't understand." Holding her in front of me, I plunged the knife into her chest. Her mouth opened under my hand as she gasped, but only a stifled moan sounded. Blood dripped onto the cold concrete floor, creating a grotesque abstract painting at our feet.

Euphoria surged in me as the weight of her body pressed against mine. The touch of another human being breathed life into me. But her own life began to fade, her touch weakening with every passing moment.

I let her gently fall to the ground, and her eyes peered up at me. "Please don't hurt my children."

She was nothing to me now. None of them were. "I'm sorry, Eleanor, but they'll share your fate."

CHAPTER 1: LAUREN

It had taken some getting used to — the quiet that surrounded our home. After months of renovations, everything was now complete. My husband and I loved our Virginia colonial in the suburbs of Alexandria. We'd taken steps to ensure the restoration returned it to its original beauty, plus a few modern conveniences.

As I prepared to lay my overcoat along the back seat of my car, I wished I'd worn pants instead of a dress on this cold winter day. I peered back at the house, admiring it for a moment. The gleaming white siding. The matte-black shutters and doors. Restored brick steps from the wraparound porch to the walkway.

"Noah, let's go, kiddo." My four-year-old son had gone back inside, having forgotten his favorite stuffed animal. "We're going to be late for school."

He bounded through the front door, closing it behind him. I walked toward it to secure the lock. As I reached for the handle, my shoulders slumped, remembering I was supposed to call the contractor about the alarm. That was when I noticed Noah's backpack. "How much did you pack in that thing?"

He glanced over his shoulder at it. "I brought Dino with me."

Dino was his stuffed T-Rex. He was a brown and tan, slightly angrier version of Rex from Toy Story. But it was Noah's favorite toy ever since his father brought it home after a business trip last month. Jacob spent a lot of time at work and on trips, so when he brought home trinkets for our son, I wasn't going to be the one to say he couldn't bring one of them to preschool.

"Okay, fine. Get in the car and buckle your belt." I walked back to my Lincoln Navigator and climbed behind the wheel. Its heated supple tan leather seats warmed my backside. February had arrived, and we'd had some recent snowfall. Nothing too crazy, but enough to make the roads a challenge. Even our driveway had turned icy.

I glanced back at Noah, double-checking the harness on his booster was secured. "You ready?"

He brushed away a few strands of his curly blond hair. "Ready, Mommy."

We drove through our neighborhood, the roofs on each home dusted in a sea of white. Cars warmed on the driveways, emitting puffs of white smoke from their exhausts. The sun had just begun to peek out from behind the clouds, casting rays that glistened off the melting snow. It was moments like these that made me happy. Finding comfort in the mundane routines of life. And my life was the very definition of mundane.

"Noah, what do you think about making a snowman this evening, if there's enough snow left?" His imagination had always been so vivid and pure. I did all I could to encourage it.

His face lit up. "Can we really, Mommy?"

"Of course." I glanced at him through the rearview mirror. "We'll make the biggest snowman ever!"

Noah clapped his hands, his laughter filling the car.

His preschool was only minutes from our home, but every moment spent with Noah felt precious to me. We talked about his day ahead, his friends, and the projects he was working on in class.

When we arrived, I turned off the engine and reached over to give Noah a reassuring squeeze on his knee. "Have a fantastic day at school, kiddo."

Noah beamed at me, his small hand reaching up to give mine a gentle squeeze in return. "Thanks, Mommy."

I nodded at one of the teachers, who ushered Noah out of the backseat and toward the building. As she held his hand, leading him inside, I felt a pang of guilt. It was to be expected, of course, but I'd chosen to return to work, which was my next stop. Accounting wasn't one of those things I'd ever desired to do for a living. It wasn't like I woke up one day and thought, *Hey, I'd like to stare at numbers all day and figure out where to code things.* But here I was, the in-house accountant for Ackerman and James Law Offices. My degree had been in finance. I thought I'd be working on Wall Street, but plans change.

I'd interned here at A&J, which was how I met my husband, Jacob. We married not long after I graduated from college. I got pregnant shortly after that. Being almost six years older than me, Jacob was now a successful lawyer at another firm, rendering my career almost pointless. But I'd always wanted to work. To each his own. That was how Jacob was, though, always wanting to move on to bigger and better things.

I stepped out of my SUV, pressing the remote to lock it as I walked toward the entrance. The sun shone brightly now, its light bouncing off the icy sidewalk. I shielded my eyes and looked up at the building. Just outside of the downtown area, it was three stories tall with a glass facade and modern finishes. It didn't fit with the heart of Alexandria's downtown area, where the brick buildings and architecture spoke of a different time.

We were a mid-sized firm that specialized in family law. Divorce was chief among the cases we dealt with, but also matters pertaining to wills, custody agreements, prenups. Not that I got involved in any of that. My job was to add up the billable hours and send the invoices. Pretty straightforward. Pretty mundane.

The office was lively with the sound of ringing phones and chatter. The receptionist, a woman only slightly younger than me, picked up a stack of invoices. With a gleeful look, she began, "Good morning, Lauren. I've got the latest batch for you."

"Gee, thanks," I replied with a chuckle. "Looks like another fun-filled day at A&J."

"That should be our corporate jingle," she replied.

"I'll be sure and bring it up in our next finance meeting." I stepped onto the elevator, riding up to the second floor with arms full of paper. My office was down the main corridor along with the rest of Accounting and Payroll. The partners were on the top floor while the associates were at the bottom. Both literally and figuratively.

I dropped the stack onto my desk and pulled open the blinds on the window behind me. The sun's rays streaked across my oak desk, illuminating the dust particles that floated above.

I quickly settled into my routine, methodically inputting data, and balancing accounts. The steady rhythm of the work was almost soothing, but it was the knock on my door that jolted me back. I glanced up to see Tammy, my fellow number-cruncher. I adored her. She was older than me — in her early forties. And I felt a sort of mother–daughter bond with her. Maybe because I didn't have a mother to speak of. I hadn't seen her since I was seventeen.

The woman had stolen my last twenty bucks, and it was the last straw for me. A lifetime of grifting, living on the outskirts of society, barely scraping by. I'd had enough of that. I wasn't going to be like her, no matter what.

"Hey, Tammy. What's up?" I asked.

Tammy walked in; her short, curly red hair neatly tucked behind her ears. She was tall, slim, but a little awkward in the way she carried herself, which she more than made up for with her warm personality.

"I came to see pictures. It's all finished now, right?"

I raised my chin with swelling pride. "Yes, as a matter of fact, it is. Sit down." I grabbed my phone and swiped open to the photos. "Take a look. They did such a great job."

As Tammy studied the photos, I heard the sound of wheels rolling across the tile in the hall. My door was open, and I looked up to see a man pushing a cleaning cart. He appeared to be in his forties, but I didn't recognize him. I smiled and he smiled back.

When he fell out of view, I leaned over my desk. "Who was that guy?"

Tammy shot around. "What guy?"

"With the cleaning cart," I replied.

"Oh, that's Gary. He works maintenance. New hire, I believe. He must be getting ready to leave for the day." She checked her watch. "Yeah, he works the night shift. Nice guy, from what I've seen."

Tammy knew everyone in the building and everything that went on, so I wasn't surprised she was in the know this time as well. "I'll have to introduce myself next time I see him." I looked back at her with an anxious grin. "So, what do you think?"

She handed back my phone. "It's gorgeous, Lauren. Really beautiful. What does Jacob think?"

I raised a shoulder. "He likes it well enough. Not that he's home much to enjoy it."

Tammy pushed off the chair. "That's the price you pay for being married to a successful lawyer. Hey, I'll see you at lunch?"

I set down my phone. "You got it."

* * *

We were lucky enough to have a wonderful neighbor who took care of Noah after school. Nancy, an elderly widow with no children of her own, watched him in our home, until I returned from work.

After showing her to the door only minutes ago, the cold from outside seemed to go right through to my bones. Since our fireplace was operational once again, I flipped the switch and the gas flame ignited. Another of the small things that brought me joy.

Noah had gone upstairs to his playroom, which was a small loft just beyond the landing. The floor of that loft was covered in Legos. Entering the playroom meant you were taking your life into your hands, as random Lego pieces nestled in the plush carpet. Each one just waiting for a tender foot to impale.

Having slipped off my high-heeled shoes, I padded in stocking feet into the kitchen, still dressed in my work clothes. This was, by far, my favorite spot in the house. I'd chosen every appliance, cabinet pull, color. They'd done a wonderful job. Tall, blue-gray cabinets with glass inserts. A six-burner stove with a pot-filler, and custom range hood. An enormous island with quartz counters and a waterfall edge. Sometimes, I couldn't believe this was the same house, or that I lived here.

Jacob had swept me off my feet, no doubt about it. He was tall, handsome, and well, let's face it, I was naïve. Barely out of college. Jacob was older than me. Now thirty-four, he was only in his late twenties when we met, but a rising star at the firm. I fell in love almost from the moment I saw him.

After my internship, I was hired on as an assistant accountant at first, but as the years progressed, I'd been promoted. Sometimes I think I was only promoted as a way to keep Jacob from taking the incredible offer at the other firm. He'd taken it anyway, and now I had no idea whether I'd ever be promoted again on my own merit.

There was no mistaking that I only had what I had because of Jacob. My job couldn't come close to affording our beautiful home. And no sooner had that thought crossed my mind than I heard the garage door open.

Jacob walked in from the garage, past the mudroom, and into our kitchen. He carried his briefcase and was dressed in an expensive charcoal gray suit. His tie undone, he was wearing it loosely around his neck, like a doctor would wear a stethoscope. "Hey, hon. You're home early." I walked toward him, raising onto my tiptoes to kiss his lips. He'd been drinking, the smell of whiskey still on his breath.

"Hi, babe. Where's Noah?" Jacob asked.

"In the loft. I was just getting ready to start dinner. Didn't think you'd be home so soon." I walked to the refrigerator. "Give me forty minutes and I'll have it ready."

"No rush," he said. "I need to answer a few emails."

"Okay, hon." I mustered a closed-lip grin before sticking my head in the fridge. Jacob must've had a rough day, what with the boozy breath. Never mind the subtle waft of floral perfume on his collar I knew wasn't mine.

CHAPTER 2: JACOB

The first thing I did when I entered the den was plop the briefcase onto my desk, then drop into my chair. Leaning back, I stretched out my legs and exhaled. This was the only place in the house they didn't touch during the remodel. I wouldn't let them. I loved my den. The cherry-wood bookshelves. My college degrees that hung on the wall behind my desk. It was my refuge. My sanctuary.

Lauren didn't get it — how hard I worked. How stressful it was being partner in a cut-throat firm like mine. Did she pick up on Maddy's perfume?

I raised my lapel and sniffed it. "Damn it." Yeah, she smelled it. The question was, would she say anything? She hadn't yet. Lauren was a beautiful woman. Long, wavy brunette hair; beautiful figure. She was great with numbers and had a razor-sharp wit. So why was I screwing one of the paralegals? *Because I'm an asshole.*

The asshole who plunked down a hundred grand renovating this house. Did Lauren even think about that — how much all this shit cost me? All the things I've had to do to give her this life.

Sometimes, it was just easier to stay at the office, but if I didn't make some effort to come home for dinner every once in a while, I'd be asking for trouble. The thing was, I loved Lauren. I loved my son. But for whatever reason . . . it wasn't enough.

"Fuck it." I grabbed my laptop and went back to work. As I scanned through the fifteen emails that had arrived from the time I'd left the office to this moment, a notification appeared in the top corner of my screen. It arrived through a secure messaging app, only breached with my unique biometrics, and demanded my immediate attention. I placed my thumb on the scanner and the message opened.

It's been two days. Payment is past due. If we don't get what's owed by the end of the week, you will hear from us again. And we won't be discreet.

The words were cold, impersonal, carrying an implicit threat I'd come to expect from these people.

"Dinner's ready."

I heard Lauren's voice echo down the hall, then the patter of footsteps on the stairs. Noah. I hadn't even said hello to him yet. I closed my laptop, and marched out of the den. Noah's voice called back to his mother. "Coming, Mommy!"

I reached the hallway and walked into the kitchen. "There's my boy!"

Noah turned around and smiled. A great big, beautiful smile. "Daddy!"

I held out my arms, waiting for him to jump up. And when he did, I raised him up high.

"Careful of the ceiling, Jake," Lauren said.

"Oh, he's fine . . . Aren't you, buddy?"

Noah laughed as I brought him back down, pulling him toward my chest. "How was your day, son?"

"Good. We made noodle hearts today."

"Noodle hearts?" I asked, raising a brow at Lauren. She shrugged in reply. "Why don't you bring it here and show me?" I set him down again and he dashed away.

"It could've waited until after dinner," Lauren added, looking slightly perturbed.

I dismissed the notion and walked over to her. "It's fine. Dinner can wait a minute." And when I scooped her into my arms, I felt a slight flinch in response. A tension that came at my touch.

"Sorry." I kissed her cheek and released her, glossing over her reaction. "Let's eat, huh?"

We sat down at the kitchen table. A small, four-seater tucked into the bay window. Our formal dining room was enormous, with an elegant table for twelve, and was only used at the holidays.

Noah excitedly showed me his noodle heart creation. Lauren served the grilled chicken she had prepared. Her smile was strained. I watched her move around the kitchen, her grace and elegance never failing to captivate me.

"And then we played Duck, Duck, Goose, and then we had to take our nap . . ."

Noah chattered away about his day at school, his joy filling the room. I listened, truly listened for the first time in a long while. His laughter was infectious.

We ate mostly in silence. A few words from our son as he picked at his vegetables. I cleared my plate. Lauren was nothing if not a great cook. And as I wiped my lips, I regarded her. "Dinner was delicious, babe. Thank you." I pushed back my chair. "I still have some work to get to."

"You don't want to bathe Noah tonight?" she asked.

I glanced at Noah, who didn't hear the word 'bathe,' by the look on his face. "Uh, you mind taking care of it? The partners wanted me to go through the monthly statements." I got to my feet.

"Yeah, sure. I'll do it."

Lauren had the ability to mask a lot, but I may have exceeded my limit tonight.

"Hey, bud. You want to get ready for your bath? I'll be up there in a minute," she said.

"Okay, Mommy. Bye, Daddy," he said, flitting off to his upstairs bedroom.

"Thanks. I owe you." I kissed the top of her head, and as I walked away, I felt her gaze on me. I knew I should've looked back and smiled. A gesture of appreciation. But I didn't, because I'm the asshole.

CHAPTER 3: GARY

In the raw night air, I stood under the covered entrance. Swiping my ID badge at the main door, I heard the click. The Ackerman and James Law Offices opened to me. The lobby was illuminated by underlighting along the reception desk, and a backlit sign mounted on the wall behind it. Emergency lighting hung down from the ceiling toward the elevators, and small LED fixtures were mounted on the walls.

The familiar scent of polished wood and chemical cleaners wafted through the air. The day crew had already done their work. I typically arrived before 5 p.m., but I'd had to ask my boss if I could arrive later tonight. A personal matter, I'd told them. It was now 9 p.m.

The silence of the office at this hour enveloped me, broken only by the soft hum of the bar fridge kept under the front desk. Come to think of it, I'd have to restock it later. Water, sodas, bottled iced teas. They were all kept inside for visiting clients.

I made my way through the lobby, where the pristine marble floor echoed with every step. The maintenance office was on the second floor, tucked far away at the back of the building. I rode the elevator up. Walking inside the office, I sat down at the desk. This was where I logged in my hours, filled out requests for additional cleaning supplies, and made notes on items in need of repair. Behind me was the storage area where we kept the carts and various supplies.

I was happy to be hired here. They were in desperate need of help, and didn't seem to mind that I'd moved around a lot, working odd jobs here and there. But this one — this one wasn't just another odd job. This one meant something, and I intended to keep it.

Eventually, I set out to begin my duties as the night janitor. I was the only one here. Of course, the firm was on the small side. I'd worked for larger companies. Only three floors with cubicles and offices. I emptied trash cans, wiped down desks, dusted bookshelves, and cleaned toilets. It hardly demanded much in the way of physical labor.

I preferred the night hours. The quiet time. The time where I could observe, learn, contemplate next steps. And the shelter was much less busy during the day. That was where I was currently living, though a liberal definition of the word.

The shelter was little more than a bunch of bunk beds in a large open space. A couple of bathrooms and only three shower stalls. There was a small kitchenette with a microwave. But it was better than being out in the cold. I'd been that route before, but got lucky when a bed recently opened up at the shelter. Still, I'd have to make my move soon. I'd already begun to plan it out, and it was the reason I'd arrived late tonight.

The gray heavy-duty plastic cleaning cart was stacked to the brim with supplies. I meandered down the hallway, pushing it along until I reached her office. Lauren Hale. She was more beautiful than I could've imagined. I only caught her gaze for a moment this morning, but the warmth in her eyes pleased me.

I stepped inside. A hint of lavender hung in the air; it must've come from the candle on her desk. I turned on the lights, my eyes temporarily stinging from the brightness, and walked toward it. Picking up the candle, I closed my eyes and inhaled the vanilla and, yes, lavender scent.

Setting it down again, I caught sight of a photo frame. Curiosity gripped me, so I picked it up and peered at the image. A smile spread wide. The picture was of Lauren, a man who must have been her husband, and a boy of not more than four or five. *Your son.*

I set down the frame again and retrieved my phone, taking a picture of the image. *So I can look at you any time I want.*

CHAPTER 4: LAUREN

Now that the house was finished, we'd fallen back into the same old routine. Jacob was in the shower when I'd awakened. It was up to me to get Noah ready for preschool and myself ready for work. All Jacob had to do was shower, grab a coffee, which I'd already made, and a bagel, which I'd also made, and he was out the door. Meanwhile, I rushed around to ensure everyone had what they needed before I could leave.

It was my fault. I could've insisted things change, but I didn't because I didn't want to rock the boat. Jacob had never laid a hand on me, nor had he raised his voice at me, but I was afraid of him, nonetheless. Afraid to lose him. Mostly because I was terrified of raising my son on my own on what little salary I earned. And the fact of the matter was, I loved Jacob. I loved my life. So I let things go, swept them under the rug because it was easier that way.

The idea he was being unfaithful wasn't one I was ready to face or believe yet, either. The time would come when it could no longer be ignored. I had not yet planned for that day.

Standing in the kitchen, my mind elsewhere, the bread popped out of the toaster. I picked it up. "Ouch. Shit."

"Mommy, you said a bad word."

I spun around to see Noah walking into the kitchen. "I know, baby. I'm sorry. I touched something that was hot. Sit down. You don't have much time for breakfast."

He climbed onto the stool at the kitchen island. I set down the buttered toast topped with strawberry jam, and a glass of milk. "Here you go. Eat up. I'm going upstairs to change."

"Okay."

As I started up the steps, Jacob appeared at the top of the landing. "Oh, hey. Are you heading out?" I asked him.

"Yeah." He walked down to meet me near the top step and kissed my cheek. "I'll see you later, hon. Have a good day."

"You too," I said, making my way to the top. I looked back at him as he entered the kitchen. I heard a brief exchange with Noah and then the opening of the kitchen door that led to the garage. He was gone. A part of me felt relieved.

As I dressed for work and made my way back downstairs, Noah had already placed his dishes near the sink. He wasn't quite tall enough to put them in the basin. I smiled. "Good job, bud. Thanks for cleaning up after yourself."

He shrugged and walked off to grab his backpack. He had no idea what that small gesture meant to me. It meant maybe I was a better parent than the ones I'd had.

My father left when I was a baby. My mother — I didn't even know where she lived anymore. When I became an adult, I got as far away from her as possible. I'd watched her swindle people out of money so many times, watched her steal things, take advantage of anyone who showed her any kindness. I wasn't going to be like her — ever. And it looked like I was proving myself right.

"Let's go, Mommy. We can't be late," Noah said, slinging his backpack over his shoulder.

"You're absolutely right. Let's head out." I swiped my phone from the kitchen counter and grabbed my coat and car keys from the foyer. As I held open the kitchen door, I continued, "After you, buddy."

We went about our usual daily routine. I dropped off Noah at school and then drove into the office. I pushed aside concerns and worries that seemed to creep into the back of my mind, instead opting to throw myself into my work. I'd learned this from an early age, and it was how I had survived.

I reached the entrance and carried on through the lobby. With my coffee in hand, I rode the elevator to the second floor. The doors parted and I walked into the hall toward my office. But on reaching it, I stopped a moment, creasing my brow. "My door's open." I closed my office door every night as a matter of habit. Not that I kept confidential information inside. It was just me protecting my work, I guess. I walked inside, flipping on the lights. Nothing appeared out of place. "Must be the new janitor."

"What's that, miss?"

I flinched, nearly spilling my coffee. "Oh, good Lord, you scared me."

"Sorry about that." He chuckled. "Name's Gary. I'm the new night janitor, and I was just about to leave when I heard you say something."

It took a minute for my heart to start again. "Yeah, uh, my door was open. I usually close it at night before I leave. Did you happen to leave it open after you cleaned?"

"I did. Gosh, I'm so sorry," Gary replied, appearing mildly embarrassed. "It won't happen again, miss. You won't have to tell me twice."

"It's okay." I raised my hand. "Don't worry about it. No harm, no foul. It's Gary, you said?"

"Yes, ma'am. And you must be Lauren."

"How'd you know?" I asked.

He aimed a finger at the nameplate on my door. "Right," I laughed. "Of course. Lauren Hale. Nice to meet you, Gary."

"And you, Lauren. I was just heading out, so have a great day."

"You, too, Gary. Nice meeting you." I walked inside and set down my things. A moment later, Tammy poked her head in.

"Hey there." She meandered inside. "Listen, it's end of month, so you let me know when you're finished with the reports, and I'll run through them."

"Sure thing." I dropped into my chair. "You free for lunch?"

She set her hands on her hips. "Always."

CHAPTER 5: JACOB

Old Town Alexandria was my favorite part of the city. My law firm was located here on King Street, alongside several other historic buildings lining the block. Red brick sidewalks, even some cobblestone streets. And there was no shortage of places to eat and drink. This morning, as I walked into the lobby, I saw Maddy holding two cups of coffee from the shop next door. "Is one of those mine?" I asked, smiling at her.

"Of course." She handed one over to me. "Just the way you like it."

"Thank you." I glanced at Joan, who sat behind the front desk. I had to be careful about what I said and around whom I said it.

Madison Price had been with the firm for about two years. A paralegal for one. We'd been working a case together last summer and had gotten pretty close. Too close. She was a young woman, twenty-three. Long blond hair she wore in loose curls down her back. Dark maroon lipstick, dusty pink rouge highlighting her sharp cheekbones, and a body that turned heads. It had started out friendly enough. I wasn't looking to screw things up for myself or my family, but it happened, and now, here I was, embroiled in an office affair. I was pretty sure Joan knew about it. She knew everything.

"I'll catch up with you later, okay?" I said to Maddy.

"Sure thing, Jake. See ya."

As I started away, I glanced back at Joan, her eagle eye trained on me. One false move and I was toast. The partners wouldn't stand for it, because I, too, was a partner, meaning I was Maddy's boss — albeit indirectly. That shit didn't fly anymore, not after the #MeToo movement. I was risking not only my marriage, but also my career. Did that mean I was going to stop? No. It didn't.

I rode the elevator to the top floor, where the partners kept their offices. Four partners, four corner offices. Only three names on the building, though. Mullen, Gossett, and Hale. The newest partner hadn't earned his spot yet. My office faced the parking lot. Victor Mullen had the best one.

My modern black desk was flanked by two tall windows along the back wall. Bookshelves lined the other walls and were filled with every law book imaginable. Case after case of precedent-setting rulings, and I'd had to learn them all. I'd come from family law, having worked at Ackerman and James, where my wife still worked. But I'd transitioned to corporate law. This was where the big money was. Blue chip companies with deep pockets. Most of the firms we represented were lobbyists hired by the big companies, who tangled with D.C. politicians. I'd come to learn that corporations pulled the strings in Washington, and it was a lucrative gig I planned to exploit for as long as possible.

As I dug into my tasks, and lunchtime drew near, I heard a knock on my door. "Yeah?" I answered.

When it opened, there was Maddy, holding a bag of food in her hand. "You hungry?"

I peered around her, searching for anyone nearby. "I told you you can't just come up here when the partners are in town."

"For your information, I checked their schedules with their assistants, and they all had plans for lunch. It's just you here."

"And our assistants," I replied in a low tone.

"Come on. You have to eat."

"Fine. Come in," I said, resigning to her, as usual.

She sauntered in, closing the door behind her. "Sandwiches from Oscar's. I know they're your favorite."

"Thanks, Maddy."

We ate, exchanged some light-hearted banter. And when we were done, I knew what was next. Maddy stood up and walked around to my side of the desk. She straddled me in my chair.

Her touch was electric, her fingers tracing the contours of my face. Her lips inching closer to mine. The scent of her perfume made me drunk with desire. This wasn't the first time we had found ourselves inextricably entangled, but something about today felt different.

The weight of our secret bore down on my shoulders. I was playing a dangerous game, risking everything for stolen moments of passion and pleasure. But the allure was undeniable, impossible to resist.

Maddy's lips finally met mine, and fireworks erupted between us. Her kiss was like a drug, addictive, and exhilarating. I pulled her closer, my hands caressing every inch of her body. Our affair had become a refuge from the reality of fatherhood, being a husband, and breadwinner.

As our bodies intertwined, I wondered how long we could sustain this. We were walking a tightrope, constantly teetering on the edge of exposure. The risk was part of the thrill, fueling the flames of our passion, but it also tugged on my conscience.

One careless move could bring everything crashing down. The consequences would be catastrophic.

But in that moment, all rational thoughts evaporated. The world outside this space ceased to exist.

She unbuttoned my dress shirt, her hand pressing against my chest. Every touch sent shivers down my spine, igniting a fire within me that burned hotter with each passing second.

Time seemed to stand still as we lost ourselves in each other. But even in the depths of passion, reality had a way of seeping through. The distant ringing of a phone cut through the haze, jolting me back into the real world of responsibilities.

Maddy's lips lingered on mine for a moment longer before she reluctantly pulled away. I reached for my phone, heart pounding in my chest, and answered the call. "Jacob Hale here."

"Just a friendly reminder about our meeting later. Make sure you're not late." The line clicked.

I froze, the phone still at my ear, his words echoing. This was new. They were calling me at work, which was cause for concern. I set down the phone and looked at Maddy, the mood having evaporated.

"Everything okay?"

I lifted her off me. "I should get back to work."

* * *

It was five o'clock and I'd just arrived at Mill Landing, a local bar I wouldn't normally ever set foot inside. But today, my presence here wasn't dictated by personal choice or preference.

Inside, stale beer and desperation intermingled. Shit. Maybe I deserved to be here, after all.

I loosened my tie, sitting down at a wooden table on uneven legs. A brief check of my phone revealed no calls or messages that the meeting had been rescheduled. No, I wasn't going to get that lucky.

The door swung open with a groan, and two figures stepped over the threshold. The first was a man known to me as Bushnell, his face hard and unyielding. His companion, who I hadn't had the pleasure of being introduced to, appeared in stark contrast: a wiry build, and eyes that darted around with unsettling quickness.

"Evening, Jake," Bushnell's voice rumbled. He dropped into the chair.

The other man sat down next to him. A henchman? I grinned at the thought.

"Something funny, Jake?" Bushnell asked.

"Nope." I raised my hand for the server. "You two want a beer?"

"Don't bother," he replied. "We won't be here long enough."

I waved her off apologetically. "Sorry. We're good here for the moment."

Bushnell tilted his head, a silent question hanging in the air between us. "So, are we good?"

Small talk seemed out of the question, so I reached into my suit pocket and retrieved the envelope. "Here you go. All there."

"All of it?" He snatched the envelope and ripped it open.

"Well, no. Just what's currently due."

His lips curled into a crooked smile. "You mean, what's past due?"

"Yeah, I guess I do."

Bushnell counted the money right there at the table. I surveyed the thin crowd, but no one paid any attention.

Appearing satisfied, he handed the money to his partner, never breaking eye contact with me, ensuring no room for misinterpretation. "Miss a payment again, and it won't just be money on the line. We clear?"

I licked my lips, provoked by his threat. But who was I kidding? "Crystal."

CHAPTER 6: LAUREN

As I prepared to leave for the day, I examined my desk. It didn't look much better than when I arrived this morning. Invoices still piled high. Reports sat in folders ready to be reviewed. I had two more days until the end-of-month reports were due, but it still wasn't enough time.

Regardless, I was already leaving later than usual tonight. It was almost five thirty and I'd texted our neighbor, Nancy, that I would be home late. In fact, I might even pick up dinner on the way, so I didn't have to cook.

I turned off my computer and locked my filing cabinets. We kept timesheets and call logs in my office so I could reference them for billing, but for some reason, I felt I should lock them up. Maybe it was because my door had been left open last night.

While I retrieved my laptop bag, I heard a knock. My door already open, I glanced up to see the janitor. "Hi, Gary. Sorry I'm still here; I was actually just leaving. How are you tonight?"

"Doing well, thank you." He walked inside. "A long day for you then, huh, Miss Hale?"

"It's Mrs. Hale, but please call me Lauren. And yes, it's the end of the month, so you'll come to find out this is pretty typical. I'll get out of your hair." I grabbed my things and realized I hadn't touched my lunch today, choosing to eat out with Tammy instead. "I don't suppose you're hungry, are you? I brought in a sandwich for lunch, but didn't end up eating it. It's just ham and cheese. Not sure if you're a fan, but it's in the staff fridge. You're welcome to it, if you'd like."

"Oh, no." He waved his hand. "I couldn't."

"Really, it's okay." Gary looked pretty thin. He could probably use the nourishment. "Please. It'll go to waste, otherwise."

He tipped his head. "All right then. Thank you, Miss Lauren. That's kind of you."

"Not at all. Have a good night, Gary. I'll probably see you tomorrow night too." I chuckled, offering a final wave goodbye.

"Hope so. Good night."

CHAPTER 7: GARY

The time had come for me to leave: 11 p.m. Janitorial duties completed, though my shift didn't end until 1 a.m. I'd planned my move, and this was the first step. It was best not to clock out. No way to trace my comings and goings. Exiting through the rear, where cameras were noticeably absent, was the best route. I'd had access to the security room and knew where each camera had been placed. Their oversight was my advantage.

The night air felt brisk, piercing through my long-sleeved shirt as I slipped out the back door of Ackerman & James. The city streets had grown quiet with only the sound of the occasional vehicle passing by. I pulled on my coat, raising the hood to obscure my face as I walked to the bus station three blocks away. Buses ran until midnight. I had cut it close.

Traveling by bus wasn't ideal, but it was the only source of transportation I had for now. Something that would soon be rectified. As the lone rider, I stared through the window at the passing landscape. Barren trees. Dusty white roads and sidewalks. Streetlamps every so often.

The city lights soon gave way to rows of suburban houses, each one offering shelter to their families. Lauren's house was nestled among them.

When I arrived just blocks from her neighborhood, I stepped off the bus and into another world. A world of families and friends. Dinners and birthday parties. I felt at home.

Among the shadows of hedgerows and brick walls, wood fences, and ornate mailboxes, I walked. As I approached Lauren's house, delight and tension played a game of tug-of-war in my gut. I eyed the long driveway and the stately home perched at the top. I had spent many nights imagining this moment, wondering what it would be like to finally cross the threshold into her world.

The porch light bathed the door and front steps in a warm glow, calling out to me. But I had to remain in the shadows while I worked out what would be my way inside. It would not be through the front. Not yet.

I'd taken the time to study the beautiful colonial home. Learning its secrets, researching its weaknesses. I circled the perimeter, my eyes scanning for additional vulnerability, careful to avoid security cameras. But there were none. An error during the remodel, no doubt, but one I couldn't take for granted. And then there it was — my way in.

A large dormer vent at the top of an easily scalable metal trellis, whose vines lay dormant in this harsh winter. This was where I would call home for the foreseeable future. A home with a family. My family. And I would love them, just as I have loved all the others.

CHAPTER 8: DETECTIVE COLLINS

If I could just punch these guys in the face, I'd feel a whole hell of a lot better. Yeah, I was a cop, and they were my coworkers, but if I had to listen to them drone on about how their team lost the Super Bowl, I was gonna lose my shit. It was three weeks ago! A lot of women liked football. I wasn't one of them. I'd had enough, especially when I was at my wits end with this Tomlin investigation. Maybe that was the real reason for my frustration.

Nah, it was these losers. "Hey, y'all mind talking football somewhere else? Some of us have jobs to do."

"Sorry, Collins," Lockhart replied.

I'd been assigned this shit investigation a month ago, after the previous detective jumped ship. So far, I'd exhausted all my leads. A family had been murdered in their home in the northern part of the city. Two young kids, a boy and a girl, and their parents. Goddamn gruesome scene.

And now, an email arrived from Forensics. New evidence had come back from some additional samples recovered from the scene. "Son of a bitch. Finally." I jumped off my chair, smoothing a few loose strands of hair that frayed from the tight bun I wore.

Heading into the hallway, I passed by the offices of top brass, and a few meandering detectives I had no time for at the moment. What I needed were results. Fingerprints. DNA. Please, God, give me something to work with.

As I arrived at the Forensics lab, the scent of bleach and chemicals practically knocked me out. Dr. Harrison, the head forensic analyst, greeted me with a weary smile. His tired eyes spoke of the countless hours he had spent analyzing evidence. And not just from my case.

"Detective Collins," he said, his voice tinged with exhaustion. "I've been waiting for you."

"I hope you found something significant, Doc," I replied, trying to keep my voice steady.

He motioned for me to follow him to a long table cluttered with various evidence bags and equipment. He picked up a glove and slipped it on, then carefully extracted a sealed plastic bag from one of the boxes labeled 'Victim 1.' She was the mother who'd been found inside a storm cellar, knife through the heart like her killer was Van Helsing. Blood everywhere. Looked like something from a horror show.

I'd insisted on a second CSI team going back to the scene after I'd discovered partial prints on the mother's earring. It had been wedged between the cracks of the cellar floor. Overlooked at first. I'm still not sure how the hell I saw the damn thing, but I wasn't opposed to believing in Divine intervention.

"I was able to complete the partial set to determine they belonged to an unknown, likely your suspect," Dr. Harrison explained, holding it up for me to inspect. "But the reason I asked you to come down was that I pulled DNA from it too."

"DNA?" I reeled back. "He left something behind?"

"Contact DNA," Harrison added. "I've run it through CODIS, but no hits."

"Yet," I raised my index finger. "No hits yet."

He returned the earring to the evidence bag. "I'm glad you can find the silver lining, Detective. I know it probably isn't what you were hoping for, but it's a start."

"You got that right, Doc. It's a step in the right direction. Thank you."

As I left the Forensics lab, defeat weighed me down. Unknown DNA was common. It meant that my suspect hadn't yet been caught for any crimes. So, until he was, how was I going to find this son of a bitch?

CHAPTER 9: LAUREN

Another day closer to the end of the month, and I'd finally begun to see progress. Now, however, I was ready to head home. Late again. If I had to look at any more spreadsheets, I might throw my computer through the window.

But there was something I needed to do first. I walked into the hallway and headed toward the kitchen. Just a small area where the employees could microwave their lunches or store them in the refrigerator. The coffee was always on, thanks mostly to Tammy. She monitored when a new pot needed to be brewed.

I opened the fridge and retrieved the plastic container. Inside was last night's leftovers. Pasta and chicken. Nothing special, but I figured I'd offer it to Gary. It seemed he ate the sandwich I'd left for him, and I was pretty sure he needed it. He didn't look like he had much — of anything, really.

As I closed the fridge again and returned to the hallway, I headed back to my office to close up for the night. When I approached, I saw him inside. "Gary?"

He turned around, seemingly embarrassed I'd caught him looking at my desk. "Miss Lauren, how are you tonight?"

"Well, I was just getting ready to go home." I cocked my head. "What are you doing?"

"Oh, just getting a jump on emptying the trash cans. I figured you were gone until I saw your computer up and running. Didn't mean to intrude on your work," he replied.

"You didn't. I actually wanted to bring you something before I left." I held out the container.

He smiled, leaning closer with noted interest. "What you got there?"

"Pasta and chicken. We had so much left over last night, I didn't want to throw it out. Of course, don't feel like you need to take it." I laughed awkwardly.

"Oh, I wouldn't pass this up. Not a chance." Gary took the container from me. "This will make for a delicious dinner. Thank you very much, Miss Lauren. You really are a gem."

"Don't mention it." I walked around to my desk and gathered my things. "You have a good night, Gary, and I'm sure I'll see you tomorrow night too."

I started toward the hallway again and glanced back, watching Gary pry open the lid and inhaling. It felt nice helping someone, even if it was only a small gesture.

CHAPTER 10: GARY

She was exactly as I'd expected. I dabbed my lips with a napkin and set down my fork. It was almost 11 p.m., and I'd just finished my dinner — a delicious pasta dish cooked by Lauren Hale. If she was this wonderful, I could only imagine what her husband and son were like. I'd find out soon enough.

When the world went quiet, I would continue to set up my new home, soaking in the love of the Hale family. Adoring them as if they were my very own.

I set off back to my duties. Back to cleaning the toilets, wiping down the employee kitchen, emptying the trash cans. If this was what it was going to take to get close to Lauren, then that was fine by me.

Within another hour, I was ready to get down to business. I'd brought in a few things tonight. A small duffel bag with my clothes and essentials. That was the extent of what belonged to me. But soon, the Hales would belong to me, too.

I retreated through the back, as I had before. A borrowed vehicle awaited me in the parking lot next door. 'Borrowed' might have been putting it politely. I'd stolen it. Hey, the guy shouldn't have left it unlocked in the apartment complex in the first place.

I'd parked it next door to avoid any assumption that it was mine, replacing the license plates to keep the cops on their toes. I jumped into the small two-door white coupe and headed north to the suburbs of Alexandria. I took care not to tighten my circle so much that the police might pick up a pattern of movement, should suspicions arise. This wasn't my first rodeo, though if all went well, it would be my last. That would be up to the Hales, of course.

Another left turn and I'd arrived. One street over, of course. I wasn't crazy enough to park outside their home. I could take it by foot from here.

As I stayed hidden in the shadows of the trees, I reached their home. Stunning, even in the night, with its architectural lighting and subtle fixtures placed on the porch and garage doors. The absence of light inside indicated the family had retired for the night. Now, to make my way in without detection.

The side of the house was where I was headed. To the trellis that led up to the attic dormer. As I approached it, a cold breeze wrapped around me, but I remained steadfast, feeling invincible. A steady foot on the lattice, I began to climb. Each step bringing me closer to my destination. My palms burned as they gripped the icy metal framework.

Once I reached the dormer, I paused for a moment to catch my breath. The soft glow of moonlight illuminated the scenery, casting ominous shadows across the roof.

The attic dormer was slightly ajar, as I had left it the night before. Carefully, I pushed it open wider and slipped inside, stepping softly onto the plywood floor. The air in the attic was stale, filled with dust and cobwebs. I took a moment to steady my breathing.

I looked around at the partitioned space. Some of the lumber appeared new, a product of the remodel I'd come to learn about. My steps were careful, deliberate until I reached the area that I had already begun to call my own. A small door that led to a separate storage area.

Inside, shelves lined two of the walls, but remained empty. It appeared to have been cleaned out and was the perfect spot. Hidden. Secret. I would live among my new family without leaving any trace of my existence. I'd be at work while the family prepared to retire for the night. I'd stay silent in their attic until they left for work and school in the morning. It was far better than the shelter, the perfect scenario. I was home.

The anticipation of being so close to Lauren, weaving myself into her life until she couldn't imagine a world without me — it excited me.

My mind wandered to the future I had planned. The breakfasts together, the laughter shared at the dinner table, and the late-night conversations about hopes and dreams. Every detail was carefully imagined, meticulously constructed in my mind.

I unzipped my duffel bag and pulled out a small but warm blanket, unfurling it onto the floor. It no longer felt strange to be setting up camp in someone else's home. I'd been at this for a while. And I reminded myself that it was only temporary. Soon enough, the Hales would become my family, and this house would become my home.

CHAPTER 11: LAUREN

My eyes snapped open, and as my vision cleared, I noticed our bedroom was still cloaked in darkness. I turned to see the time on my bedside clock. One in the morning. I was sure I'd heard something. A door closing. A thump on the stairs. What was it?

I looked over to see Jacob on his side, snoring lightly. It was in times like these that I wished we had a dog. Now, I would have to investigate this myself.

Leaving the warmth of the bed, I slipped out from under the covers and padded toward the bedroom door. The floorboards moaned lightly beneath my weight, causing me to freeze in place. Even though we'd remodeled most of this house, it still creaked on its old bones. I held my breath, straining my ears for any other sounds. Silence enveloped the house once again.

Determined to discover the source of the noise, I made my way downstairs, using the handrail to steady myself. Each step felt like an eternity as I descended into darkness. The only light came from the moon filtering through the windows, leaving a slight glow around the closed blinds.

As I reached the bottom of the stairs, a sense of foreboding washed over me. The air felt heavy, charged with an unknown presence. Pushing aside my unease, I continued on.

I would start in the foyer, checking that the front door remained locked. It had. Now, I moved onto the living room. As I approached, I noticed a faint glow. When I entered, reluctance nearly putting an end to my investigation, I saw nothing. The light had come from the clock on the cable box. No sound. No movement. Nothing.

I snickered. I'd lived here for years now, and this old house always creaked and shifted and settled. Why had it forced me out of my bed this time?

Might as well grab a drink of water before returning upstairs. I carried on into the kitchen. All the blinds were drawn, and the curtains closed. I couldn't see outside. My imagination tended to go into overdrive, especially since becoming a mother. I supposed that was where Noah garnered his imagination. It was hereditary.

Thoughts of my own mother sprang to mind. Her utter disregard for me or my safety. She was hardly around at all, leaving me to deal with things that went bump in the night. Never mind now. I was grown up. I had a child and a husband.

I returned to bed, climbing in as quietly as I could, but it seemed I'd disturbed Jacob. He shifted a little, finally opening his eyes. "You okay, hon?"

"Yeah, I was thirsty and went downstairs for a glass of water." I laid down, pulling the covers over me. "Sorry to wake you." And then I felt his hand on my hip. He rubbed it gently, sliding it down to my backside.

I arched my back slightly, inviting his touch. His warm hand on my skin felt soothing, erasing any lingering unease from my late-night investigation.

Jacob leaned in, his breath tickling my ear as he whispered, "No need to apologize." The husky tone in his voice sparked a passion within me, and I couldn't help but crave his touch even more.

With a gentle, yet firm grip, Jacob pulled me closer to him, our bodies pressing against each other in the darkness. He nuzzled his face into the crook of my neck, scattering light kisses along my skin. The sensation of his warm lips against my flesh made my body tingle. Jacob's touch always had a way of sending a lightning bolt through me. I surrendered myself completely to the moment.

The room filled with the sound of our ragged breaths and soft moans, drowning out the reality of our troubled marriage. The intensity of his touch overwhelmed me, sending waves of pleasure through my veins. I bit down on my lower lip to stifle a moan as his fingers moved higher, inching closer to where I needed him most.

Jacob's lips found mine once again. Our bodies pressed tightly together, a perfect fit. And then I remembered . . . I wasn't his only one.

* * *

The calendar marked the beginning of a new month. The final few days were proving hectic, but nothing out of the ordinary. The concerns of my home life were swept under the rug, glossed over while I spent the weekend clearing out the remaining construction debris in our house.

Jacob had escaped to work on Saturday and indulged in his love of golf on an unusually warm Sunday. I was left to entertain Noah for a playdate at the local indoor activity center. Our weekends had become predictable and routine, while I lived in denial of the truth.

I'd been surprised the other night by Jacob's advances. It had been weeks since we'd made love, and he seemed particularly interested that night. I'd given into him, as usual, pretending that our marriage was perfect.

Now, however, I was back at work. It had become my refuge. A place where I felt like myself — just Lauren — not wife or mother to anyone. And as I noticed the time, I headed into the break room to grab my lunch. The lasting aroma of reheated food and brewing coffee greeted me as I entered. The scent of citrus was discernible just beneath the surface, a remnant of the cleaner used to wipe down the counters.

"Hey, there."

Startled, I turned around to see Tammy. "Perfect timing. Care to join me?"

"Absolutely. I'm starving," she replied, yanking open the fridge to retrieve her own lunch.

I had great admiration for Tammy. Divorced with a son in college. Her boldness and confidence amazed me. She always held her ground, unapologetic about her needs.

We settled at our usual spot near the back, away from prying eyes and ears. As I unwrapped my sandwich, Tammy leaned in closer. "How's things with Jacob? Now that all the renovations are finished, everything settling down again?"

I hadn't told her of my suspicions. Some things weren't meant to be shared, in my opinion. Not until certainty came into the equation. But by the tone of her question, Tammy clearly had her own suspicions. "Yeah, sure. It's been great having the house to ourselves again. No more contractors knocking on the door at 6 a.m. It's quieted down a lot, but I'd like to plan a family weekend away soon."

Tammy raised an eyebrow. "You know, I always thought Jacob was a hard worker. Very ambitious guy. At least, he was when he worked here. I imagine that hasn't changed much now that he's a partner at his firm. Sometimes, that can be hard on a marriage. But I'm glad you're happy."

She was good, I could admit that. Her answer was neutral, yet insightful. She was trying to dig deeper, but I wasn't prepared to go below the surface. Not right now. And not here. "We've gone through some rough patches lately, but now that the chaos at home is over, things will return to normal."

Tammy placed a comforting hand on mine, her eyes filled with empathy. "I don't need to tell you that communication is key, but I'm here. Just so you know."

I took a bite of my turkey sandwich, letting her words settle around me. After dabbing my lips with a napkin, I regarded her. "You should come over and check out the house this weekend."

Tammy smiled, picking up on my clever attempt to change topics. "Sure. I'd love that."

CHAPTER 12: NOAH

Mrs. Hammond picked me up from preschool every day. She drove really slow all the way back home. She lived next door and parked her car in her driveway, then we walked over to my house. I got to spend all afternoon with her, until Mommy got home from work. This was my favorite part of the day, because I knew I was gonna get snacks and juice. I unbuckled my booster seat and grabbed my backpack. Mrs. Hammond always made me wait for her to open my car door, so I did.

"Just sit tight, young man, and let me help you down."

Mrs. Hammond was so slow. She was old with lots of wrinkles and white hair. But she was always nice to me. Gave me lots of cookies and candy, even though my mommy doesn't like it when she gives me unhealthy treats.

"Thank you." I took her hand and jumped down, running to my front door, waiting for her to hurry up and unlock it. It was cold and my coat was inside my backpack. Now, I was freezing.

I tried to be patient. Mommy says I have to work on that. Mrs. Hammond finally caught up to me at the door. It took her a few more seconds to get the key into the lock and open it. When she did, I rushed inside our warm house, dropping my backpack on the floor.

I ran into the kitchen and opened the refrigerator, pulling out a juice box. I heard Mrs. Hammond's footsteps behind me. I turned around, showing her the juice. "Can I have this, please?"

"All right. Sit down and I'll get you a snack."

I smiled, jumping onto the kitchen stool, and waiting for my snack. I had a grandma. Daddy's parents lived close by. But Mommy told me her parents died before I was born. Mrs. Hammond was like a grandma to me. She didn't have grandchildren, and she was alone. Mommy said her husband went to heaven last year. Sometimes, I think she was meant to be my grandma. I loved her, especially when she gave me snacks.

"Here you go, Noah." Mrs. Hammond set down a plate of cookies for me.

"Thank you." I gobbled them up pretty quick cause I was starving. And when I was done, I wiped my mouth with my shirt sleeve. "Can I go upstairs and play now?"

She raised her eyebrow at me. "Go on. Go play."

"Thank you." I hopped down and ran upstairs to my playroom. Mommy and Daddy made it so nice when we had all those people here fixing the house. I got my own TV now.

I plopped down on the squishy bean bag chair in front of it, excited for my favorite cartoon to start. The room was filled with toys, and books. Plenty of Legos in boxes all around. Mommy got mad when I didn't pick them up, but she wasn't here right now.

I turned on the TV, flipping through channels until I found my cartoon. I sang the words to the theme song and got comfy in my chair.

The TV was quiet for a minute, and some commercial came on. That was when I heard a strange noise from the ceiling, somewhere over in the corner. I got up and walked to the spot I thought it came from. It was like a thumping sound above me.

I listened for it again, but I didn't hear anything for a while. "Oh well." I walked back to my chair and my cartoons, but then . . . there it was again. I turned around. "Who's making that noise?"

CHAPTER 13: LAUREN

When I'd gotten home, our neighbor was in the living room with a book in her hand. "Hi, Nancy. How are you?"

She slowly rose from the sofa and tugged on her oversized top. "Doing just fine. Noah's upstairs watching TV and playing Legos. I checked in on him just a few minutes ago."

I glanced up the staircase. "Wonderful. Thank you so much, as usual." I helped her pull on her coat and walked her to the door. "We'll see you tomorrow, then?"

"Of course." she looked up, cupping a hand near her mouth. "Night, Noah. I'll see you tomorrow."

"Good night, Mrs. Hammond," he shouted back.

I closed the door behind her and heard Noah jogging down the steps. "Hey, there, kiddo. How was your day?" I opened my arms, and he ran into them.

"Hi, Mommy. It was good. Mrs. Hammond gave me cookies."

"I'll bet she did." I kissed his cheek. "I suppose I should start making dinner. You can go back to your cartoons if you want."

"Okay."

He disappeared upstairs as I made my way into the kitchen. I'd have dinner ready in about an hour, and just as I set out to begin cooking, a text arrived on my phone. I read the message from my husband.

I've been called into a last-minute meeting with the partners. I'll be home late.

"Yeah, I'll bet." I set down my phone on the kitchen island. "Guess it's just dinner for two tonight."

The good news was that I could make chicken nuggets and mac and cheese and be okay with that.

I understood when he'd made partner that there would be times like this. Times when he'd have to cozy up to clients, taking them out for dinner and drinks. I got that. After all, I'd seen the partners in my firm doing the same thing. But I never expected it to be so frequent, which made me question his truthfulness. I could only ignore the obvious for so long. But just exactly how long would that be?

"Noah, come get some dinner now, sweetheart," I said, placing two dinner plates on the breakfast table. He'd run in so quickly that his socked feet slipped on the wood floor in the kitchen. "Careful now."

"I'm okay," he said, laughing.

"Then come and eat." I pulled out a chair and joined him at the table. The sun had set, and the long winter night had begun. I poured myself a glass of red wine, hoping it would smooth out the edges. I wasn't a big drinker, but I turned to wine on nights like these. Unfortunately, they'd become more frequent, so maybe I should reassess my habit. "How was school today?"

"Fine." Noah picked up his chicken nugget and dipped it in ketchup. "We didn't get to play outside, though, because it was too cold, they said."

"It was pretty cold, but I'm sorry to hear that. Did you get to go into the gym and play games?"

"Yeah. It was fun." He took a bite, leaving behind ketchup on the corners of his lips.

I reached across the table and gently wiped it away with a napkin. "You've got a little something there." I grinned. "There we go, all clean."

We continued eating in comfortable silence. Noah enjoying his dinner while I pondered tomorrow's work to-do list.

"Mommy?"

"Yeah?"

"I made a new friend today."

"You did?" I regarded him with curiosity. "That's great. What's his name?"

"He said I could call him whatever I wanted, so I named him Billy."

"You named him Billy." I set down my wine glass, tilting my head a moment. "Is this friend in your class at school?"

"No, I don't know where he goes to school," Noah replied, still plunking nuggets into his mouth.

"I'm confused, honey. How did you meet Billy? Where?"

"Oh, he lives in the walls."

I chuckled. "Billy lives in the walls . . . of our home?"

"Yeah. Of course. Where else?" Noah stared at me for a moment, deadpan in his expression. "He said he's always lived here and that we could be friends."

This no longer seemed funny. "Noah, are you making this up?"

"No, Mommy, I promise," His eyes widened, pleading for me to believe him. "Billy is real."

Not wanting to stifle Noah's imagination, I simply smiled. "Okay, sweetie. If Billy makes you happy, then that's great. But just remember, he's not real like you and me."

Noah nodded obediently, but his eyes held a flicker of defiance. It was as if he knew something I didn't — an unspoken secret that left me feeling unsettled. "Why don't you finish your dinner, and then we'll get ready for your bath?"

CHAPTER 14: GARY

The boy wasn't supposed to hear me. I should've been more careful as I prepared to leave for the night, leaving too late, as it turned out. Still, he was young, and I'd been around the young ones plenty. They were easy to persuade. They believed anything and everything. So we talked for a short while. I was careful not to reveal too much, even gave the boy an opportunity to give me a name. Billy. I liked it.

I'd arrived at work on time, managing to see Lauren for a moment or two. We exchanged a few pleasantries. I was careful not to pry. Didn't want to seem too interested. She didn't have any leftovers for me this time, but that was okay. I just wanted to see her face.

I'd gone about my regular duties, cleaning up after these people I cared little about. Only one mattered. And just being in her office, feeling her presence around me, it kept me going. She made me happy.

My shift soon ended. I could return to the Hale home. My home. I left the office, as I usually did, through the back, and without clocking out. My supervisor had yet to ask why I'd forgotten to clock out at night. To be honest, I don't think he really cared.

I could usually count on the indifference of others. It was how I'd gotten away with this for so long. People didn't question things. They took me at face value. Their mistake. And the best part about all of it was that the police, should they come around, would have no pattern to follow. That was how they solved things, right? Finding patterns was the key to finding their suspects. I had figured out how to make that harder for them.

I stepped out into the darkness, the light breeze piercing my skin, and walked down a block. That was where I kept the car I'd boosted. Every few days, I'd put on new plates. I had a stash of them, thanks to a new style they'd come out with recently. A friend of mine had access to such things. It wasn't free, of course. Nothing ever was.

So, I slipped behind the wheel of the older white coupe when the light patter of rain began to dot my windshield. The rain intensified as I pulled out onto the road, but I couldn't let the weather dampen my spirits. I had a goal in mind, and nothing would stop me from accomplishing it.

The rain continued to pour, creating a symphony of rhythmic droplets against the car's roof. The scent of stale cigarette smoke still lingered inside as I drove on.

I took a moment to adjust the rearview mirror, catching a glimpse of myself in the dim light. My reflection revealed tired eyes with deepening wrinkles. Sharp features that made my cheeks appear gaunt. I knew I was too thin, and Lauren knew it, too. How kind she was, in this world that lacked compassion. But this lifestyle was catching up to me. I looked older than my forty-seven years. I'd been neglected, forgotten in this world, and I couldn't let it stand. Lauren would see that, too.

CHAPTER 15: DETECTIVE COLLINS

This case, so far, had two major components. One, the suspect managed to gain entry into the Tomlins' home without their knowledge. Two, he had to have been there long enough that they'd grown suspicious. Mrs. Tomlin was murdered in the cellar, so either she investigated her growing concern, or she happened to have stumbled upon him and it was bad timing. The rest of her family, murdered in the home. All I had was a partial print and an unidentified contact DNA sample.

I leaned back in my chair, staring out into the bullpen where my coworkers kept their heads down, investigating their own cases. I needed to understand the suspect's M.O. How did he choose his victims? Were they known to him or were they random?

My attention was drawn to my laptop when a notification sounded. I peered at the screen. "Holy shit." When I'd first been assigned this case, I'd entered relevant information into ViCAP, the national database used by FBI and local authorities. It was how suspects were connected to other crimes. Similar signatures, or markers. And I'd just been notified of a hit. Multiple hits — actually. I'd also double checked the DNA sample Forensics had entered into CODIS, praying for a match. Nothing yet. But things were looking up.

"Where the hell was this information when I first entered the case details?"

"What's that, Collins?" Detective Dixon passed by my desk on his way to his own. The veteran detective was tall, thin. Had a hitch in his step from a gunshot wound a few years back. Handsome, in a sort of rugged way.

I glanced up at him. "Nothing." As I read on, it appeared there were two other families in addition to the Tomlins whose cases were strikingly similar.

Reviewing the details, I realized why these others hadn't shown up before. Both families were within a twenty-mile radius of Alexandria, along the outlying suburban areas, an unsettling revelation, and had happened over the course of eighteen months. Then, I spotted my error. "Son of a bitch."

I felt Dixon's stare and looked at him. "I entered the wrong dates."

"Where?" he asked.

"ViCAP." I shook my head in disgust. "I took on the Tomlin case at the beginning of January and didn't change the date from the previous year when I input the information, so it didn't pick up the others."

He tilted his head. "I don't take your meaning."

"It wasn't until I added the detail of the DNA sample that the dates reset, and now, I got two hits." I slammed the side of my fist against my desk. "Goddamn it."

"Who was assigned those other two?"

I scanned through the information. "Lockhart got one of them, but it was moved to the Cold Case unit late last year. The first investigation goes back eighteen months. Kevin and Dana Godfrey, and their unborn baby."

Dixon glanced away. "Christ."

"And then the Pitzers. About a year ago. And again, it was moved to cold cases in January — after the Tomlins were murdered. How the hell did that happen?"

"Sloppy paperwork, I'd guess. So you got three similar investigations over an eighteen-month span. Hard to confirm whether they're connected. I'd suggest talking to Lockhart and the guys in Cold Case. But unless those cases name any potential suspects," Dixon added, "it doesn't move the needle much. All you can do is take the ball and run with it from here."

Detective Lockhart's desk was only steps away from mine. He wasn't there, but I knew where he'd most likely be. "Appreciate the advice, Dixon. Thanks." I got up and headed into the breakroom.

Stepping inside, I spotted him. "Lockhart?"

He looked back at me, holding a steaming cup of coffee and a bagel. Eugene Lockhart had been with Alexandria PD his entire career, having started as a patrolman. He was about my age, at around thirty-five. He wore a permanent five o'clock shadow and kept himself fit.

"Collins, what's up? Was I talking too much football again?"

I headed toward him, wearing a smile. "Thankfully, not this time. Listen, what do you remember about the Godfrey investigation?"

He glanced up, seeming to think about the question. "Kevin and Dana Godfrey. I remember. She was eight months pregnant."

I noticed the regret in his eyes.

"Why are you asking?" he continued.

"Got a case that has a lot of similarities. To yours and another that was sent over to the Cold Case unit. What can you tell me about how their killer got to them?"

"Did you read the file?" He raised his hand. "Sorry, I don't mean to sound like a prick. It was a tough case, you know?"

"Yeah, I get that. But this one I'm working now . . . the one Harding dropped into my lap."

"Still can't believe he took the job with the NYPD," Lockhart shook his head.

"What are you gonna do, right?" I replied. "Anyway, the suspect got to the wife in the cellar of their home. We figured he was already there because the cellar door was easily accessed. Then, he managed to get into the house and murder the husband and their two kids while they were in bed. That's where I'm stumped, because no one's found signs of forced entry."

"Sounds a lot like what happened to the Godfreys."

"Exactly. So, did you ever figure out how their killer got into the house?"

"At the time, best guess was he got in when they weren't home. No signs of breaking and entering, though, so we couldn't figure it out. Same as you. Leads ran dry pretty quickly. Probably doesn't help you much."

"More than you might think. Sounds to me like they are connected. Hey, I appreciate the help." I headed out of the breakroom.

"Collins, you need anything else, let me know," Lockhart added. "Check with CCU too, yeah?"

"Will do, thanks." I made my way back to the bullpen, mulling over the idea this killer just magically appeared in his victims' homes. Of course, I knew it wasn't magic, but I needed something to work with.

Returning to my desk, I began to review these other cases in more depth. "How's this guy getting into these houses at night while the families are home?"

"Could be during the day — when they're not." Dixon, still at his desk, had heard me.

"During the day." I nodded. "I can buy that, but I still don't know how."

"First of all, he'd have to have known when his victims would be out. Work, or school, or whatever," he added.

My mind ran through various possibilities. "Was he watching them? Learning their schedules? Maybe. But this guy — he had to know the layout of his victims' homes, too. You can't go sneaking around inside a house, looking for bedrooms and shit. You'd be discovered before anything happened."

"Could be onto something there," Dixon replied. "You've already hit up friends, family, coworkers, I assume."

"Yeah. Turned up squat." I noticed his wheels spinning. "Why? What are you thinking?"

"Well," he shrugged. "I'd maybe take a look at the neighborhood's nearby shelters. Encampments. You're talking about someone outside the family's circle with that kind of knowledge of his victims. So, could be someone who has time to observe. Someone who doesn't want to be on the radar, you know?"

"Transient?" I asked, feeling a spark of optimism.

"It's worth a look, Collins. That's all I'm saying."

Plenty of homeless encampments had popped up in the suburbs over the past year or more, so I grabbed my jacket and snatched my keys.

"What's your plan?" Dixon asked.

I regarded him a moment, feeling grateful for his insight. Dixon had been on the force longer than me. He knew his stuff. And I could see he wanted to help. A good detective didn't turn down help from a better one. "Figured I'd hit the streets near the Tomlin residence to see if anyone's willing to talk."

"You want some backup?" he asked.

"Let me check it out first. See if the theory pans out. If it does, I'll give you a heads up."

I headed out of the police station and slipped into my gray newer model Ford Fusion — the department had picked it up at auction.

I headed back toward the suburbs, toward the neighborhood where my victims — the Tomlins — had lived. I knew of two nearby encampments. Hard to say how many people were there this time of year. The nights got damn cold.

A brutal wind blew through the streets today, the clouds rolling in fast. I had no idea if this was the right move. But I was dealing with three families and a total of ten victims; damn if I didn't need to pull a lead out of my ass quick. I was going to have to take this to the captain. And I didn't want to do it empty-handed.

Ahead of me, I saw it. Blue tarps being used as makeshift tents. Camping tents that looked like they'd been pulled from the dump. A few fires burned in trash cans as people huddled around them for warmth. Men, women. A few kids. Sorry sight to see.

I parked my car across the street from the commons where the encampment had spilled over into. Stepping out, I pulled my coat tightly around me to ward off the frigid air. That was when I saw a group of weary faces turn toward me as I approached. They knew I was a cop. These guys got harangued on a daily basis.

"Morning. I'm Detective Collins. Alexandria PD." I showed them my badge. No one seemed impressed.

I set my sights on the older man. What little hair he had was gray and disheveled. His clothes, worn out. "How long have you been out here, sir? Can I ask your name?"

He looked me up and down. "Long enough to know you ain't been around here before. Who you looking for, Detective?"

Straight to the point, with a question I wasn't sure how to answer. "Wanted to know if you might recall a man, possibly around twenty-five to say, about forty." I pulled that out of my ass based strictly on statistics, not fact. "Could've hung around a while. Interested in the neighborhood. Maybe packed up and moved on after a few months."

"Lady, you just described most of us out here." He scoffed. "You got anything more specific?"

I glanced around at the faces staring back at me, searching for a glimmer of recognition or a flicker of a memory. "Probably did a good job of keeping to himself. Might've taken off during the afternoon, or evening hours, showing back up in the mornings."

As I surveyed the few people around me, not one seemed remotely interested in helping. Maybe they didn't know anything, but if they did, there wasn't much incentive to speak up. The older man's gaze bore into mine, a deep-seated mistrust beneath it.

"Sorry, Detective. I ain't seen anyone like that. At least, not anyone who stood out."

"No one who mentioned having family nearby or that you noticed had access to a car?"

The old man ran his finger under his nose and set his sights on me again. "Like I said, Detective, we ain't seen anyone like that. Good luck to you, though."

CHAPTER 16: GARY

The house was quiet now. The husband left for work, then Lauren, who took Noah to school first. I was alone in here, in this small storage space tucked away inside the attic that seemed to have been forgotten in the efforts to improve the home.

The air felt like tiny needles pricking my skin, leaving it chilled and tingling. Each breath I took seemed to freeze inside my lungs, forcing me to cough up the block of ice impeding my airways. I pulled the blanket tighter around me, covering my ears with my wool hat. A hint of light seeped in through the dormer vent from which I'd entered. Dust particles were captured in the gray light, floating along without a care in the world. Aside from my sinking body temperature, that was how I felt in this moment. Someone with no cares. But the feeling wouldn't last. It couldn't.

My desire to learn more about my new family compelled me to leave these frigid surroundings, knowing I could take shelter within the warmth of their walls. I stood from the floor, dropping the blanket, and carried on toward the attic scuttle several feet away. What I needed was a shower and a fresh change of clothes. I would be alone for the next few hours, until little Noah returned from preschool with the elderly neighbor.

I descended the ladder and found myself in the hallway between the upstairs bedrooms. The smell of fresh paint and new wood floors lingered. I walked through the corridor toward the hall bath, passing family photos mounted on the walls along the way.

Lauren was too young, it seemed, to have a child, but I supposed some people wanted to start early. The husband — I stared at him in the photo. His hands were cupped over Lauren's shoulders while she held a baby Noah in her arms.

From what I could see in this picture, I already disliked the man of this house. Overbearing. Controlling. Demanding. That was what I saw in his eyes, his hands practically clutching at Lauren. I'd hoped not to have to rid the family of him, but the husbands weren't as welcoming or understanding of my presence. Of course, I'd thought Eleanor would be different, too. She wasn't.

I made my way into what appeared to be Lauren and her husband's bedroom. "What is your name, husband?" Nothing in here would likely reveal that information, but that didn't prevent me from looking. I placed my hands on the mattress, still warm from their bodies.

The room was decorated in soft, earthy hues. Thick blankets on top of the bed. Large, fluffy pillows. Overstuffed side chairs perfect for curling up on with a good book. "You have good taste, Lauren." Good taste was made easier with enough money. I could see the family had no lack of it.

As I moved through their private sanctuary, I noticed the walk-in closets were filled with clothes. Suits on one side. Casual business attire on the other. Perfectly folded sweaters resting in velvet-lined drawers.

In the corner of the room was a small dresser with a few personal knickknacks resting on top of it. A photo of Noah's first birthday, as evidenced by the cake in front of him. A souvenir, perhaps from a vacation, and a wooden box with an inscription that read, *Jacob and Lauren.* "Jacob." I smiled, opening it. Inside was a collection of small trinkets that must've meant something to her.

Ahead, next to the closet, was a luxurious bathroom. I turned on the lights. A claw-footed tub. A shower made for two. Exquisite marble vanities. "Yes, this will suit me just fine."

I let my clothes drop to the floor, turning on the shower until steam arose. It had been days since I'd showered. The hot water soothed me, washing away the grime of the attic, warming my bones. But I couldn't linger. Still much to do. I stepped out, drying myself with one of Lauren's towels, and dressed once again.

I had to continue my exploration, ensuring I knew every inch of the Hale home. Returning to the hallway, I found Noah's room. The joyful innocence enveloped me. Bright colors on the walls in varying shades of blue. Shelves full of toys, books, and drawings.

Noah's clothes were hung neatly in the closet, organized by size and color. Tucked into a corner, I noticed a small, worn teddy bear, who appeared as if waiting to be found by its rightful owner. That was when I knew I had to make this work. This time would be different. This family would come to love me.

The rumbling of my stomach pulled me back into the moment. I jogged downstairs and into the kitchen, which was near the front of the house. It was large with modern finishes. Hues of gray and blue with gleaming white counters.

I assumed the refrigerator would be well-stocked and as I peered inside, I could see I wasn't wrong. I pulled out a carton of eggs, a package of bacon, and fresh bread that had been tucked into a bread box on the counter.

I'd already made myself at home, and it was a wonderful feeling. As I sat down to eat, I made note of the time. Still early, but things had been known to go awry before. I couldn't afford to loiter, no matter how much I'd wanted to relish my new family's life.

Without further delay, I stuffed myself with what remained on my plate and cleaned up the mess. Everything would have to be returned to its precise location, leaving no trace of my presence. Would they miss a few eggs? Probably not.

Realizing the boy would be home soon, I'd retreated to my secret cavern, feeling refreshed and invigorated. Noah was the key to my success. Gaining his trust would ensure my position inside the Hale home. So that was what I'd set out to do.

It wasn't until another hour passed that I heard a car outside. I rushed over to the dormer vent and squinted through the slats. "He's here." Moments later, the sound of young Noah's voice reverberated through the air vents.

As I listened, I reviewed my plan, confirming how best to continue our newfound friendship. Our first conversation had been brief, but had gone well. Below me was the playroom. It was the place where Noah would be most comfortable and where I could begin to earn his trust. I'd learned through my earlier exploration that it was filled with all kinds of games and gadgets, a treasure trove for someone of his age. Patience was now required. Waiting for the perfect moment to strike up another conversation without frightening him.

It was a bold move. One I had not undertaken before. Never had I been so moved by any family as this one. Befriending the boy was my way in.

I stood near the vent that exited through to the attic furnace. These old systems allowed sound to travel easily, so I waited for his voice, or the television from his playroom. Finally, I heard him call out. "I'm going to watch cartoons now," he said to the old lady.

Sound from the television soon arose. Then came the clinking of toys being played with and occasional laughter from Noah.

I smiled at the sound of his voice. So young and innocent. Full of hope, not knowing anything of the real world that awaited him. I almost envied him.

"Hi, Noah." I waited a moment. Had he heard me? I soon got my answer.

"Billy?" Noah asked.

"Yep, I'm here. How was school today?"

"Good. Where are you? Do you live in the attic?"

The boy was curious. Smart. I had to be smarter. "Of course not. I live all around you." The last thing I needed was for Noah to tell Daddy that he had a friend living in the attic. No, I had to make this seem like I was a figment of his imagination.

"Oh, okay. I thought maybe you were just hiding up here." Noah said, with a startling dose of reality. Maybe I wasn't as smart as I thought.

"I wanted to make sure you didn't miss me too much during your time away." I hesitated a moment, knowing I had to cut through the chitchat and get down to business. "Tell me about your daddy, Noah. I'd love to know more about him," I said. "What's his name? Is he fun? Do you play catch with him?"

"Oh, my dad is the best! His name is Jacob." I heard the excitement in his voice. "He works a lot, but that's because he loves me and Mommy so much."

"He sounds like a great dad." I didn't hear any more for a minute, but then Noah continued.

"Billy, do you think we'll ever meet?"

I wavered, unsure of how to answer. "Well, Noah, I guess that depends on you."

CHAPTER 17: LAUREN

Some days, the only thing I looked forward to was going home to see my son. I supposed I looked forward to that every day, but there were times it was the only thing that got me through my work.

As I prepared to leave for the evening, I retrieved the leftovers I'd saved for Gary. I'd come to appreciate the way he stopped by just before five to say hello. Something about him made me think he was a good person. Someone who thought of others before himself.

On returning to my office, I shut down my computer and heard the cart in the hallway. I looked up and there he was. "Evening, Gary. Are you just getting started for the night?"

"Sure am, Miss Lauren."

I liked how he called me Miss Lauren. "Well, you know I brought you something." I walked over to him, noticing the friendly expression on his face and his kind eyes. "I made some spaghetti last night. Thought you might like it."

"That's so kind of you," he said, examining the contents of the Tupperware. "This looks like it'll make for a fantastic dinner. Thank you." A smile arose on his face.

"You're welcome. Enjoy. I'm heading out, so maybe I'll see you tomorrow."

Gary stepped away from my door. "I certainly hope so, Miss Lauren. You and yours have a good night."

"Same to you." I walked out, heading into the lobby and eventually making my way into the parking lot. I climbed into my Lincoln and headed straight for home.

The dusky skies mixed with thin clouds and made for an ominous drive. A storm appeared to be heading our way. I turned up the music to drown out the whistling wind. Some pop artist I didn't know, but it was catchy, nonetheless. I wasn't blind to the fact that plenty of women my age were single. Had no children. Lived a party life. But I'd been forced to grow up quickly. Barely scraping by in college. No time for anything except my studies and work. But when I looked at my son, I regretted nothing.

When I arrived home, and opened the garage door, I noticed Jacob wasn't home, not that it came as much of a surprise. He could be any number of places right now. It was a thought I didn't want to waste another moment on.

Instead, I walked through the door from the garage into the kitchen. "Hello, I'm home." I'd expected to see Nancy sipping on a cup of coffee at the table. Instead, the kitchen was cast in the shadow of a setting sun.

I carried on through to the living room. "There you are." She sat perched on the sofa, reading a book while the fireplace burned.

"Lauren, hello." Nancy closed the book. "I didn't hear you come in. How was your day, sweetheart?"

Nancy often treated me as though I was her daughter. Couldn't say I minded too much, though. "Same as always." I shed my coat and set down my laptop bag. "Where's Noah? How's he been for you today?"

"A peach, as always. He's upstairs watching cartoons, and playing, I suspect." She grunted as she got to her feet. "I'll be heading home, then."

"I appreciate you looking after Noah," I said. "See you tomorrow?"

"Of course." She rubbed my arm a moment. "Have a good night, Lauren." Her gaze drifted up toward the staircase. "Good night, Noah."

"Good night," he called out from beyond the stairs.

I showed Nancy to the door, closing it behind her. "Noah, come down and say hi, would you?" I heard a mild groan before the sound of his footsteps traveled from the landing, and I spotted him on the stairs. "Did you have a good day today?"

He reached the bottom step and wrapped his tiny arms around my neck as I leaned over. "It was okay. I talked to Billy again today."

"Billy?" I asked, pulling upright again. "That's your new friend from school?"

He swatted the air like I was out of my mind. "No, Mommy. Billy is my friend who lives in the walls. Remember?"

* * *

Something pricked the back of my mind as I hovered over the cooktop, the aroma of onion and garlic wafting before me. Noah's new friend sparked reminders of my mother's mental state when I was young. I'd told Noah she passed away before he was born, as had his grandfather. The reality was, I had no idea where either of them were now, nor whether they were still alive. Was there a hereditary element to her behavior? Could it have been passed down to Noah? Or was I simply overreacting to a boy who'd made up a friend?

Headlights flickered through the breakfast nook window as Jacob pulled into our garage. I heard the car's engine rumbling before he turned it off. Should I tell Jacob about Noah's friend? Our marriage seemed to always be perched on a ledge, ready to teeter in either direction at any moment. On the one side, happiness and love. On the other, irritation and annoyance at one another. Which side was on tonight's menu? Especially if I led the conversation with the idea that I believed our son might share some of his grandmother's traits?

Jacob walked inside, his tie already loosened, carrying his briefcase.

"Hi. Did you have a good day?" I only glanced at him, keeping my attention on the cooktop while continuing to make dinner. His dinner. But it didn't take a genius to see that tonight, it would be annoyance and irritation on the menu. The subtle rolling of his eyes at me indicated as much.

"Fine. Just busy." He glanced down at the stove. "What's for dinner?"

"Grilled chicken and vegetables. Roasted potatoes. Should be ready in about twenty minutes. Will you be joining Noah and me at the table?"

"Of course I will. Christ." He stormed off toward the stairs.

His footsteps sounded heavy as he stomped up to our bedroom. I shook my head, letting out a deep sigh. How I wished he was still the man I'd met only a few years ago. So eager to please me.

But time had taken its toll on both of us. The weight of our responsibilities had eroded the passion and tenderness we once shared. I stirred the vegetables absentmindedly, lost in my thoughts — Noah's imaginary friend among them. A persistent itch that refused to be ignored. Maybe it was just harmless imagination, but my history had left me wary.

While the chicken rested, I set the table for three. The sound of Jacob's footsteps descending the stairs made my heart sink. I braced myself for another tense evening, unsure of how to broach the topic of Noah's make-believe friend.

Jacob slumped into his chair at the head of the table, his face etched with exhaustion and frustration. He avoided making eye contact with me, instead staring at his plate. The silence between us was suffocating, heavy with unspoken words. I mustered the courage to break through the tension, to bridge the growing divide that threatened to consume us.

"Jacob, I'm a little concerned about Noah."

He looked up at me. "Concerned how?"

"Well, he's been talking about an imaginary friend." I sat on the edge of the kitchen chair. "And he insists this friend lives here."

Jacob's shoulders slumped even further. "Look, Lauren, let the kid enjoy being a kid, okay? It's perfectly normal for boys his age to do that. Don't create a problem where one doesn't exist."

Frustration knotted my gut, but I knew I needed to quickly change the subject as Noah arrived. "Hi, honey. Why don't you sit down? It's time to eat." He pulled out his chair and climbed into it while I dished out the food.

Noah's eyes sparkled with excitement as he settled into his seat, unaware of the tension that swirled around the table. However, his excitement evaporated the moment he saw his dinner. "Chicken?"

"Sorry, buddy. No pizza tonight." I planted a forced smile. "Isn't it nice that Daddy's having dinner with us? Why don't you tell him what you did at school today?"

Noah's face lit up as he launched into a lively retelling of his adventures, spouting off a long list of activities. I noticed Jacob watching our son with genuine interest, despite his weary expression. It was clear he was grappling with his own internal conflicts, ones that had made him blind to my concerns. And in a risky move I knew could blow up in my face, I asked the question. "Noah, why don't you tell your dad about Billy?"

"Who's Billy?" Jacob asked, seeming oblivious of our conversation only minutes ago.

"That's my friend that lives here with us," Noah replied.

"In our house?" Jacob asked, taking a sip from his glass of water. "Listen, kiddo, no one else lives in this house but you, me, and your mom."

Noah cast down his gaze, appearing defeated, and poking at his food. "Okay, Daddy."

"Good." Jacob cleared his throat as if that was the definitive ending of the conversation. "Then let's eat this delicious meal your mom cooked for us."

CHAPTER 18: GARY

The bright fluorescent lights inside the diner pained my eyes. My shift over, I stopped by the twenty-four hour spot for a cup of coffee. It would be the last warm thing I would have before retiring to the bitterness of a cold and unpleasant attic. That was where I would warm myself only with the thoughts of my family resting peacefully beneath me.

The smell of coffee and fried food had seeped into every surface here. The black vinyl booths. The checkered curtains on the windows. I was sure the walls would bleed grease if they could.

I'd positioned myself in a booth next to the window. It was the middle of the night, and few people were around. The occasional car passed by outside in a blur of light.

Inside, along the back corner, a young man and woman dressed in a strangely dark, gothic manner were whispering to one another. Their hands laced together. Their eyes like glass. A look I'd see often when forced to shelter among the damned, as I had when I couldn't be with my families.

At another booth, a lone man sipped his coffee, mesmerized by the contents on his phone. I glanced through the window and noticed the big rig in the parking lot. It surely belonged to him.

I'd decided on the young couple. A new love? Maybe so. I'd never known such a feeling. Oh, I thought I'd come close once, only to be disillusioned by the end. But this couple, they intrigued me. I wondered how much they loved each other. Would they protect one another if threatened, or would they be selfish, looking out only for themselves? I was about to find out.

I finished my coffee, waiting for several more minutes before the young lovebirds slid out of their booth. As they walked toward the exit, the woman caught my gaze. I smiled. She sneered. Things weren't off to a good start.

With an eye on the parking lot, I paid my tab with cash, leaving a small tip. I respected the woman who served me. She had a family to support, speaking about her children earlier. I'd never been given the chance to know what that was like.

I zipped my coat as I stepped out of the diner. My frosty breath was visible in the night air. I followed the couple, who had almost reached their car that had been parked to the right of the big rig. I looked back into the diner. No one paid me any attention.

When they reached their car, I was still a few yards away. This game was best played in close proximity, but I'd had to wait for my bill. Nevertheless, the woman . . . she glanced over her shoulder at me. There seemed an air of urgency about her now. She sensed who I was, and what I was. I quickened my pace, catching up to them just as they were about to enter. "Excuse me."

The woman looked at me, more like a frightened girl now. "Don't I know your parents?" I asked her.

"What?" Her lips curled at the sight of me.

Could I blame her? A middle-aged man with gaunt features and frayed hair. I'd be afraid, too.

The young man, who stood on the driver's side, stared at me. "Sorry, buddy. You got the wrong person. Her parents don't live here. She doesn't know you, so mind your business, yeah?"

I fixed my gaze on her. "What a shame. Family is so important. The only thing that matters."

"Fuck off, creep." She stepped into the car.

I heard the door lock when she closed it. Her eyes aimed straight ahead, not giving me a second look. But I stared at her, knowing she feared me. Could I still touch her? Feel her warmth? Invoking emotion in another human being propelled me. It meant I wasn't invisible. I was part of this world, whether or not they wanted me to be.

"I just want to talk to you," I called out to her.

When the man stepped into the driver's side, closing his door, I loomed toward the passenger window. "Look at me." I tightened my fist and began to pound on the glass, making her jump in response.

"Drive, Eric. Drive away!" Her muffled voice dripped with panic.

I slammed my hands against the window, pressing my face close to hers so she could see every twisted emotion etched into it. "Don't leave me." I pulled away again, hammering on the glass with all the force in my throbbing hands.

The engine revved, almost drowning out the girl's screams, driving me further into a frenzy as I watched her cower in terror. "I know you. I know where you live. I'll find your family."

Her screams grew louder as she yelled at her boyfriend. "Go! Drive!"

The wheels spun, and smoke drifted from the tires. The car shot off like a bullet. I watched it fade in the distance.

For the moment, I smiled, having filled the void with their fear. It empowered me. It was the control I craved. They lived among the loved, and I was left only to observe that love from a distance, never to have it for myself. But that would soon change.

CHAPTER 19: DETECTIVE COLLINS

The noise of the station house was usually easy for me to tune out. Not today. Today, every noise grated on my nerves. I'd struck out at the homeless encampments. I suppose I wasn't expecting much, especially without some kind of physical description of the guy I was looking for. But a part of me still believed there was something to the theory Dixon presented. So how else to go about learning where this killer came from? How had he known about the families? And why had he decided to kill them?

Where was I supposed to go from here? I needed the evidence to talk to me, and right now it was saying, *Good luck, bitch. You ain't going nowhere.* I laughed at myself, drawing unwanted attention from my coworkers.

"You all right there, Collins?" Dixon asked as he eyed me from behind his desk.

"Yeah, I'm all right. Just ready to pull my hair out, you know?"

"I do." He walked over to me, standing in front of my desk with his hands in his pockets, nodding the way he always did when he knew something that I didn't. "So, uh, what happened yesterday? Did you strike out?"

"Jack shit happened. No one there knew anything — or if they did, had no interest in talking to me." I tossed the file onto my desk. "Got any other ideas?"

He picked it up, quickly scanning its contents. "No hits on your contact DNA."

I leaned back in my chair, folding my arms. "No prints in the system. Evidence isn't turning up shit for me. And I was up all last night re-examining those two other investigations. They didn't turn up squat, either. Lockhart doesn't have any more details."

"You got ten people dead and nothing? Yeah, that's not going to cut it with the captain." Dixon raised an eyebrow, the skepticism clear in his eyes. "Not trying to tell you what's what, but did you rule out your unknown DNA sample against other relatives of the Tomlins? Collect any of their DNA? This happened near the holidays. Any family pay them a visit around that time?"

I rubbed my forehead. "I've talked to all of them. Didn't get samples, but they all had solid alibis. They're cooperating, but if you think it's worth my time to get them down here . . ."

"It's your case; you gotta run it the way you see fit. Go with your gut." Dixon studied me for a moment. "I might be able to put in a call or two. See if I get anywhere with the Cold Case unit. Still could be something there that'll tie this thing up for you."

"I reached out. They're looking again, but I'm not going to hold my breath."

"Let me see what I can do." He raised his finger. "Have you checked the security cameras in the area? Ring cameras from the neighbors?"

"No offense, Dixon, I appreciate your input, but I been down that road already. Harding had been down that road too, according to his notes." I sighed, rubbing the back of my neck. "I've gone through their friends, family, and coworkers. Everyone has an alibi. None of the families had enough money for that to have been a motive. Shit, I don't know."

Dixon returned the folder to me. "Listen, you gotta work the case. I know you know how."

I raised my palms. "What am I missing? Putting all these cases together makes this guy a goddamn serial killer. Maybe I need to ask the captain if we should bring in the feds for help. I mean, who the hell is this guy?"

Dixon perched on the edge of my desk. "You don't need the feds. We don't need them. Someone doesn't just decide to take out entire families while they sleep." He rubbed his smooth chin. "Send me all three cases. Let me take a deeper dive and see what I can turn up."

"You saying you want in on this?"

He raised the corner of his lips. "You saying you don't need the help?"

CHAPTER 20: GARY

Why was he still here? Jacob should've left for work thirty minutes ago, yet I hadn't heard the garage door open, or seen his car emerge from it. I'd meticulously tracked the Hales' schedule. Lauren and Noah had kept to their routine. Something was wrong. Did Jacob suspect Noah had been telling the truth about me? Had I risked too much by attempting to befriend the boy? He was my way in. The only way I could be certain Lauren would come to love me.

A muffled voice echoed from below and drew my attention. I stepped away from the dormer vent and tiptoed across the plywood floor, mindful of the creaking noises. I knelt down, leaning an ear toward the ground where Jacob's baritone voice reverberated. "He's on the phone."

The manner of his voice was almost unrecognizable. Soft, kind even. Not like the brash, harsh tenor I'd heard him speak to his wife and child in the mornings before leaving for work. When I heard him laugh, that was when I understood. "A woman."

A woman was on the other end of the call. I was certain of that. But who? Not his wife. I'd learned enough about their marriage to realize that much. Was Jacob flirting? Oh yes, flirting most certainly, but could it be more?

I felt heat rise in my chest, flushing my cheeks with anger. How could he do this to his family? Who was this woman, and had he been cheating on Lauren?

The thought of Jacob betraying his family was too much to bear, and I wasn't about to let him get away with it. I continued to listen, straining my ears to catch more snippets of their conversation.

". . . I can't wait to see you later," Jacob's voice echoed. My heart ached for Lauren as Jacob revealed his true self. How long had this been going on? How many lies had he spun to keep his secret hidden?

If Jacob was having an affair, I needed evidence to expose him. Lauren and Noah deserved to know the truth, even if it would shatter their world. And if it served my purpose, then all the better.

Several minutes passed before I heard the front door close and an engine rev. I hurried to the dormer and craned my neck toward the driveway. Jacob was backing out. "Finally." I retreated to my little corner of the attic to gather my things.

A piss and a shower were what I needed first. It would give me time to devise a plan of action. Jacob would not get away with betraying Lauren like this.

After I readied myself, the time had come to search for the truth. I walked into Jacob's den, full of law books, and smelling of too much cologne. I searched for something that might point to who he had been speaking to earlier. Who was this woman? Did he work with her? Was she a client?

Jacob's desk was clean, almost obsessively so. But something did appear prominent. I smiled, picking up one of the cards from the stack neatly placed in a silver holder. "Jacob Hale, Partner. Mullen, Gossett, and Hale." I tucked the card into my pocket for later reference.

The desk drawers were locked as I tried to open each one. The file cabinets too. What I'd now come to understand was that Jacob didn't trust Lauren with anything relating to his business. I supposed that extended to his apparent work-related side piece too.

Minutes ticked by and still nothing. I stepped back, giving the room another once-over, in the event I had missed something. But Jacob kept his secret well-hidden. Maybe nothing was here at all, and I'd put my focus on the wrong location.

The clock was about to run out, and I had to make a decision before Noah returned from school. Would I continue to explore our relationship, molding the child to believe what I wanted him to believe, or was it best to act now? Moving forward with my plans as a result of Jacob's misdeeds?

Maybe there was another way to get answers. And when I had them, I could be better equipped to offer them to Lauren without pulling the veil from my own intentions.

I returned to the attic, snatching a granola bar and bottle of water from the kitchen pantry. After finishing my snack, I'd reached my decision.

"Time to go." I climbed through the slatted door of the dormer vent, stepping down onto the trellis to begin my descent. Each metal rung pressed against my palms. But it was the chill of the winter air seeping through my jacket that kept me alert. I was mindful of passersby, and nosy neighbors, though most were probably working. Except the old lady. She would leave soon to pick up little Noah. I had to be quick.

As I reached the ground, I surveyed the area. The neighborhood was quiet, save for the distant sound of a leaf blower. Satisfied that I hadn't attracted any attention, I set off down the street.

I walked two blocks down, where I kept my car. Jumping inside, the warmth of the heater finally took hold. Jacob's office was my destination, knowing I could learn more about his female caller if I simply waited.

I navigated the now familiar streets. This neighborhood had already begun to feel like home, and I feared losing that. It occurred to me I was taking risks I never had before.

The gray clouds above reflected my mood as they hung low in the sky, threatening to unleash at any moment. Raindrops soon trickled down the windshield, almost keeping time with my racing thoughts. Double-checking the address on the business card, I drove on.

Jacob's office was located in the heart of downtown Alexandria, wedged between a bustling coffee shop, and an old antiques store with a restaurant above. The building, itself, complemented the historic area, its brick facade blending seamlessly with the others on the street. But I wasn't here for a history lesson. I needed answers.

I parked my car several yards from the front of the law offices, stepping out and draping the hoodie over my head as the rain continued. I reached the building and walked around to the parking lot on the side. There it was — Jacob's shiny black Porsche. A beautiful car that symbolized wealth and power. Everything Jacob wanted to have, and be. Yet it seemed his actions may have put it all on the line. Not unlike my own.

CHAPTER 21: LAUREN

How was it possible to still be miserable after spending nearly one hundred thousand dollars renovating my colonial home? When I'd embarked on the remodeling journey, I recalled Tammy telling me that my home would be beautiful — all the old parts repaired or replaced. But it wouldn't fix things. I knew what she'd meant. Even if I kept things from her, she knew.

And it seemed she was right. I had a beautiful home, but I still felt empty and alone. Now I had my son creating imaginary friends. I'd begun to think that he'd picked up on the strains of his parents' marriage, and this was the end result.

I glanced at the time, realizing it was noon and Noah would be home from school soon. The thought of him brought a smile to my face as I sat behind my desk, staring at a spreadsheet full of numbers that had begun to meld together.

The buzz from my phone snapped me out of my trance. An incoming text message from Tammy. "Speak of the devil." I read her message confirming our lunch date and typed my reply. *Yes, absolutely. I'm ready when you are.*

I needed the break from work, and the intrusive thoughts, so I snatched my things and headed into the hallway. Tammy was still in her office when I arrived at her door. Moments passed without her noticing my arrival. "Well? Are we getting out of here, or what?"

Tammy got to her feet. "That bad, huh? Let's go then." She circled around her desk, making her way toward me. "What do you feel like today?"

"Sushi?" I asked.

"Perfect."

We carried on outside and headed down the street. A great local sushi bar that catered to the business crowd was located only a few hundred feet away.

On our arrival, it appeared busier than usual, but we got a table. I followed the host and slipped into the booth. Tammy slid in across from me. When we placed our orders, I peered through the window that overlooked more buildings and tree-lined sidewalks.

"You want to talk about it?" Tammy asked, clearly sensing my somber mood.

I sighed; my gaze still fixed on the bustling street outside. "It's just . . . everything feels so off lately. The distance between me and Jacob. I feel alone. And now it looks like Noah has imagined himself a friend . . . one he says lives in our house."

Tammy was quiet for a moment, sipping on her Diet Coke.

"What is it?" I asked.

She peered down a moment, as if considering her words carefully. When she captured my gaze again, she continued, "Lauren, I hate seeing you so unhappy. I know you'd hoped that the renovations would change things — somehow make you and Jacob whole again, but I think we both know that hasn't happened."

"No." I unwrapped the paper from my chopsticks.

"And clearly, Noah is having a hard time too. He's picking up on your stress."

The server set down our sushi rolls and quickly dismissed herself.

"He made up a friend." I shook my head. "Gave him a name and everything."

Tammy raised a brow. "Sounds like he's looking for attention. I mean, look, my kid's obviously older now, but I do remember when he was Noah's age. And yeah, they got pretty creative with their stories, but I think this is something you need to keep an eye on with Noah. I know you have your neighbor looking after him until you get home, but maybe consider getting him into a sport or some other activity for kids his age."

"When am I supposed to take him to stuff like that, Tammy?" I asked, feeling that all this rested on my shoulders. Which, I knew it did.

She leaned back in the booth. "I know it's tough. I remember. Between work and trying to maintain the house, it feels like there aren't enough hours in the day. Maybe you can find a way to reorganize your schedule or ask for some flexibility at work. It might be worth exploring."

Her suggestion struck a chord. I had been so caught up in my own struggles that I had neglected to fully consider Noah's needs. Tammy was right — he needed an outlet, a way to channel his energy and emotions. Something that would make him forget about imaginary people.

I took a deep breath, feeling a glimmer of hope. "Yeah, you're right. I need to prioritize Noah. I'll talk to Chuck. Maybe he'll work with me."

"You never know. He gets it more than you think he does." She aimed her chopsticks at me. "But don't let Jacob off too easily, you hear me?"

I raised the corner of my lips into a smile. "I hear you."

CHAPTER 22: GARY

Jacob rounded the corner of his office building, heading toward the parking lot. Dressed in a dark suit, his gray peacoat flapped in the cold breeze. He secured a button and carried on toward his car.

I kept an eye on him from inside my stolen ride, laying low to avoid being seen. My goal was to follow him to see where he was headed. Could've been going to a business meeting for all I knew. But given the lunch hour, I suspected he used his break for other, more nefarious reasons.

He stepped into his expensive Porsche SUV, and I waited for him to pull out of the parking lot. When he did, I trailed him, careful to remain undetected. I was no super-sleuth, but I knew how to remain covert in my movements. I'd been doing it for a long time.

As he drove along the busy city streets, I followed. My eyes constantly scanned for any sign of being noticed. I was determined to catch him doing Lauren wrong, but even I could admit, I'd taken this farther and risked more than I should. Nevertheless, this was for the sake of my family, Noah and Lauren, and the future that I wanted for them.

Jacob slowed down as he pulled into a parking lot. I turned in, heading the other direction. When I stopped, I gazed through the rearview and watched him step out. Before he closed his car door, he reached inside and picked up a bouquet of flowers. Interesting.

Ahead was a restaurant. Quaint, rustic, as though dining in a cozy cottage. The outside was adorned with empty flower-pots as winter stifled new life. He cast around his gaze appearing to search for someone. Then, without another moment's hesitation, Jacob entered.

I wasn't going to get to the bottom of this without further investigation. So, I took my chances and stepped out of the car. Jacob didn't know I existed, so a disguise was a little pointless. Still, I pulled up the hood of my jacket and walked toward the entrance. Windows lined the wall facing the parking lot, and that was when I saw them. Jacob kissed her on the cheek and sat down next to her in the cozy booth. A young woman with long blond hair and a bright smile. "So you're the reason for the flowers." Now, I was angry.

What could I do? What evidence could I garner, and present to Lauren anonymously? "Only one way to find out." I stepped inside and found a seat on the opposite end, remaining obscured behind a large wooden column in front of me.

"Afternoon."

I drew my gaze upward to see the server.

"What can I get for you today?"

She was an older woman with a friendly smile. I gave her my attention. "Just coffee for now, please." She rolled her eyes at me and walked away. Not so friendly after all.

The server wasn't my concern at present, Jacob Hale and his mistress were. I leaned to the right for a better view. They talked and laughed, their conversation flowing easily between them. I couldn't hear their words, but I could see the warmth in their interaction. They seemed to know each other well. But I still didn't know anything about her.

Who was this woman? And more importantly, what did it mean for Lauren and all I was trying to accomplish? The Hales were supposed to be different. They were supposed to be the ones. Now, Jacob might have to be removed from the equation.

After an extended lunch, the two walked out of the restaurant. I'd paid my bill and waited a moment to follow them.

Outside, I noticed the woman stepping into her car, and Jacob getting into his. It was her who I needed to follow. Her origins would be revealed to me then. And to no one's surprise, I followed her straight back to Mullen, Gossett, & Hale. Jacob's law firm. Now, to find out exactly who she was and what threat she posed to my family.

My shift was set to begin in less than two hours. Not much time to learn more about the blond harlot, who compromised my very existence. I couldn't miss visiting Lauren. I had to arrive in time to see her off for the evening. But if I wanted answers, I'd need to wait for the woman to leave. Could I stick around long enough without jeopardizing it all? I had an idea how to make that happen. I picked up my phone and made the call.

"911, what is your emergency?"

I peered through the windshield. "Someone walked into the office building at 917 King Street and left a duffel bag inside. It's still here, and he's not. Please . . . send some help. I don't know what it is."

"What is your name, sir?"

I ended the call, setting down the cell phone that couldn't be traced back to me.

Within minutes, the office building emptied. People rushed out to escape the chaos I had created. I took another look at the throngs spilling out of the front door. My eyes skimmed the evacuating crowd for any sign of the woman or Jacob. I had pushed this to the point of no return.

The sirens grew louder, so if I was going to do this, it had to be now. I opened my driver's side door and stepped out into the parking lot. I made my way toward the greens where everyone from the building now waited.

No one would ask why I was there, only assuming I'd worked inside. That was my cover. I meandered toward Jacob as he navigated through the crowd, until eventually moving in toward the blonde.

I came up behind them, listening in on their conversation while sirens wailed in the distance. I had but moments to learn her identity before being forced to make a hasty exit.

Jacob wore a smug look, like he had the upper hand in this whole situation. Like he was in control. Far from it. I had the power here.

The blond harlot, whose name I still didn't know, appeared nervous but excited, her eyes darting around for eavesdroppers. "Well, well, well. I wonder who arranged this little meeting."

Jacob shrugged, a smirk creeping onto his face. "Don't look at me. If this was a prank, then whoever did it might have committed a federal crime. My hands are clean."

I watched Jacob as he casually placed his arm over her shoulders, not drawing too much attention to their closeness.

She snuggled up next to him, but only briefly before gauging the reaction of others who surrounded them. "Then I should thank whoever made the call."

I looked on while another woman approached them. She eyed the blonde.

"Maddy, I heard this was a prank. You hear anything?" the woman asked.

"No, nothing," she replied.

Maddy. Her name was Maddy. Short for Madison, Madeline? Hard to say. This was a good start, but my time was up. I just wanted a little more information. Just a few more moments before I made my exit amid the rumbling crowd.

When the other woman walked away, Maddy turned back to Jacob. "She seems suspicious."

Jacob pulled in close. "Maddy, if word gets out about us . . ."

She raised a preemptive hand, "I know. I know."

There it was. Confirmation, at least, as much confirmation as I needed. I had a name and the fact that the two were involved. I made my escape, slipping away from the crowd and back into the parking lot where I jumped into my car.

I drove through the city streets, making my way to see Lauren. Beautiful Lauren, who was being deceived by her husband. Betrayed by the man she loved. How would I make this known to her? The sound of sirens still echoed in my ears, a reminder of the bedlam I'd left behind. Every moment, worth its weight in gold.

As I entered the parking lot of Ackerman & James, I searched for Lauren's car. Relief swept through me at the sight of it. "You're still here."

From the confines of my vehicle, I hurriedly changed into my coveralls. Soon, I emerged and headed toward the entrance, where some of the staff was already heading home for the night.

Dusk had settled with traces of light spilling in through the windows of the lobby. I carried on inside, nodding to the assistant behind the front desk.

"Evening, Gary," she said.

"Evening, Karen. You have a good night." I swiped my badge and walked on without turning back for a response. I had places to be. I had to see Lauren.

I rushed to the maintenance room that doubled as my office. Clocking in, I noticed the time. "Damn. I'm pushing it." I began to gather supplies for my cleaning cart, knowing I'd have to be quick to catch her.

With my back against the open door, I guided my cart out into the hallway. Take a breath. Slow down. Don't look panicked. I told myself this over and over until I felt my pulse return to normal. Eventually, I reached Lauren's office.

There she was. Innocent. Unknowing of her husband's infidelity. But how was I going to pull this off? "Evening, Miss Lauren."

She looked up at me, setting down her pen. "Oh, is it that time already?"

"Time for you to go home? Yes, I think it is," I said, smiling at her. "Must've been another busy day for you, huh?"

"No busier than usual. I've got a few things to wrap up, Gary. You don't mind coming back in a bit, do you?"

"Not at all. You do what you need to do." I started off when I heard her call my name. Her voice was the sweetest sound I'd ever heard. I walked back, leaving my cart several steps ahead. "Yes?"

"I'm afraid I didn't bring any leftovers for you tonight," she said with guilt masking her face.

"Now, don't you think twice about that, Miss Lauren. I got plenty of food here to eat. Don't get me wrong, I appreciate what you do for me, but you shouldn't go through the trouble, all right?"

"It's no trouble." Lauren wore compassion in her gaze. "I'll make a double recipe tonight, so I have enough to bring in." She raised her hand at me as I prepared to speak. "I won't hear it. I'm bringing it for you to taste. I thought I might try a new recipe. I could use the input."

I loved her. I loved everything about her. Warm, kind, compassionate. My God, she was a dream. "Thank you, Miss Lauren. I won't turn you down. Good night."

"Good night, Gary."

CHAPTER 23: DETECTIVE COLLINS

The night shift was clocking in, and noise and chaos surrounded me. From my desk, I entered the commands into CODIS for the third time today, praying a DNA match would somehow appear. Instead, more of the same, which was nothing. No matches to the single DNA transfer sample we had in the Tomlin file. The other cases didn't even have that much. I should've counted myself lucky.

"Hey, Collins, you okay?"

I peered over at Detective Dixon. "Still hoping for a miracle."

"No breaks yet, I take it," he replied. "Unfortunately, my efforts haven't yielded much either."

"Just keep hitting a brick wall, man." I couldn't contain my frustration as I slumped back in my chair. "How the hell has no one seen this guy? Nothing on security cameras. No car that I've seen."

"Oh, I imagine his victims saw him, but were murdered shortly thereafter," Dixon replied.

"Fair point." The case weighed on my mind. The gruesome images of the murdered Tomlins flashed through my thoughts once again — their bodies sprawled across their beds, the walls splattered with blood. The mother, who seemingly realized too late what was about to happen.

"What more can I do to pitch in?" Dixon asked.

I forced myself from my chair and walked over to the murder board. Hands on my hips, I stared at it. "Nothing for now. Something will break and when it does . . ."

"I'll have your back," he jumped in.

The board was covered in photos of the crime scenes. Images of items left in the homes. Theories representing every lead I had pursued. I'd added the other families now as well. Captain was pissed we only just discovered the connection. And as I glanced at the clock on the wall, I realized my shift was over.

I knew I should go home, but what awaited me there, except an empty apartment? I could read a book. Order take-out. Meanwhile, a killer roamed free, probably staking out his next victim, if he hadn't already. So, was I going home? No. To hell with that.

I turned back to Dixon, raising my index finger. "Maybe there is something more you can do."

"Name it." He got up and joined me at the board.

I walked closer to it, examining each note that I'd pinned to it. "The home where the Tomlins were killed . . . You feel like running out there with me?"

"Now?" He checked his watch. "It's gonna be dark soon."

"I know. The house still has power."

"Okay, so what are you thinking? Forensics has scoured the place, twice, from what you've said. So has CSI. What do you think they missed?"

I couldn't help but feel a tug on my lips. "Come with me. I have an idea."

"Well, all right."

I grabbed my things and waited for Dixon as he prepared to leave. I had to figure out how the killer got inside the Tomlin home. How he remained undetected. If what the friends and relatives of this family had said was true, then either this killer was a goddamn ghost, or he was one stealthy bastard. And if I could figure out which, then maybe it would open some doors for this and the other cases.

We jumped into my Ford sedan and headed north on Richmond Highway, then west toward Mount Vernon Avenue. Took about forty minutes, thanks to rush-hour traffic, but we'd arrived in the area known as Potomac West. I drove down Mosby Street and parked along the curb in front of the Tomlin home. The sun was long gone, leaving behind a bright moon and clear skies. But along with that came the bitter cold. I reached into the backseat and grabbed my coat, eyeing Dixon. "You ready?"

He stepped out to join me. "You got keys to this place?"

"Of course I do." I walked to the front door and retrieved the key.

Dixon clenched his square jaw. "Where'd you get that?"

"I have friends in high places," I snickered. "And I am the lead detective."

He gestured outward. "After you, Lead Detective."

I opened the door, stepping inside the darkened home. A light switch was on the wall just inside the entrance and I flipped it on. It illuminated a scene frozen in time. The furniture, once neatly arranged, now appeared in disarray. The smell of death clung to every surface.

Dixon followed closely behind me, his footsteps echoing in the silence. His hand instinctively gripping the butt of his sidearm. "He left behind some damage. Means someone fought back."

"I figured it was the dad," I replied. "The kids were fairly young, and the killer probably went for them after the mom. Then, he took a shot at Dad. Maybe Dad put up a fight, or maybe the killer left things this way to make it look like he did."

We moved farther into the house, and while I was careful, I also knew the house had been swept multiple times. I wasn't going to get lucky enough to find more evidence, as I had with the earring.

Family photos still adorned the walls. They looked happy. But the rest of the house told a different story, altogether. A chilling tale of savagery. The thought of it was unsettling, and any detective who denied this shit got to them was lying.

"Where the hell did he get in if he'd been out in the storm cellar?" Dixon asked.

"That's what we're here to find out," I replied.

We moved from room to room, searching for clues and overlooked details. The silence was disturbed only by the faint creaks of aged floorboards beneath our feet. Each step we took felt like trespassing over a gravesite.

"If we can find out how he gained access and if he managed to hole up in here somewhere, chances are, we'll find crucial evidence," I said. "Short of that, I'd be happy with a better take on this guy's M.O."

"Something to open this thing up for us." Dixon nodded. "The cellar. You said the mother got it first. She found him in the cellar."

"We cleaned that out pretty good, in fact, I found the earring there. I didn't see anything else, but another set of eyes can't hurt."

"The front door was never unlocked," he continued.

"I see you did read the file." I turned back toward him. "Yeah, so, then how did he reach the main house? No windows were broken. No locks busted. The guy didn't break in. He was already here. He had to be."

"Then there's a way through the cellar. Makes sense," Dixon added. "You know these old houses. I mean, what's this place? Damn near a hundred years old or more?"

"About that. Let's look for a passageway, then."

As if on cue, a low creaking sound echoed through the house, causing us both to freeze. We exchanged a glance, my instincts suggesting we were no longer alone.

"Did you hear that?" Dixon brandished his weapon.

"I heard it. It came from this way." I motioned for him to follow me as we headed toward the source. It was coming from the back of the house, down the hallway and past the kitchen. I held out my hand to stop him, then listened for the sound to come again. Just as I started . . . "Shh. That's it." I aimed my finger ahead. We walked down to the end of the hall where a door appeared. It shifted as if caught in a breeze. "This is the utility room. We searched it already."

Dixon stepped inside. "Let's take another look. There's air coming through here. It moved the door. If there's a secret passageway into the cellar, I'll bet it's in here."

A washer and dryer lay pushed against the wall. Something in me knew, if a secret passageway existed, it would be behind here. "Check this out." I walked over to the washer. "There's a draft coming from here. Help me move this thing."

Dixon stepped in, grabbing one side while I pulled on the other. The metal feet with rubber ends slid with some resistance. "This would've had to be moved when no one was home. It's making too much noise," I said.

"Oh, yeah. Son of a bitch is heavy, too." He tugged a little more. "There. Look there."

I stood on tip toes and leaned over the back. "What do you know? This must've been a trash or laundry chute back in the day."

"Going straight into the cellar, no doubt." Dixon looked at me. "You going in or am I?"

"You aren't getting in there, no offense. Which means our killer isn't a big guy, despite having to move this thing out of the way each time." I slipped around the machine, crouching low as I reached the opening. "He came in through here after he killed the mother. Take a look at the metal door." I aimed my finger at the metal panel next to me. "I don't know how we didn't see this."

"Would've been easy to miss, Collins," Dixon added. "It's a laundry room with an access behind the washing machine."

"Maybe." I carried on, crawling through the opening. It was too level to be a chute. No drop in elevation. It could've been used as a transport of some kind, maybe alcohol. "Meet me in the cellar," I called out. "There must be a hidden entrance in there."

"Got it," he yelled back.

As I made my way through the dark tunnel, barely large enough for me, I noticed a hint of light seeping in. "The cellar. I see it. Are you there, man?"

I waited for Dixon to reply but realized he must not have made it yet, so I continued. The narrow passageway was brick-lined. The brick on the floor was chipped and cracked, years of decay had taken its toll. It was clear to me now that this was how the killer got in and out of the home. How Eleanor Tomlin discovered him, I had no idea, but there was no doubt in my mind that she had been the first to be killed.

"You coming out, or what?"

It was Dixon, his voice bellowing through the tunnel. "Almost there," I replied. I soon reached the end and crawled out to find him holding a blanket with gloved hands. "What's that?"

"Found this over there." He tossed a nod toward the back. "This blanket, a small pillow, and a candle."

"Holy shit." I examined the blanket. "He lived here, at least until Eleanor discovered him. Or he feared she would."

Dixon wore a broad smile. "We might get lucky enough to pull DNA off these things."

"I hope you're right. But if not, we know his M.O. And I'll bet we'll find similar set ups in the other victims' homes." I set my hands on my hips, still eyeing the blanket and pillow. "We're getting closer now."

CHAPTER 24: GARY

When I'd returned to my family in the early hours of the morning, every fiber of my being yearned to storm into Lauren's bedroom and confront Jacob, to rip the life from his eyes. But I knew it would tear apart the fragile bond I'd just begun to develop with her and Noah. Nevertheless, I would find a way to make Jacob pay for what he'd done to my family.

Now, as the Hales went about their daily routines, I found myself sequestered in the cold confinement of the attic, biding my time for the opportune moment to set my plan in motion. The sky outside slowly brightened, casting a pale glow through the dusty space.

When I was certain I was alone, I went through the motions of my morning routine. The warm water of the shower did little to soothe my nerves, instead offering only warmth to my skin.

I'd gone downstairs and turned on the television. Keeping on top of police efforts to find me was essential to my survival.

The comfortable sofa beckoned me as I made myself at home. Soon, this would be my home. The morning news broadcast traffic conditions around the city. "Come on. Just get to the headlines." Several minutes later, they'd begun to repeat the top stories. "Okay. Now we're talking." I took on a defiant stance.

"*We have a major breakthrough in the case of the Tomlin family murders*," the anchor announced, her voice tinged with morbid excitement.

"*According to Alexandria police, the family of four, brutally murdered in their home back in December, had been the victims of an intruder. This intruder, we now know, had already been inside the home, waiting for the family. Possibly, taking shelter there for some time. Police say they are still awaiting forensics results. They've asked the public for information on anyone they might have witnessed around the Tomlin home at the time of the murders . . .*"

I stood on trembling legs, anger filling my chest. I looked down at the coffee table, snatching the candleholder on top of it. With all my weight behind it, I threw it against the fireplace. The high-pitched sound of shattering glass crashing against the tile surrounds echoed. "No!"

No, this couldn't be. I'd been so careful. Had they found where I'd hidden? It was possible, even if they'd left out that juicy detail. Wasn't that how the cops operated? Not giving away too much?

Several minutes passed while I ran through the various scenarios I'd concocted in the event I needed to flee. But then I looked at the mess I'd created. "For God's sake." I spun around, peering through the front window. Noah would be home soon.

I rushed into the kitchen in search of a broom. I'd broken Lauren's candleholder. How could I hide that? She would see that it was missing. "Noah." He would be home at any moment, and I would be discovered. I wasn't ready to end his life or the old lady's. I didn't want to. It was a measure of last resort. "For God's sake, what have I done?"

Time slipped through my fingers as I hurried to wipe away all traces of my anger. I held a kitchen bag, sweeping the glass into it. Now, to dispose of the bag before it was too late.

I caught sight of movement from the window. A car had driven by. Was it the old lady? I stood in the middle of the living room, television on, holding a bag of broken glass. This would've been comical had it not been so damning. I scanned the room in search of the remote, spotting it on the sofa. I turned off the TV, taking care to place the remote exactly where I'd found it.

There was no time to take away the bag. If I didn't retreat to my attic, I would be discovered, and I wasn't ready to lose Lauren, or the boy. "Run."

Taking the stairs two at a time, I reached the landing. The attic scuttle was only steps away, but I still had to climb the ladder. I pulled it down, disregarding the creaking hinges because I was still alone for the moment.

Holding the bag, I climbed. The broken glass clinked against the steps. As I reached the top, I hoisted it up. The bottom edge of it scraped against my pants, piercing my skin. "Goddamn it." I cringed, closing the scuttle, and hurrying to my corner.

I stood frozen, panting, adrenaline pumping through my veins, forcing blood to soak my pants from the laceration in my leg.

And then, the moment arrived. The sound of footsteps echoed in the walls and through the vents as Noah ascended the stairs. Had I forgotten anything? Left any trace of my presence? If I had, no doubt the police would soon arrive. But I waited. No urgent phone call from the old lady. It seemed she suspected nothing.

I let out my breath, knowing I'd made it, and realizing my reckless mistake. Noah might not have known I was here, but Lauren would suspect something strange had happened when she noticed her missing candleholder.

Never mind that now. I was safe for the moment. As Noah made his way to his little game room in the loft, I positioned myself near the vent, straining my ears to catch the faint sounds of his favorite cartoons emanating from the television below. Could I compose myself well enough to press on with my plan?

Summoning all my acting skills, I adopted a soft, child-like tone as I spoke through the vent, my voice carrying a hint of familiarity and lightheartedness. "Hi, Noah. I'm so glad you're home. How was school today?" I held my breath, waiting for a response, praying he had come to think of me as a friend.

Several moments elapsed in silence, causing a knot to tighten in my gut. "Are you there, Noah?" I asked, growing desperate for a response.

"I'm here."

I closed my eyes and exhaled with relief. He hadn't dismissed me as his new, albeit imaginary friend.

"Did you have fun today at school?" I asked again.

"I guess so. Where are you?"

His voice seemed to carry a hint of suspicion. "I'm all around you, silly. We're friends, remember? You gave me a name and everything."

"Yeah, I know. I was just checking."

His voice wavered with uncertainty. I had pushed too far. This could easily unravel at any moment.

"What do you look like, Billy?"

Noah's question caught me off guard. He was looking for assurance as though he attempted to reinforce the nature of our connection.

"Well, what do you want me to look like?" I asked. "I guess I look a little like you. We could be brothers, Noah. Wouldn't that be fun?" Had I managed to salvage the relationship, or had I pushed the boundaries so far even a four-year-old couldn't suspend disbelief?

I was out of time, and chances. Now was the moment before I'd lost him completely. "Hey, Noah?"

"Yeah?" he replied.

At least he was talking again. I leaned closer to the vent. "Could you tell your daddy something for me?"

"My daddy?" I heard confusion in his tone, yet he continued, "Okay."

And in as casual a voice as I could muster, I added, "Tell him that I know what he's done."

Noah couldn't possibly comprehend my meaning. I had to work harder to convince him to relay my message so that Jacob would understand.

"What did my daddy do?"

"He'll know. Just tell him exactly what I said. It's really important, okay?" I waited a moment. Maybe I'd already lost him. "I'll be your best friend if you do. Don't you want to be my best friend?"

"Yeah."

CHAPTER 25: DETECTIVE COLLINS

At last, after endless leads and dead ends, a breakthrough in the case had been made. The pieces fell into place, and I finally knew how the killer had accessed the Tomlin home.

Dixon and I had searched every inch of the small alcove where the killer had sheltered. It was barely big enough for one person, let alone a grown man. This discovery told me that our culprit was not a physically imposing individual — he relied on surprise and vulnerability to carry out his brutal murders. It would have been nearly impossible for him to overpower the father, who had been a strong and commanding man.

Now, we pushed for finding a DNA match to the unknown genetic material on the earring. We had the killer's blanket and other items that I'd turned over to Forensics first thing this morning. Hair, fibers, anything that would give us another DNA sample to compare.

This new revelation brought with it a new path for me to take. The killer chose this family for a reason. If I could find that reason, I might learn where he intended on striking next. But what was even better was that I had a description of this killer. Not much, but it was something.

Now, I needed to find out who had access to the family home in the months leading up to their deaths. A tradesman? Landscaper? Handyman? I still couldn't rule out the possibility of a transient. I could then cross-reference that information with the other cases. I might get lucky enough to find a match. Someone each of the victims had known in some form or another.

My attention was drawn to Dixon as he returned to his desk.

"It'll take Forensics days or weeks to pull DNA. What's the plan in the meantime?" he asked.

I rolled back in my chair. "We know the killer is a small to medium built man, not particularly strong."

Dixon nodded. "Patient. He waited for the right opportunity."

"And we have no idea how long he stayed concealed in the house before carrying out the murders. That's why I want to focus on any visitors the family may have had in their home over the few months prior to their murders."

"I can help with that."

I snatched the report from my desk and handed it to him. "Information on the Tomlin neighbors. Interviews conducted when it happened. This was before I took over the case but see if anything pops out at you. I'll check again with friends and relatives. See who else they know that might've had access to the home."

CHAPTER 26: LAUREN

When it was time to leave the office today, I had somehow managed to miss Gary. But I hadn't forgotten my promise. I'd brought him plenty of leftovers and placed a sticky note on the Tupperware dish with his name on it. I'd left it in the employee fridge, and then walked to Maintenance to leave a note for him on the desk.

Now, as I prepared dinner for my family again after a long day at work, I wondered if he'd seen the note. He'd been so kind to me, and he clearly needed the food. In fact, did he even have a permanent roof over his head? So many people now worked multiple jobs and still didn't have enough for rent.

And here I stood, cloaked in the drama of my own life. A distant husband, who I suspected was having an affair. Financial resources far beyond what I could ever need. A stunning home that served as a testament to my prosperity. And a son who had made up a friend to compensate for something I hadn't yet discovered. It was moments like these that reminded me of the importance of perspective. Gary, with his unwavering kindness, most likely lacked the basic necessities.

Noah's footsteps echoed through the house as he descended the stairs and ventured into the kitchen. "Mommy, is dinner ready yet?"

I appreciated the hint of anticipation in his tone — then again, he didn't know what I was cooking. "Almost. Are you getting hungry?"

"Yeah. Is Daddy having dinner with us tonight too?"

I looked at Noah for a moment. He wore an expression I hadn't seen before. Dread? No, it couldn't be. But his big brown eyes revealed a strange reluctance. "Let me see if he sent me a message." I grabbed my phone from the kitchen island. Sure enough, Jacob had sent a text that read he was heading home. "Looks like he will. That'll be nice, won't it? Having Daddy here for dinner?"

I would've expected a smile, but instead, I was met with a simple nod.

"Okay. I'm going back upstairs till dinner's ready."

"All right." I should've been happy he asked if his dad was joining us. It wasn't a question I often heard. I should remind Jacob of that fact.

As for the lingering doubts that threatened to unravel the fabric of our marriage? I left them in their place, under the rug, waiting for the right moment when my courage and preparedness to leave was strong enough.

The minutes ticked by. The sound of the garage door opening drew my attention. Jacob was home. I steeled myself in preparation for the dinner ahead. The words that would remain unspoken. Speaking to one another as though we were simply roommates, rather than husband and wife. Pretending to love each other deeply in front of Noah. At least, we were on the same page where he was concerned.

Jacob walked inside, closing the kitchen door behind him. "Hey."

"Hi. How was your day?" An innocuous question to keep this ship steadily on its course.

"Good. Finished early. Thought it'd be nice to sit down and eat with my two favorite people."

Jacob slipped his hand around my waist as I stood at the stove. He kissed my cheek, and I smelled neither booze nor women's perfume on him. The evening was looking up.

"Well, we're glad you're here." I glanced at him with a pleasant smile. "Dinner will be ready in about ten minutes, if you want to settle in first."

"Great, thanks, babe." He carried on through the kitchen and disappeared up the stairs.

I finished preparing our dinner of pork tenderloin, wild rice, and Noah's least favorite vegetable, Brussel sprouts. For him to eat this meal would probably require an act of God.

Within moments, I'd plated the food and set down the dishes at each of our usual spots around the dinner table. "Time to eat, guys."

Noah bounded down the steps and rushed to his seat. He looked up at me and flashed a bright, warm smile. Until he saw tonight's meal. He took one look at his plate and rolled his eyes as if I was serving him prison food.

Jacob descended the stairs, a soft smile on his lips as he took in the scene before him. "Hey, kiddo." He placed his hand on Noah's back before taking his seat. "How great is this, huh? The three of us sitting down together for dinner?"

"It's really great, Daddy," Noah replied.

I exchanged a glance with Jacob, the implicit words hanging between us. And then I turned to Noah, who poked at his food, not having taken a bite of anything. "Hey, bud?"

He looked at me. "Yeah?"

"Are you okay?" My question drew Jacob's attention as we both regarded him.

"I'm okay. It's just . . ." He drew in a deep breath. "I was talking to my friend earlier — when I got home."

"Oh yeah?" Jacob cut in. "Which friend was that?"

"Billy."

Jacob shot a look at me as if I had control over what came out of our son's mouth. "And what did Billy have to say?" I asked.

Noah chewed on his lower lip and kept his eyes on his food.

"It's okay, sweetheart. You can tell us." Why was Noah so hesitant to talk about his imagined friend? I was the one who seemed troubled by it, without actually saying as much to him. It was Jacob who seemed completely on board, writing it off as a boy's imagination.

It was then that Noah peered at his father. "Billy said he knows what you did."

Jacob set down his fork. "I'm sorry, what's that now?"

I could see the anger building in Jacob's chest. The rise and fall of each breath growing deeper and deeper. I turned to Noah. "That's a strange thing to say."

"I didn't say it, Mommy. Billy did," Noah shot back as though he was about to get in trouble for speaking.

"Okay." I raised my hands. "Okay, but what did Billy mean by it?"

Jacob threw down his napkin onto the table. "All right. Enough of this. Noah, go to your room."

"But I didn't do anything." His eyes reddened.

"Jake, don't get upset with him," I said. "We have no idea what this is even about."

And that was when Jacob looked at me. Really looked at me, and what I saw in his eyes was guilt.

A sinking feeling deep in the pit of my stomach took hold. The atmosphere in the room turned heavy, filled with the weight of secrets. "Noah, sweetheart," I said softly, trying to maintain a sense of calm. "Why don't you go to your room for a little while? I'll fix you up a plate of chicken nuggets. You don't have to eat this. Daddy and I need to talk."

Noah hopped out of the chair, his gaze lingering on his father before slowly retreating from the room. As soon as he left, the silence settled in like an uninvited guest.

I already had a hunch about what Noah's imaginary friend was referring to. The frightening part was what that signified — that Noah had seen or heard something his father had done, and even at his tender age, must've understood to a degree what it meant. "Jacob, did something happen in front of Noah?"

* * *

Whatever I had built up in my mind for the evening had blown up pretty quickly. Noah believed he'd been in trouble for asking the question. Jacob grew defensive by the implications of it.

But it was clear to me Noah had no idea what he was asking, or if he did, there was some subconscious element to it. Maybe he'd picked up on parts of conversations Jacob and I had had over the past several months. Either way, it required a gentle touch.

I'd asked Jacob what the question meant, even though I wasn't sure I'd wanted the answer. Rather than wait for it, I had excused myself from the table and went upstairs to bathe Noah. We had played a few games first and I had assured him he was in no trouble at all. But I hadn't pushed him on his question. Or how Billy became involved in it.

Somehow, I figured Billy was Noah's way of dealing with the growing trouble he clearly had picked up between his father and me. So here I was now, lying next to my husband in our pitch-black bedroom. Neither of us having addressed the situation further.

My eyes remained open. My head muddled with thoughts traversing through without making any kind of sense. I glanced at Jacob's sleeping figure beside me. Of course, he'd been able to sleep.

Noah's innocent question had stirred something inside me, a hidden truth that I had been avoiding for far too long. It was as if his imaginary friend, Billy, had become a vessel for all the unspoken tensions and unresolved issues between Jacob and me. I couldn't ignore it any longer: we needed to have an honest conversation.

Gently untangling myself from the sheets, I got out of bed and tiptoed toward Noah's room. The soft glow of his nightlight illuminated his peaceful face as he slept soundly. I leaned against the doorframe, watching him for a moment, overwhelmed by a love so fierce it brought tears to my eyes.

And then I heard it. A distant thud of some kind. It sounded like it had come from the ceiling. I knew our old house often creaked and squeaked, but this didn't sound anything like that. This was a definite thud.

It seemed I wasn't the only one to hear it. Noah roused from his sleep. "Mommy?"

I walked into his room. "It's okay, buddy. Go back to sleep."

There it was again. The furnace? Maybe. It did feel slightly colder in here than usual. Maybe it had gone out. "I'll bet that's the heat. I'll wake up Daddy to have him take a look."

"No," Noah cut in. "It's just Billy. He can be noisy sometimes."

I tilted my head. "What? You think it's your friend, Billy?" I sat down on the edge of his bed. "Honey, you have to understand that Billy exists only in your mind. It's what kids do. They have pretend friends. It's perfectly okay."

"No, you don't understand." Noah sat up against his headboard. "Billy told me to ask Daddy that question. I don't know why. Billy wouldn't tell me. He lives in the house, Mommy. I already told you that."

My heart thumped firmly in my chest because now it seemed a real possibility someone was inside our home. But I had to take caution with my words. "Noah, baby, what do you mean Billy lives in our house?"

Noah's small shoulders shrugged. "He just does, Mommy. He talks to me sometimes."

A wave of concern and curiosity swept through me as I absorbed my son's words. Was this simply an overactive imagination, or was there something more at play here? I had always encouraged Noah's creativity, but this felt — disturbing.

"Have you ever seen Billy?" I asked, trying not to think about the noises I'd just heard.

"No. He never comes out."

What was I supposed to do with that? Was someone in our home? That seemed impossible to consider. Billy was Noah's make-believe friend. He had to be. But fear gripped me, and I had to act. "I'll go wake up Daddy and we'll have a look around, okay?" I held out my hand, waiting for Noah to take it. "Come on."

I led the way back to my bedroom, walking toward Jacob's side of the bed. I gently shook his shoulder as he lay on his side. "Jake? Honey, wake up. There's a noise."

Jacob stirred, his eyes fluttering open. "What is it?" he mumbled, his voice heavy with sleep.

Noah stood next to our bed. "Daddy, we have to find Billy."

I glanced at Noah and then back at Jacob, unsure of how to proceed. The whole situation seemed absurd, but there was an undeniable sense of unease in the air. "I heard a noise that sounded like it came from the ceiling."

Jacob sat up on the edge of the bed. "Okay. It's probably the furnace in the attic."

"That's what I figured, and then we heard it again. Sorry, but could you go up and take a look?" I pretended as though we hadn't had our earlier conversation. As though everything between us was completely fine. That was partly due to Noah and partly due to the fact that I was a little terrified at the moment.

"Fine. Yeah, okay." Jacob rose from the bed and stepped into his slippers. "It feels warm in here, so the furnace must still be working. Maybe something fell."

"I'm sure that's all it is," I said, hoping to reassure Noah.

"Mommy doesn't believe me. I told her it was Billy."

Jacob swung around, aiming his index finger at Noah. "That's enough of that, you hear me? I don't want to hear that name again, all right? Billy is a figment of your imagination. Nothing more." He stomped off toward the attic scuttle in the hall.

Noah and I followed and when Jacob had climbed the ladder, I heard something else, only it didn't come from above. "Did you hear that?"

"What?" Jacob shouted down.

I let go of Noah's hand. "Stay here, okay?" I walked toward the end of the hall where I was certain the noise had come from. It sounded like it had come from outside this time. I peered through the window but could see only darkness. "That's it. We're calling the police."

* * *

It was three in the morning. Jacob had searched everywhere. He didn't want me to get the police involved, but I couldn't ignore what I'd heard. Now, Jacob and I sat on our sofa, two officers standing feet away with their little note pads, asking us questions.

I held Noah in my arms while he slept.

The officers exchanged a concerned glance before focusing their attention back on us. "Can you describe the noise you heard, ma'am?" one of them asked, his pen hovering above the notepad.

"It was like . . . a thud," I replied, struggling to find the right words to convey the unsettling sensation. "I heard it twice. Woke up my husband to check it out. That was when I heard a noise outside."

Jacob leaned forward, resting his elbows on his thighs, and appearing exhausted. "I walked around the house twice. Didn't see anything. It could've been a stray cat for all I know."

The second officer scribbled notes while the first one nodded. "And you mentioned, Mrs. Hale, something about a boy named Billy?"

I hesitated, not wanting to add fuel to Jacob's frustration earlier. But the truth needed to be told. "Our son has an imaginary friend. He insists this Billy is the one who made the noise."

"Has your son ever seen Billy?" the officer asked.

"No, sir," I replied. "He says Billy talks to him through the walls." The officers traded glances, and I knew then they had no intention of taking this seriously. Maybe Jacob was right, and it was a damn cat or something. I'd begun to feel like I was wasting everyone's time.

The first officer cleared his throat before speaking, a sure sign he was about to patronize me. "Mrs. Hale, I understand you want to keep your family safe, and you did the right thing. But I think your husband is on the right track. It was probably an animal you heard, and not an imaginary friend come to life. We'll take note of this incident, but unless there are any other signs of trouble or suspicious activity, there isn't much we can do at the moment."

How could I argue? They had a point. And they'd searched the perimeter too, coming up with nothing. I looked into Jacob's eyes, silently pleading with him to say something more convincing. But he remained silent. "I understand, Officer. I'm sorry to have wasted your time."

CHAPTER 27: GARY

What choice did I have but to return to the office? Staying inside the Hale home would've ensured my discovery, and I had only just made it out before Jacob climbed the ladder. How could I have jeopardized all of it with my own negligence? I had accidentally kicked my work boot, sending it tumbling across the attic floor in the dead of night.

And to confirm whether I had awakened the family, I pressed my ear against the vent, straining to listen. Lauren's muffled voice drifted through.

I had hurriedly gathered what few things I owned, fleeing down the trellis in the nick of time. As my feet had touched solid ground, panic had surged within me. I had to distance myself from the house, certain Jacob would search the area.

Mercifully, luck was on my side. I had seized the opportunity and sprinted toward my car. But the damage was done. Lauren would be suspicious of every noise from now on. I was going to have to rethink it all.

CHAPTER 28: DETECTIVE COLLINS

With much needed forward momentum on the Tomlin investigation, I arrived at the station this morning, holding out hope Forensics would find DNA on the evidence we recovered in the cellar. And that we'd get a match.

On my way to the front desk, I caught sight of a couple uniforms who looked to be going off shift. "Morning."

"Detective," one of them replied with a nod. The other tipped his hat at me.

They continued their conversation as I walked by. I overheard a portion of it, and it stopped me in my tracks.

I spun around and walked back to them. "Hang on, did you say you had a call last night with a family who believed they'd had an intruder?"

"Yes, ma'am," the officer replied. "Apparently, their young son believed it was his imaginary friend making all the noise they'd heard. The husband had searched the perimeter by the time we'd arrived. But we made another pass to keep the wife happy. Came up empty."

Was this a coincidence? Should I dig a little deeper, or was this a big fat nothing? More importantly, could I afford to treat it as such? "Hey, uh, you mind sending me a copy of your report?"

The officer shrugged. "Yeah, I guess. Sure. Can I ask why?"

I raised my shoulder. "Call it a hunch."

CHAPTER 29: LAUREN

Discussing what had happened last night with Jacob had been nearly impossible. He believed I had made a fuss by calling in the police. God forbid. They had found nothing, neither had Jacob. But something gnawed at me. This imaginary friend of Noah's . . . why had he suddenly come into our lives? And why had Noah insisted the noises last night were from this friend? He didn't fear Billy. And now, here I was, trying to make sense of it all. The imagination of a four-year-old, notwithstanding.

Maybe Jacob was right to brush it off. It could've been a raccoon, squirrel, or even a cat.

It did put my mind at ease knowing the cops hadn't suspected anything unusual. No recent reports of burglaries in our area. That was comforting.

As I contemplated last night, my drive into work went by in a blur. I hadn't been able to go back to sleep after all that had happened, and I was feeling the effects of it. Now, I had to prepare myself for another busy day.

A light mist hung in the morning air. Dark, clouded skies reminded me of winter's dismal hold as I arrived at the office. I stepped out of my Lincoln, the cold haze clinging to my hair and coat. Inside our warm building, I brushed off the dampness. "Hey, Nicole. How are you this morning?"

Nicole was interning here while she worked on becoming a Certified Public Accountant. "Good morning. I'm doing all right." She glanced outside. "Nice weather this morning, huh?"

"I can't wait for spring. I'll put it that way." I snickered. "Good to see you." The elevators were only steps away, and I rode to the second floor. When the doors parted, I continued down the hall and toward my office. "Oh no." I came to a halt, my shoulders sinking. With everything that had happened, I'd forgotten to pack up leftovers for Gary. "Damn." I glanced at my watch, realizing I didn't have enough time to run back home before my first meeting of the day. Gary would have to fend for himself, it seemed. The thought nagged at me, but he would understand.

I was happy to see that he'd remembered to close my door last night, and as I entered, I flipped on the lights. Something on the floor near my desk caught my attention. A business card. I reached for it, flipping it over as I stood again. Right away, I noticed the company name. And then . . . "Madison Price. Paralegal Specialist. What the hell is this?" I shot around, marching back toward the hallway, craning my neck left, then right, expecting someone to be there. It was empty.

The card was from Jacob's law firm, and I had no idea who Madison Price was, or why her card was on the floor of my office. First thing I needed to do was sit down. My chest tightened. Thoughts swirled in my mind. Suspicious thoughts. "Who put this here?"

"You talking to yourself again?"

I glanced up, coming out of my swirling thoughts. "Hi, Tammy, good morning. Yeah, I guess I was."

She continued inside, seeming to have picked up on my distress. "What's going on? You all right?"

I held the card between my fingers, turning it over and over. "I don't know. I found this on the floor near my desk when I came in." I handed it to her.

Tammy examined it for what seemed like an eternity. Then I saw the look in her eyes as she handed it back. "She works with Jacob, I take it."

I shrugged, feeling the sting of tears behind my eyes. "I guess so."

Tammy wore a look I'd seen plenty of times. The look that reminded me to stay calm. "Listen, Lauren, before you jump to any conclusions, let's think about this logically. There could be a perfectly reasonable explanation for why Madison Price's card ended up in your office."

Defiant, I crossed my arms. "I can't imagine what that could be."

"We've known each other for a long time. It's not like you haven't thought these things before, but like I said, before you go blowing up your life, make sure you're right about this first." She held my gaze a moment. "I gotta go. I have a meeting to prepare for. Listen, I'll catch up with you later?"

Tammy walked out of my office, leaving me with her words of wisdom, knowing the decision was mine. What I couldn't wrap my head around was how this woman's card ended up here. It wasn't there last night when I left. No one had been in here since I arrived this morning, except for Tammy, so how? But more importantly, why?

There was someone I could ask, but I doubted he was still here. My new friend, Gary. He might have answers. He worked last night. But the question would have to wait until this evening when his shift started, leaving me to stew in my own toxic imaginings. And then I felt a sudden, steely determination. "Maybe not."

I got up from my chair and headed into the hall, making my way to my boss's office. Chuck was the senior partner and former colleague of my husband. He was a good man who was left with a bad taste in his mouth when Jacob quit. It had taken me a long time to get back into his good graces, but now that I was, I needed to ask him a question.

"Morning, Chuck, how are you?" I walked inside and noted his relaxed demeanor. He must've been having a good day so far. He was a mousy sort of man. A bald spot on his crown. Wire-rimmed glasses over full cheeks. Older, at about fifty-three, and probably the most decent guy I'd ever met.

"Good morning, Lauren. I'm all right and you?"

"Well, I was doing all right, but I just got a call from the school. Turns out, Noah's not feeling well. I need to pick him up and take him home."

"Oh yeah, of course. Do what you gotta do."

I offered a grateful smile. "Thank you. I really appreciate this. I plan on coming back unless he's really not well. Our neighbor watches him in the afternoons, so if he's feeling up to it, I'll have her take over for me a little later."

"Whatever you need, Lauren. It's fine by me."

I nodded, turning to leave. As I walked back to my office, I stopped at Tammy's door and leaned in. "I'll be back later — maybe." The look in her eyes suggested she had an inkling of what I was about to do.

Finally reaching my office again, I grabbed Madison's business card along with my purse and laptop bag. I wanted to come back so that I might catch Gary and ask him if he'd seen anyone in my office. But for now, I'd take everything in case things went south, like the plot of many a Lifetime movie. Usually, it was the wife who got screwed, so I wasn't holding much hope of another outcome.

I pushed through the lobby doors, squinting at the sun that broke through the earlier clouds. The mist had dried up but had left small puddles on the asphalt. As I walked through the parking lot, heading toward my SUV, I checked the time. Barely 9 a.m. I climbed inside and drove on until I reached Jacob's office.

The parking lot was around the back and that was where I headed. I immediately spotted Jacob's Porsche parked in one of the spots reserved for the partners.

I parked a few spaces away and took a deep breath, the anticipation making my heart race. My plan was simple, though the risk was great. As I stepped out, the brisk morning air brushed against my skin, cooling the anxiety that gripped me. I squeezed Madison's business card, feeling its edges digging into my palm.

Walking toward the entrance of Mullen, Gossett & Hale, I pushed open the heavy glass door and entered the lobby. A sleek electric fireplace burned on the back wall at the seating area. The receptionist looked up from her desk. She recognized me.

"Lauren, what are you doing here?"

"I . . . I — Jacob forgot something. I thought I'd bring it to him. Is he in a meeting or his office?"

She checked her computer and looked back at me. "He's in a meeting with a big client, actually. All the partners are there. You want to leave it with me, and I'll make sure he gets it?"

I clearly hadn't thought this through. I had nothing of Jacob's on me. I simply wanted to find Madison's office and learn who she was. "Would it be all right if I took it to his office?" I leaned in, a spark of genius hitting me. "It's personal. He would be embarrassed if anyone else knew."

"Oh." She leaned back, appearing uncomfortable. "Of course. I understand. Please, go on up. You know where it is."

"Thanks, oh, and don't mention this, okay? Jacob might think I told you and you know, it would just get awkward."

She raised her hands. "You have my word."

"I appreciate it." I spun around and headed toward the elevators. Jacob's office was on the top floor along with the other partners. I wouldn't find Madison Price there. I'd been here a few times and their set up wasn't much different from my office. Support staff would be on the lower levels. Madison was a paralegal, so I'd try the third floor, below the partners.

As the elevator doors closed, I slowed my breathing to calm my nerves. These were dangerous waters, but the feeling of betrayal propelled me. What if Madison, herself, had left the card? Snooping around to learn more about her lover's wife? The idea nauseated me.

When the doors opened, I found myself in a spacious hallway adorned with sleek, modern artwork. The atmosphere was different here. A sense of power and authority lingered in the air. Their clients were wealthy corporations. Money flowed freely.

I navigated through the maze of corridors, glancing at office names engraved on polished plaques. The sound of subdued voices drifted from behind closed doors. As I carried on through the halls, hoping to tamp down suspicions, her name appeared on neither an office door nor any desk that I could find. It seemed this was where the junior partners worked.

Undeterred, I returned to the elevator, heading down one more floor. So far, no one took any notice. A good thing, considering several people around here knew I was Jacob's wife. Although, I was invisible to most people while in his presence.

Finally, my gaze landed on her name, etched in elegant script on a door plate. Madison Price, Paralegal Specialist. I stared at the plate for too long. She could be behind the door right now, possibly aware someone stood outside her office. The question loomed in my mind; would I enter? No. No, I couldn't do it. Uncertainty swelled in my chest. My resolve crumbled.

I turned around, defeated, embarrassed by my actions. Returning to the elevators, I stepped inside as the doors parted. Tammy's words echoed in my head like a mantra, "Don't jump to conclusions." But that was exactly what I'd done.

Staring at the numbers above, I could think of no logical explanation as to why that card would have been in my office. Who had planted it there? The possibility existed that someone in our circle, either at my office or his, had seen Jacob and this woman together. And maybe this was how they chose to tell me.

The doors opened into the lobby, I hurried out, offering a dismissive wave to the woman at the front desk.

She looked surprised by my abrupt departure. "Bye, Mrs. Hale."

I could only imagine how unhinged I must have looked, fleeing from the building as if it was on fire. Once safe within the confines of my car, I pressed the ignition. My fingers white-knuckled around the steering wheel. What could I possibly do with this information that felt like a noose around my neck?

CHAPTER 30: DETECTIVE COLLINS

The responding officer's report was sparse, almost barren of detail. "What is this shit?" I slammed my laptop shut.

"You doing all right, there?" Dixon had arrived at his desk, holding a paper bag that looked to contain his lunch.

"Yeah, fine." I eyed the bag. "Got anything in there for me?"

"You should've said. I would've picked up something for you." He took a seat, pulling out the cheeseburger and fries. "What are you looking at anyway?"

"I overheard Henderson and Williams talk about a call they got in the early hours this morning. Noises in some family's house. Anyway, something in me clicked and so I asked them about it. I'm looking at the report now. I gotta say, they could've been a little more thorough."

"How so?" he asked.

"It's just the basics. The thing is, the mother claimed her son insisted the noises came from his friend. An imaginary friend — inside the home. Something that makes me believe this could be the guy we're after."

"Wow. That's quite a leap." He wiped his mouth with a napkin. "You're gonna have to give me more than that to go on."

I rolled my chair toward him. "Pull up last night's call log. I'll show you which one it is. Take a look and tell me what you think." I waited while he retrieved the file. It only took a moment or two before I noticed the look on his face.

"It's thin, I'll give you that. But I hear what you're saying." Dixon leaned back. "Still, it's a hard sell." He looked again at the report, scanning the words carefully as if trying to decipher a hidden message within them. "Even the mom wavered, so it's hard to say. Husband didn't appear on board at all."

"Take a look at her statement again." I pointed to the screen. "She said the kid's been talking to his friend, Billy, for the past several days. So I assume before that, there was nothing." I held up my hands. "Not trying to jump the gun, here, but that kind of timing strikes me as more than coincidental."

"You're sounding desperate," Dixon added. "But if you want to take a pass at these folks, let's do it. Rule it out and move on."

CHAPTER 31: GARY

The cut on my shin was deeper than I'd realized. In my hurried attempt to descend the trellis before Lauren discovered me, my foot had slipped. I'd carved a sizable gash down the shin of my right leg that had caught on a broken piece of metal. It made the cut from the broken candleholder seem like a mere scratch.

It was mid-morning now as I approached the neighborhood where the Hales lived. I had no idea whether the police had been called or if they'd found my spot inside the attic. When the elegant Hale home appeared in the distance, I saw no sign of the cops. No sign that anything out of the ordinary had happened last night. Even better — no indication anyone was home right now. Noah was still at school, Lauren at work. Jacob doing whatever it was Jacob did, and with whomever he did it.

I'd been lucky to escape, injury notwithstanding. If I hadn't already raised Lauren's hackles, this definitely had. Had Noah delivered my message to Jacob? If so, what had his reaction been? I brought this on myself. Risked everything for Lauren.

I couldn't live without her or Noah. I needed my family, so I would take the odds and try again. But not right now. I only needed to confirm the house wasn't under some sort of police surveillance.

I would leave Noah be for a while, until things settled. It might be days before Lauren felt safe and secure once more. However, all was not lost. In fact, this respite would offer a chance to better plan a future with my family. Getting rid of me wouldn't be so easy.

Soon, I would see Lauren again. I pondered whether she'd spotted the business card. No doubt, she had, and it had set off a series of events that would force a reckoning in their marriage. It hadn't been easy to get hold of Madison Price's card.

I'd paid another visit to Mullen, Gossett, and Hale yesterday after the chaos settled and they'd all gone back inside. Returning only an hour later to the front desk, hat in hand. I'd explained to the receptionist that I'd accidently scratched a vehicle in the parking lot. Suggesting that I thought it belonged to Madison Price because I'd seen her in the building before. But I was too embarrassed to face her head-on.

After promising to make things right, the young receptionist had taken pity on me. She offered me Madison's business card so I could call her and settle things that way. People had the capacity for kindness, but few displayed it. This young woman had. I felt hopeful Lauren would also carry kindness in her heart for me — sooner or later.

Now that the wheels were in motion, I would prepare for tonight's shift — to see Lauren again and gauge her mood. After all, I couldn't stay here any longer. Little Noah would have to get along without me, but it wouldn't be forever. I would return to my home soon enough.

CHAPTER 32: LAUREN

I was a coward. A coward who couldn't confront the woman I was sure had been screwing my husband. Did I have proof? No. And that was my excuse. Tammy insisted I not jump to conclusions, so I heeded her advice. Even if it was a little too late. That was my story.

I'd returned to work, tail tucked between my legs, feeling as though I'd lost control of everything. My son's imaginary friend seemed to know about my husband's affair. Why else had Noah said Billy knew what he'd done? It was only now that it had started to make sense.

The idea my son knew about his father's transgressions sent a ball of rage rumbling in my gut. Jacob's reaction to Noah's comment was about as much proof as I needed.

"Stop." I rubbed my forehead, trying to clear away the intrusive thoughts. It was then that I noticed the time. "It's five already?" I could go home, but go home and do what? Would Jacob be late again? Would he come home at all?

My eyes burned with tears again. I grabbed my phone and made the call. "Hi, Nancy, it's Lauren. Hey, I need to work a little late tonight. Would you be available to stick around and look after Noah? He could even go to your house if it would be easier."

"How late do you think?" she asked.

"Oh, I imagine I'll be home by seven, or seven thirty. Is that too late?"

"No, that should be fine. Honestly, I'd rather stay here since all of Noah's things are here. I'll see you later, Lauren."

"You're a lifesaver, Nancy. Thanks and I'll see you later." I ended the call and shut down my computer. I wasn't going home. Not yet.

I heard Gary's cart rolling down the hall. Right on time. My new friend brought a smile to my face as he stopped outside my door. "Evening, Gary. How are you?"

"I'm doing well, Miss Lauren. And you?"

"Doing all right. Getting ready to leave for the day." I cocked my head. "Hey, can I ask you something?"

"Go right ahead," he replied.

How could I phrase this? I supposed just coming out with it was the best way. "Did you happen to notice anyone in my office last night or early this morning before I came in?"

Gary raised a thoughtful gaze. "No, ma'am. I don't recall anyone here at all. Why?" He marched inside with purpose. "Did someone steal something from you?"

I waved my hand. "No, no, it's nothing like that. Never mind. It's not important." I glanced away, feeling embarrassed. "I'm afraid I didn't bring you any dinner tonight. Will you be okay?"

"Of course, I will. I got plenty here. I do thank you for all you've done, Miss Lauren. But you should go on and go home. Spend some time with your boy."

I tightened my brow, an inquisitive smile tugging at my lips. "How'd you know I have a son?"

Gary pointed at the photo on my desk. "Forgive my curiosity, Miss Lauren, but I noticed this picture a while back. I just figured that was your boy."

"Oh, right. Of course." I picked up the frame. "This was taken last summer while we were on vacation."

"Well, I should let you get back to it. Good night, then."
He started away.

I got up from my chair and caught up to him at the door.
"Gary?"

He stopped and turned back. "Yes, ma'am?"

"Are you okay?"

He smiled at me, tilting his head a little. "How do you mean?"

"I see you're limping. Did you hurt yourself?"

"As a matter of fact, I did. Slipped on some ice on my steps when I went home early this morning. It got pretty icy after that rain," he replied.

"Yes, it did. Well, you take care. See you tomorrow," I added.

"I certainly do hope so."

He disappeared around the corner, and I returned to my desk. Just talking to him made me feel better. He hadn't seen anyone here last night, so that left the question of the card unanswered. Never mind. Someone left it, and it was someone who wanted me to know the truth I'd denied for too long. So, while I'd lacked the courage to confront this woman, I didn't lack the curiosity to see whether she would be with Jacob tonight in his office. Alone. Doing things he stopped doing with me a long time ago.

I made a beeline for the lobby, not stopping to say goodnight to anyone, not even Tammy. She'd let me hear about it in the morning, but that was a problem for another day. I hurried through the rising icy winds, heading toward my car in the parking lot. Dusky light surrounded me. The streetlamps flickered on, and the outside of the building lit up.

I climbed into my Lincoln and fired up the engine. With traffic, I could be there inside of twenty minutes. Whether I would find Jacob still at his office depended on what excuse he'd managed to concoct. So far, I hadn't received any messages from him. If he was there with her, well, I wasn't sure what I would do.

I sped through the busy streets, my thoughts fueled by images of them together. Anger, jealousy, and desperation waged a war in me. I had to know the truth. To see it with my own eyes.

As I pulled up to Jacob's office for the second time today, my pulse raced. I surveyed the parking lot and noticed his Porsche. "Still here." I'd told Nancy I'd be home by seven or so, giving me time to wait them out. Would I catch him with her? Would I do anything about it this time, or would cowardice prevail?

I'd cut the engine and now felt the cold air seeping into my vehicle. Twenty minutes had gone by and still nothing. My mind came up with various scenarios of Jacob and that woman having sex in his office. On his desk, or on the conference table, or anywhere my mind could wander. The rising anger at my growing imagination made me want to scream. But I couldn't. I had to sit here in silence, hoping to prove to myself that the man I'd married was a liar. A painful realization I wouldn't wish on anyone.

Finally, the front doors of the building opened. There he was. Jesus. There was Jacob smiling and placing his hand on a woman's back. That had to be her — Madison. Oh my God, what the hell was I going to do now? "Follow them."

I whispered those two words to myself, the command echoing through the empty car. The decision had been made. I started the engine once more, leaving off the headlights.

As Jacob and Madison walked toward his car, I carefully maneuvered my SUV out of the parking spot, making sure to keep a safe distance between us. The darkening streets masked my presence, allowing me to trail them. Every turn he made, every traffic light he stopped at, my heart pounded in my chest, fearing he would notice me.

The tension grew with each passing minute as he weaved through the maze of city streets. Doubt flickered in my mind, but I refused to let it take over this time. I had come this far; turning back wasn't an option.

They eventually arrived in front of the Regal Hotel. My face felt drained of color. "Are you serious? You're bringing her here? Where we spent our anniversary?"

In that moment, I'd wanted to fling open my door, march toward my husband, and confront them. But I didn't. Instead, I watched them approach the entrance, and walk inside — together. "What more proof do you need, Lauren?"

CHAPTER 33: JACOB

That euphoric feeling had passed. Those few moments after sex when I lose myself in her, in the moment, in everything. I even forgot that she wasn't my wife and that I had a family waiting for me at home.

But that feeling quickly evaporated, and the guilt set in. I was in that moment now as I lay next to Maddy. Her head was tucked into my chest. Her wavy blond hair tickling my forearm. And now I knew I had to tell her. What happened with Noah meant that he'd seen or overheard something and that was why he'd said what he'd said. Billy, some figment of my son's imagination, knew what I'd done. And I knew exactly what he'd meant when Noah said those words to me.

No matter how hard I denied it to myself and to Lauren, Noah knew. And now this so-called friend of his was living in the walls of our home? Could I really blame Lauren for believing the noises she heard were connected? Of course it was ridiculous, but I had no choice in the matter when she'd called the cops. The cops, for Christ's sake.

My world was on the verge of unraveling, and I had to tell this woman, who I now held in my arms. "Maddy," I whispered.

"Yes?"

She looked up at me with adoring green eyes. "Listen, uh, something happened last night with my son . . ."

"What is it?" She pulled up onto her elbow. "Is he okay?"

"Yeah, he's fine," I cut in. "It's just that I think he knows. Either he overheard something, or I don't know what. But that means that Lauren probably knows too, or suspects. I guess I already figured that but didn't want to admit it."

"What are you saying, Jake?" Maddy's face was masked in concern, and maybe a little fear.

"I'm saying that I think we need to cool it for a while. You know, take a step back until I can figure things out."

Her eyes widened with confusion and pain. She instinctively retracted her hand from my chest. "Take a step back? Jake, what does that even mean? Are you breaking up with me?"

I sighed, feeling the weight of guilt on my shoulders. "No, Maddy, it's not like that. I just need some time to sort things out with my family. We can't continue like this while my son is dealing with issues I created."

Tears welled in her eyes as she sat up, distancing herself from me. "So, I was just some distraction for you? A way to escape your problems?"

"No, Maddy, it's not like that either," I pleaded, reaching out to touch her arm. "You mean a lot to me, but right now I have to prioritize my son."

Her lips trembled as she pulled away from my touch. "Are you being serious right now?"

I sat up to join her. "I think this is the way it has to be, but only for a while."

She jumped off the bed, pulling the blanket over her. "You're an asshole, you know that?"

This was not news to me. "Maddy, come on."

"No. No way." She wagged her finger at me. "You think you can just toss me aside?" A strange laughter came out of her as she walked toward the end of the bed, still holding the blanket around her. "You listen to me, Jacob Hale. I know all your dirty little secrets, you son of a bitch."

I raised my hands in surrender. "Maddy, babe, be reasonable." By the look on her face, I quickly realized that was the exact wrong thing to say.

"I'll be reasonable, Jacob." Anger heated her otherwise pale face. "I'll tell the partners how you've been skimming from them. How you inflate your hours, just in small increments. How you tell the clients about our so-called extra charges, which is money you tack onto their bills after the partners sign off on them. You want me to tell them all that?"

I jumped off the bed, naked as a jaybird. "Maddy, listen to what you're saying."

"You really think I won't do it?" She raised an eyebrow, a smirk forming on her lips. "You underestimate me, Jacob. I'm not just some distraction; I'm your partner, your confidante. I know everything about you, and I'm not afraid to use it."

My throat tightened as I tried to come up with something, anything that would make her see reason. "Maddy, please, don't do this. We can work this out. We can find a way to make things right."

She scoffed, shaking her head. "Oh, now you want to make things right? I'm not an idiot, Jacob, and I'm not going to let you get away with it."

Without her help, I wouldn't have gotten away with the billing extras. But even she didn't know about the money I owed them, making payments every two weeks to keep them off my back. Whittling away gambling debts I'd amassed over several trips to Atlantic City. Trips I'd also happened to illegally write off as business expenses. Somehow, though, if I mentioned that part, also insinuating I would expose her, too, everything would be out the window. No, this had to be on me. I had to find a way out of this before I lost her, my wife, and my son.

My mind raced as I tried to come up with a plan she could accept. "Maddy, you're right. I've been deceitful, and I never meant for it to come to this."

She eyed me with warranted suspicion, her face still heated. But I could tell she was also weighing her words, considering whether it was worth it to go through with her threat.

"Okay, listen." I approached her. "Babe, just give me a few days. That's all I ask. If Lauren finds out, it's over anyway. The partners will find out. They'll fire me. And you and me? We're through. I don't want that. Do you?"

She closed her eyes a moment. "No. I love you, Jake."

She'd said the L word. I didn't love her, but I sure as hell wasn't going to admit that in this moment. "So, can you give me those few days? I'll smooth things over with my wife. Make sure Noah's okay. And then we can go on as normal. We'll put all of this behind us. No need to blow up everything, okay?" If this didn't work, I'd find myself behind bars pretty quickly, or with at least a broken leg or two, not to mention losing my family. Madison Price knew I'd siphoned money from the partners. I had to find a way to get her to see reason. That money . . . it was my lifeline. The only way I was able to stay afloat. I couldn't let her take it away from me.

"Okay," she said. "Fix this, Jake, or everyone will know everything."

CHAPTER 34: LAUREN

In the end, I didn't have the courage to wait for Jacob to emerge from that hotel. The very same hotel we'd spent our sixth anniversary. Instead, I came home, relieved Nancy had pretended in front of my son that everything was fine, regardless of the look on my face.

It was okay that Noah had an imaginary friend, who somehow knew Jacob was having an affair. It was okay that I'd heard noises in the night and Noah insisted it was his friend, Billy. And now, it was okay that I'd watched my husband walk into a hotel with his mistress.

It was all O.K.

Except it wasn't. I walked upstairs to find Noah in his playroom. "It's time for bed, sweetheart."

He glanced back at me as he played with his Legos. "But I haven't had my bath yet."

I checked the time, realizing Jacob would be home soon. He'd gone through the trouble of texting me a little while ago, mentioning how he'd had to work later than he thought and could I put a plate of food in the oven for him. Of course I could.

"I know you haven't, but Mommy's not feeling up to it tonight. Can we skip it for just one night?" He looked at me with a sort of understanding on his face. Of course, he couldn't possibly have understood.

Noah pulled himself off the floor. He slowly picked up his Legos and placed them into the bucket, milking the process for all it was worth.

"Come on, buddy. Let's get moving." I would've enjoyed his antics had I not been about to confront his father about the affair. Noah was too innocent. He didn't deserve this.

What I had yet to decide was whether I would actually leave Jacob. People out there would say that if they were in my shoes, it would be a no-brainer. But no one knows what they would do in this sort of situation until it happens to them. No one.

I watched the sulking Noah carry on to his bedroom. I'd wanted to smile at him, knowing he would not be like this forever. Nonetheless, I was in no mood to smile.

Noah crawled into his bed, fidgeting restlessly. He glanced at me, his eyes pleading. I could see the thoughts racing through his little mind. *Maybe I should go to bed now? No, maybe me and Mommy could talk some more.*

But I didn't have the energy for Noah's company tonight. My thoughts were consumed by the image of my husband with his mistress, and all the emotions that came with it. The anger, the sadness, and the fear. What will happen to us now?

I realized then that I had to make the most difficult decision of my life. Do I stay and fight for the sake of my son, or leave it all behind and start over? I could feel the weight of it all pressing down on me, threatening to push me below the surface, from where I might never emerge again.

I walked back into the living room, sitting on the couch, the weight of my decision hanging over me. The room felt suffocating, filled with the remnants of a love that was slowly disintegrating. Everything seemed to be closing in on me — the walls, the memories, the unanswered questions.

Headlights passed by the front window and turned onto the driveway, disappearing into the garage. Jacob had arrived.

My shoulders raised, my jaw clenched. He would walk inside in mere moments, and I still didn't know what to say to him.

The kitchen door opened, the swoosh of its thick metal core reverberating through the house. I stared at the television, which was nothing more than a dark, blank screen. My stomach was in my throat and my mouth had dried. I quickly took a sip of water from the glass on the table.

"Evening, babe. Sorry I'm late."

Jacob walked over to me, leaning down to kiss my cheek. I didn't turn to look at him. He pulled upright again, and I felt his eyes on me. The silence in the room became unbearable as I continued to avoid his gaze. I clenched my fists. How could he act as if everything was normal? As if he hadn't shattered our world?

I could sense Jacob's apprehension as he stood before me, his eyes searching for any sign of what I might do. I kept my gaze fixed on the television, refusing to acknowledge him. It was as if every unspoken syllable hung in the air, begging to be released.

After what felt like an eternity, I finally found my voice. "Late again, huh?" I said, my tone dripping with bitterness. "You always have an excuse, don't you?"

Jacob shifted uncomfortably on his feet, a sheepish look crossing his face. "I . . . I got caught up at work."

"Work. That seems to be your favorite excuse these days," I snapped back, unable to hold back the venom in my words.

There was a heavy silence again, punctuated only by the igniting of the furnace as heat spilled through the air vents. I could feel Jacob's desperation. I finally turned to face him. "You think work is a good enough excuse? Well, let me tell you something, Jacob. Your precious work isn't more important than our marriage."

Jacob's shoulders slumped. "I know," he whispered.

"I want a divorce." There, I'd said it, almost unexpectedly so. The words that could change my entire life, and the life of my son. I felt nauseous and exhilarated all at the same time.

Jacob walked toward me. I could almost hear his breathing. He leaned in. Now, I could feel his breath on my neck. "If you think I'll let you keep your son if you divorce me, you're sorely mistaken."

CHAPTER 35: DETECTIVE COLLINS

If I suspected a killer lurked inside the Hale home, then relaying that to the family without a shred of evidence would erode any trust I might have been able to garner. Dixon was right, it was a leap. That wasn't going to change my mind until I had another look for myself.

In the light of day, however, Mr. and Mrs. Hale, along with their son, wouldn't be home. They'd be at work or school, so I discovered where the wife worked. She was the one who made the call and would be the most receptive to my visit.

Standing from my desk, I secured my weapon in its holster and glanced over at Dixon. "Do you want to come with me to talk to the wife?"

With uncertainty in his gaze, he replied, "What are you going to tell her? We can't be sure of anything — not yet."

"You're right. But if we say nothing, and something happens . . ."

"It's your call." He got to his feet and pulled on his suit coat. "We'll take her temperature and see what we're up against."

I walked through the busy corridor, past the bullpen, and into the lobby. All three case files, I'd shoved into my carrier bag and slung over my shoulder. I didn't want the Hales to be added to the body count.

Dixon was steps behind me as I pushed outside into the cold morning air. It had taken some leg work to learn the details of Mr. and Mrs. Hale, but this was worth my time and theirs — I hoped. Then again, this might just scare the shit out of the young wife and mother. A prospect I didn't relish.

She wasn't expecting us, possibly making matters worse. But what exactly was I supposed to say? *Uh, excuse me, Mrs. Hale, but I believe you have a killer living in your house somewhere.* That wasn't the best approach to this, and after twelve years on the job, I knew of a better, more palatable way of handling this, if there was such a thing.

We jumped into my car. I waited for Dixon to fasten his seatbelt before pulling out of the station's parking lot. "It's best if we discuss this outside of her office, don't you think?"

Dixon eyed me, appearing to consider the question. "If we talk to her around her coworkers, they'll be asking her questions. So yeah, I'm thinking we ask to speak to her outside, preferably out of view of those she works with."

"Then we agree. And from what I learned; Mrs. Hale is some sort of accountant. I'm gonna assume she's pragmatic. Hopefully not prone to panic."

"We'll see," Dixon shot back. "Anyone who hears what you're about to say isn't going to sit back and take it lightly."

"Copy that."

Several minutes went by without Dixon and me saying much to each other. We understood the gravity of the situation and the need for kid gloves. And when we arrived at the law offices of Ackerman & James, the time had come to see how far we could get with Mrs. Hale.

I cut the engine and turned to Dixon. "We'll head straight for the reception desk. I'll ask if they can call her down and then we'll usher her outside."

"It's cold," Dixon added. "We should insist she bring her coat."

"Good point." I stepped out of my car and waited for Dixon to join me. We walked ahead in silence until reaching the double glass doors. "Here we go." I opened one side and stepped into the lobby. Marbled floors, large windows, a modern glass and iron staircase, and elevators.

I plastered a smile on my face and, with Dixon at my side, headed straight toward the desk. "Good morning. I'm Detective Collins. This is my partner, Detective Dixon. We'd like to speak with Mrs. Lauren Hale. Would you mind calling her down?"

"Lauren?" The woman's face suddenly became etched with fear. "Is everything okay?"

I donned a smile. "Yeah, of course. We're here regarding a situation going on in her neighborhood. Figured it was best to speak to her first. She's not directly involved." It was a feeble attempt, but the woman seemed to accept it as fact. "Oh and ask her to bring a coat. We'd like to speak to her outside."

"Yes, ma'am. I'll call her down right now. One moment."

I stepped aside with Dixon, rolling my eyes. "Close one."

"We aren't over the hump yet," he added. "Hard to say how she'll react to this."

I looked over toward the elevators as the doors parted. "I'll bet that's her."

"Why do you say that?"

"Because she looks guilty of something."

Dixon chuckled. "She hasn't done anything."

"No, but whenever someone says the cops want to talk to you, kind of makes you feel like you've done something wrong." I extended my hand and walked toward her. "Mrs. Hale?"

"Yes, that's me." She accepted my greeting. "What's this about? Is everything okay?"

I glanced over my shoulder and noticed the receptionist had an eye on us. I turned back to her. "Would you mind stepping outside? I know it's cold . . ."

"It's fine. Nicole said you wanted me to bring my coat." She slipped it on. "After you."

We headed toward the double doors once again. Dixon held it open, and Mrs. Hale stepped out first. I followed her. "Thanks."

"No problem." He let go of the door and caught up to Mrs. Hale and me as I walked out of sight of the windows.

I glanced around for eavesdroppers, but no one was dumb enough to be standing outside in this weather, except us. "Mrs. Hale, I'm Detective Collins. This is Detective Dixon. I need to tell you something that isn't going to be easy to hear, but it could involve your family."

CHAPTER 36: LAUREN

As soon as the detective hinted at my family's potential involvement in something troubling, my mind immediately jumped to Jacob's transgressions. I tightened my grip on my coat, bracing myself against the biting cold and the unsettling news that was about to come. "Okay. What is it you want to tell me?"

"I understand you called the Alexandria police out to your house the night before last?" Detective Collins asked.

"Yes, I did. I thought someone was lurking around my property," I admitted, trying to keep my voice steady. "Did you find someone?"

"No, ma'am."

She responded with an eye on the immediate area around us, seeming in search of a place to go, while clutching a folder in her hand. "There's a table over there for smokers. Should we sit?"

"Actually, that's not a bad idea," the detective replied.

We walked over to the smokers' corner — a small concrete table with bench seating next to a towering trash can topped with an ashtray. The acrid smell of stale smoke wafted around us. As we sat down, anxiety gnawed at me; I knew the other shoe was about to drop. "Okay. So if you didn't find anyone, why are you here?"

She placed the file folder on the table, her partner taking up a seat beside her. I eyed the folder, my curiosity piqued.

"I've been investigating a case for some time now, Mrs. Hale." She opened the folder to reveal an image of a house wrapped in police tape. "A family lived here. Not too far from your home."

I felt a chill that had nothing to do with the weather. "What happened to them?"

Collins shared a glance with her partner before turning back to me. "They were murdered in their home while they slept."

The words hit me like a punch to the gut. I covered my mouth, shock rendering me speechless for a moment. "Oh my God . . . When did this happen?"

"A couple of months ago," she replied in a matter-of-fact tone. "And we're of the belief two other families shared the same fate over the past eighteen months. Leads have been running dry until your call came in the other night."

My brow tightened. "What do you mean? What does any of that have to do with me and my family?" Detective Collins' words swirled around me like a fog.

"You told the responding officers that you believed someone had been inside your home. In fact, you said your son had a make-believe friend, reinforcing that idea." The detective rummaged through her papers with an air of detachment. "Uh, I believe you said your son called him Billy."

I felt a shiver run through me. "That's right."

She closed the file again with a soft whoosh that echoed in my ears. "Mrs. Hale, given the proximity of my other investigation, and the fact that we now know with certainty the killer laid in wait for his victims . . ."

"There's a chance the same thing could be happening to you," Detective Dixon cut in abruptly, seeming to sense my impending reaction. "But we need to know more."

This couldn't be happening. Not now. Not while I was already dealing with the fallout of my crumbling marriage and my husband's threat to take away my son if I dared to divorce him. And now these cops were telling me that my son's imaginary friend was real . . . and deadly?

A wave of nausea swept through me, threatening to pull me under its weight. I cupped my forehead, leaning heavily over the table as if it could anchor me to reality.

"Mrs. Hale, are you okay?" Detective Collins reached out, placing her hand on my shoulder.

"No, ma'am. I'm not okay." I looked up, my gaze shifting between the detectives. "You're telling me a stranger is living in my home and that he's made friends with my son. And he wants us dead."

"I'm saying there's a small possibility an intruder may have tried to do the same thing. Whether your son's imaginary friend is real, or related, I have no idea. None of this is certain, Mrs. Hale. We're here to rule it out," Collins replied.

I raised my hands in a futile gesture of desperation. "Then what the hell am I supposed to do?" The detective's stern features were softened by a pair of sympathetic eyes. I wondered if she herself was a mother and could relate to my distress.

"Your son . . . If our assumption is correct, then the possibility exists that, yes, someone could be sheltering in your home. And maybe your son happened across him, believing he was imaginary." Collins grabbed the file again. "I read that your son is four?"

"That's right."

"Then he probably has an active imagination," she continued. "But in order for us to rule all this out, we'd like to conduct a thorough search of your home. Leaving no stone unturned. If he's there, we'll find him, or at least some evidence he may have been there at one time."

"And if you don't find anything?" I asked. "If you turn up empty-handed, what then? Are we safe?"

Dixon, a tall man with graying hair and an air of quiet authority, eyed Collins before he began. "There's a possibility we're wrong about this. In fact, this case right here in the folder is the first we'd discovered that someone was very likely living in secret with this family . . ."

"We didn't find the same evidence associated with the similar investigations," Collins shot back quickly. "So, like my partner said, we could be wrong. But I'd rather that be the case, frankly, than ignore what happened to your family altogether."

"We'd like to search the property," Dixon continued. "And then, with your permission, speak to your son about this friend."

I felt a knot tighten in my stomach. What would Jacob say to all this? Noah was so young; his world consisted of playdates and cartoon characters. "My son is only four. I can't allow you to frighten him like this."

Collins raised her hand. "I get what you're saying, Mrs. Hale. I do. Let us start with a thorough search first, and we'll take it from there. It would be very easy for us to rule out the possibility altogether. That's what we want. And I know that's what you want."

My mind was a whirlwind of thoughts, each one scarier than the last. "Yeah, okay. I can agree to that, but I'll have to tell my husband." If only they knew how that conversation would go down. "And if he agrees, then you can have at it."

"Why would he not agree for us to just take a look?" Collins narrowed her gaze.

"He's a lawyer," I replied with a weak smile. "It's just how he is."

* * *

This was going to be a delicate balancing act. Managing Jacob's irritation over a notion he was sure to dismiss and trying not to terrify my son. Jacob and I were already grappling with our own demons. This new development was unlikely to be well-received.

As the day waned, and Jacob's secretary finally relayed my urgent message to him, the familiar ringtone echoed through my office. His name illuminated my phone screen. "Hey," I answered.

"What is it, Lauren?" The indifference in Jacob's tone annoyed me. "I'm buried under work right now. Can this wait until I get home?"

"No, not really." I glanced through my office window at the late afternoon sun. The street below was bathed in its shadow. "A couple of detectives stopped by my work today to talk to me."

"What the hell for?"

"It was about the other night when the police came to our house." I tucked a swath of hair behind my ears. A nervous tick I'd always had. "Detective Collins. She's a lead investigator and has been working on a murder case—"

"Murder?" he interjected.

"Yeah, I know." I paused for a moment to gather my thoughts. "Anyway, she thinks there's a slight possibility we did have an intruder around our house. And, as she described it, there are similarities to her current investigation. Jacob, she wants to have our house searched."

"I . . . I don't understand," he faltered.

I tried to steady my trembling voice. "She thinks maybe Noah's imaginary friend isn't so imaginary. And that if she's on the right track, he could be the person she's looking for." The line went quiet. I could almost hear Jacob's mind whirring, trying to manage this surreal prospect.

"When?" His voice went soft and quiet.

"As soon as possible. In fact, I don't think we should even go back to the house until they've searched it. If someone's been in our home . . ."

"It's okay, Lauren," Jacob cut in, seemingly trying to soothe my frayed nerves. "Let them search. I don't believe for a second that anyone's been in our house without us knowing about it. The idea is absurd, but if this will make you feel better, let them."

"Okay. Thank you. I'll call her back and they can go out there today."

"What about Noah?" he asked. "I don't want him there while they do this. It'll only scare him."

"I agree, so I'll ask Nancy to watch him at her house for a while." I hesitated before adding, "Listen, uh, with everything going on between us, if you don't want to be around for this, I can—"

"I'll be there," he jumped in. "You shouldn't have to deal with this alone."

Tears welled in my eyes. I felt love in his voice. A love I wasn't sure still existed. "Okay. I'll text you when they're coming. Thank you."

"Bye, Lauren."

The line went dead, and I set down my phone. Part of me was surprised he'd agreed so readily, but then again, what would've been the point in pushing back? At least this way, I'd be able to sleep tonight knowing my house was safe.

I picked up my phone again, ready to contact Detective Collins to relay the news when, from the corner of my eye, I noticed Tammy at my door. I stopped, looking up at her with a half-smile. "Hi."

She walked in, hands on her hips, wearing that look that suggested I'd kept her out of the loop. I suppose I had, but this wasn't something I wanted getting around the office. I loved Tammy — she was like my big sister, maybe even a mother — but I couldn't risk this insane notion getting out.

"It's been a couple of hours since those people came to see you," she asked, making her way inside to sit down. And when she dropped onto the chair, her fingers tapped the arms of it. "I figured I'd give you some time, but what the hell, Lauren? Who were they? Because to me, they looked like cops." She leaned closer. "Is everything okay between you and Jacob? I mean, with all that's been going on?"

I hadn't told Tammy all of it. All of what happened with Jacob, and discovering his affair. I felt ashamed, humiliated, and it was too hard to tell even her what I knew. "No, everything's fine there. We're working on things, but those people? You're right. They're Alexandria police detectives."

"Why were they here?"

I raised a casual shoulder, trying to appear light and breezy when I felt anything but. "There've been some break-ins in our neighborhood. They wanted to come check around the house to see if their suspect had been there. You know, searching for footprints and stuff around the property."

Tammy pulled back, narrowing her gaze. She didn't believe me. I could see it in her eyes. I held my breath, waiting for her response. She was my best friend and I hated lying to her.

"Okay." She nodded as though acknowledging my lie, yet seemingly willing to go along with it. "Sorry to hear that, but sounds like the cops are on top of it." She stood again. "I hope they find the thief. Hey, uh, I'll see you tomorrow. I have to leave early."

"Everything okay?" I asked, knowing a change in topic was what I'd needed.

"Yeah, everything's fine." She swatted away any notion to the contrary. "Just a dentist appointment. Hey, let me know what they find, okay?"

"Of course." I smiled. "You know I will. See you tomorrow."

When Tammy left, I let out a sigh. I might've lied to her, but until there was something to worry about, no point in worrying her as well. I grabbed my phone again and made the call.

"Detective Collins, hello. Listen, I talked to my husband and if you'd like to conduct that search, I can be home within about half an hour. In fact, I'd prefer you do it before my neighbors return from work. I don't want to draw attention and my son can stay with his babysitter."

"I can arrange that, Mrs. Hale. Thank you. I know how frightened you must be, but I appreciate you allowing us to take a look."

"I just want my family to be safe, Detective. I'll see you at the house soon."

* * *

When I arrived home, the house was quiet. I'd made the call to Nancy to keep Noah at her house for the time being. Early evening had set in, and light would grow scarce soon. If these cops wanted to look around the outside, it was best they do it while they had the light.

I keyed the lock and stepped into our foyer. Sunlight poured in through the front windows. Jacob had said he'd wanted to be here for this but hadn't yet arrived.

As I walked through the house, turning on the kitchen lights, I glanced at my phone. He hadn't called or texted. Maybe he was on his way. I would have to shelve my resentment toward him for the time being. While I appreciated him wanting to be involved in this, it felt like a desperate attempt to appease me. Would he really try to take Noah if I filed for divorce, or was it an empty threat meant to keep me at his side?

He had the legal knowledge, the money, the power. It would be all too easy for him to take my son from me. But for now, I had to push all that aside and deal with the idea my son had made a friend and the cops believed that friend was hiding in my house somewhere.

I cast around my gaze, now feeling as though I was being watched. The entire idea seemed ludicrous, but a part of me wondered if it was true. Noah hadn't been prone to the idea of an imaginary friend. The only other explanation I could summon was that it had been his way of dealing with the pressures he must've felt coming from his father and me. Certainly not that his friend had been real — and a killer.

A knock sounded on the door. I peered through the security lens. Upon opening the door, I nodded at the detectives. "Hi. Come in."

147

"Thank you." Detective Collins walked inside, and her partner trailed her. "You mentioned your husband would be here?"

I closed the door, feeling the chilly outside air against my skin. "Yes. He should be here any minute. Don't let that stop you. I have his full support."

"Okay. Good." Collins glanced at her partner. "We should take a look around the outside of the home first before we lose daylight."

"On it," Dixon replied.

As the detectives began their search of our property, I wondered why Jacob hadn't arrived. Of course, I couldn't stop my imagination from running wild. In my mind's eye, seeing him in a passionate embrace with Madison Price, laughing at me behind my back. Still, Jacob was the kind of person who would show up on time and make sure everything was in order. But as the minutes ticked by and he still hadn't arrived, my anxiety began to rise.

I paced the house, glancing at my phone every few seconds, willing it to ring. I had faith in the detectives, but I couldn't shake the fear that something had happened to my husband, or that he was incapable of showing up when it mattered most.

Finally, I heard the garage door raising. My pinched shoulders relaxed as I realized Jacob was pulling into the garage now. I waited for him in the kitchen and when he entered, he immediately raised his hands in defense.

"Sorry I'm late. I got caught up in a meeting. I saw a car out front. The cops are here?"

I would take his excuse with a grain of salt. "They're searching the outside first while it's still light. I don't know what they expect to find, but I suppose it does make me feel better."

Jacob walked over to me, setting down his briefcase on the stool at the kitchen island. He gripped my shoulders, squaring up to me. "It'll be fine. They won't find anything. This was all just Noah's imagination. And yours. I promise you."

For a moment, I felt safe. Secure. Jacob had a way of doing that for me. "I hope you're right." I stepped back just a little, enough that he knew forgiveness wasn't in the cards. Certainly not right now. "I'll feel better once they're finished."

I glanced toward the foyer when the door opened again. "That's them." I walked over to join them. "Anything?" I set my hands on my hips, waiting for a response when Jacob appeared behind me.

Detective Collins extended her hand. "You must be Mr. Hale."

Jacob accepted the greeting. "Yes, ma'am."

"I'm Detective Collins, this is my partner, Detective Dixon."

"Nice to meet you both," Jacob replied.

"Your wife tells us you're an attorney," Dixon said.

"I am, yes. Corporate law." Jacob drew in a breath. "So, did you find anything?"

Collins dusted off a light mist that had landed on her overcoat. Her dark hair pulled in a bun was laden with that mist. "You have an attic?"

"We do," I replied.

Collins glanced at Dixon and returned her attention to Jacob and me. "We'd like to take a look."

CHAPTER 37: GARY

My shift was set to start, and I'd just arrived at the office. First thing I noticed was that Lauren's car wasn't in the parking lot. She must've already set off for home. Should I have been concerned? Maybe.

I made my way toward the building's entrance when someone else stepped out of the lobby. I smiled politely, not recalling the name of this person, but knowing he worked in the building. "Have a good night." I tipped my head.

"You too," he said, continuing on toward the parking lot.

That was when I caught sight of a woman who was heading my way. Toward the end of the block were several tents that lined the sidewalk — a small homeless encampment. This woman seemed to come from that general direction. And then, even in the darkness, her features subdued, I recognized her.

Wearing a thick coat, she continued shuffling toward me, her breath visible in the cold night air. Still several paces away, I called out to her. "What are you doing out here? Shouldn't you be in a shelter where it's warm?"

She looked up at me, her face smudged. Her hair matted and dirty. The years had not been kind to her, and I should know. "It's full. You got money? Food? Hell, I'll even take a hot coffee."

"I got a few bucks." I reached into my wallet and retrieved a five dollar bill, tossing it to her. It fell to the sidewalk. "Go get yourself something hot to eat." With nothing left to say, I started on again.

"The cops are looking for you, Gary."

I stopped, closing my eyes a moment before turning to face her again. "You gonna say anything? We had an agreement."

She turned down her lips, shaking her head. "No. But uh, you still owe me. I know you got a job now, so . . ."

I scoffed, wearing a closed-lip grin. "Look, I don't have money on me. But I will soon, and I'll give you what you want. What we agreed on." When I headed back toward the entrance, it seemed she wasn't done with me just yet.

"Don't think I won't tell them if you don't come through," she said.

Something in me snapped. I spun around, marching back toward her. Gripping her shoulders, I squeezed until I saw her wince in pain. I quickly searched for onlookers, but we were in the clear for the moment. "You think I'm going to sit here and listen to you threaten me, huh?"

She tried to pull away. "Let me go, goddamn it."

I released my grip, baring a toothy smile. "Mind your business, Cheryl, you understand me? We have an agreement. Don't think you can screw me over now."

"Then give me my money, Gary," she said, her voice firm.

I clutched her face, pressing her cheeks into her rotting teeth. "I'll get you your damn money. But I swear to God, if you go to the police . . . Just know how fucking easy it would be for me to wipe you from the face of this planet. You think anyone gives a shit about you?" I let her go once again. "Now get out of here."

CHAPTER 38: DETECTIVE COLLINS

The pull-down ladder from the attic appeared sturdy enough, so I began to climb. Dixon put his hand on the ladder as if it needed to be steadied. Mr. and Mrs. Hale stood a few feet away, their eyes on me. "Did you folks do any work up here when you remodeled?"

"We had the furnace repaired, and took a bunch of things to the dump, but nothing else," Mrs. Hale replied.

It seemed a logical place to hide. And since Dixon and I had discovered the killer's belongings in an isolated location inside the Tomlin home, an argument could be made here. But would I find anything? And if I did, what would that mean for this family? More importantly, how was I going to keep them safe? "One step at a time," I whispered.

"What's that?" Dixon asked, looking up at me.

"Nothing. I'm going in." I gripped the scuttle frame and pulled myself up, eventually using my knees for balance as I made it inside, stepping onto the plywood floor.

The draft sent a chill through me. Darkness shrouded the corners of the space while a dormer vent — the vent I'd seen when we searched the perimeter, let in some light through its painted wooden slats.

I clicked on my flashlight, aiming it in search of a light switch. "There you are." I walked a few feet where a two by four stood tall from the plywood floor up to the rafters. Mounted to it was a light switch. I flipped it on and a small bulb directly above me illuminated, shedding light in a tight circle around me. Beyond a few feet, the attic remained blanketed in shadow. "Not much light up here."

"Yeah, sorry about that," Mr. Hale replied. "I've been meaning to install something brighter up there."

I noticed Dixon begin his ascent. Moments later, he brushed off the knees of his dress pants and let his eyes roam the area. "This would make for a good hiding place."

"That's what I was thinking." I aimed my flashlight toward the dormer. "If our guy is, or was here, he would've come in through there."

"Like we figured outside," Dixon added. "Let's have a look around."

As Dixon and I moved further into the attic, creaks on the plywood floor sounded under our feet. "Looks pretty well cleaned out up here," I said, shining my flashlight around, scanning the corners for any signs of our fugitive.

"Not gonna lie," Dixon began. "It's starting to feel like we're in a horror movie up here. You see any dolls come to life, you're on your own."

I couldn't help but chuckle. Dixon had seen his share of real-life horror shows, but I appreciated the comic relief. "I'll be sure and keep an eye out."

As the small circle of light from my flashlight navigated the darkened corners, I noticed what appeared to be a partitioned area. "What's that over there?"

"I have no idea." Dixon headed over. He stopped a moment, then waved at me. "Come take a look at this."

I joined him, walking around the partition to where he stood and peering inside. Our flashlights illuminated the area. "Shelves. Boxes. Extension cords. Looks like a separate storage area. Door and all."

"Yeah." He turned to me. "What do you think?"

Scanning the area again, I raised a shoulder. "If he was here, he's not now. I don't see anything."

Dixon walked around, inspecting the shelves and the boxes on them. "Doesn't look like anyone's been up here. So where does that leave us?"

"My gut's telling me one thing, but my eyes . . ." I looked around once more. I needed to be certain about this. "I can't dismiss this yet. There must be something in here."

Dixon aimed his gaze at the floor. "No shoeprints that I can see. No evidence of personal belongings, like a blanket or anything else. I don't know, Collins, it's not looking like anyone was here."

"Mrs. Hale said the attic had been cleaned out, which isn't helping us." I couldn't just uproot this family based on a hunch. No proof to be found anywhere. But damn if my gut wasn't screaming at me right now. "Shit. I got nothing." I turned back to Dixon. "Guess I was wrong."

CHAPTER 39: LAUREN

Jacob and I stood there in the middle of our hallway, wondering what the police might find up there in our attic. The only time I ever climbed in was to pull down the Christmas decorations. Maybe bring down one of the plastic totes where I kept Noah's old clothes. It seemed I always had a friend who was pregnant and in need of baby clothes, so I kept everything of his.

I could admit that having the police here made all of this too real. Too frightening. The idea someone might have been up there, talking to Noah. Befriending him. It terrified me.

"They're coming back down," Jacob said, nudging me back into the moment.

I waited, anticipating the worst. And when they reached the bottom again, I searched their expressions, looking for a hint of revelation. "Did you find anything?" At this, Jacob wrapped his arm around me. I wanted to pull away, but keeping up appearances in front of the cops was probably the wiser move.

"We didn't, Mrs. Hale," Detective Collins replied. "Nothing we found indicated anyone was coming in or out of your attic. I would, however, suggest sealing that dormer vent as a precaution. The door on that thing moves easily."

"I can do that," Jacob added. "What happens now? I mean, what about our son and his imaginary friend?"

"I don't know what to say, except, if it would be all right with the two of you, maybe I could talk to him?" Collins asked. "Bring up the topic casually. I mean, look, nobody's here. And that's the good news. But that doesn't mean he wasn't here. Maybe when you called out the officers the other night, it scared him enough to move on."

"You're saying he was here?" I pressed.

"I can't honestly say that, no," she continued. "We're focusing on proximity, accessibility."

"Well, what about our neighbors then?" Jacob asked. "Shouldn't you warn them or something? For God's sake, if there's a killer out there getting into people's homes . . ."

Collins raised her hands. "I understand your concern. And we are monitoring the area." She turned to me. "Is your son available to speak to?"

"I don't want you to scare him," I pleaded.

"We are trained in these things, Mrs. Hale," Detective Dixon added. "And you'll be right there with him. Both of you."

I glanced at Jacob, who seemed to silently agree with me. "Okay. Yeah. He's next door. Should I get him?"

"The sooner we understand this, the better," Collins replied. "So, yes, please do."

I wriggled out from Jacob's clutch of my shoulder. "I'll go next door." And when I walked downstairs, he followed me.

"I thought I'd come with you," he said.

"You should probably stay with the detectives." I opened the front door and turned back to him. "I don't want to leave them alone in our house." While that was partially true, the reality was, I didn't want Jacob with me at all right now. My head swam with fear about this entire situation, and I quickly realized I'd just stood my ground with him. It felt good.

Moments later, I arrived at Nancy's home. It was a single-story, sprawling older home, pale yellow siding, gray shutters. From what I'd understood, it had been in her husband's

156

family for generations. Now, she lived here alone, and I wondered who helped her maintain it.

Light had faded and the streetlamps flickered on amid the darkening skies. As soon as the door opened, I saw my son in the living room and smiled. "Hi Nancy. Thank you so much for looking after Noah. I hope he was no trouble."

"No, not at all." She peered over her shoulder. "Noah, time to go home, honey. Get your book bag." She turned back to me. "I haven't fed him any dinner, but he's had plenty of snacks and treats. I hope that's all right."

I smiled. "Of course it is. I can't tell you how much I appreciate this."

She tilted her head, regarding me with that look only a grandmother could give. "Is everything all right?"

"Of course. Yeah. Jacob and I had a few things to take care of but everything's fine." I noticed Noah running toward me with his backpack slung over his shoulder. "You ready, bud?"

"Yep." He stepped outside.

"Thanks again, Nancy, and we'll see you tomorrow. Have a good night."

"Good night, Lauren. And good night, Noah." She waved at him.

"Night," he replied.

When her door closed, Noah had already begun to sprint toward the house. "Hey, buddy. Wait up, okay?" He stopped and I quickly caught up to him. "Listen, there's a couple people inside who want to talk to you."

"Who are they?" he asked.

"Police officers. They want to ask you some questions about what happened the other night and maybe about Billy too."

"Again?" He rolled his eyes at me. "Didn't we already talk to the police?"

"We did. But these are different police. It'll just be a few questions and then I'll make some dinner. Or better yet, maybe I can convince Daddy to run out and pick up some McDonald's. Would that be okay?"

He nodded and smiled, hurrying toward the house. I picked up my pace and on reaching the door, I opened it for him. "We're back."

Inside the living room, the detectives waited. Both were sitting on the sofa. Jacob emerged from the kitchen with bottles of water in his hands. "Everything okay?" I asked.

"Fine." He looked down at Noah. "Hey, buddy."

"Mommy said you can get us McDonald's for dinner tonight."

Jacob eyed me. "She did, huh? Well, then I guess that's what we're going to have. But only after you talk to the police officers. Did Mommy tell you?"

"Yeah. It's okay." He dropped his bag in the middle of the foyer and ran into the living room.

I reached down to pick it up, preparing to hang it on the nearby coat hook when Jacob touched my arm.

"You're sure about this?" he asked. "I don't want him to think every imaginary friend he has is coming to kill him."

"I hope it won't be like that. I hope, after they talk to him, we can just end this whole thing. Be done with it and get back to normal." I wasn't sure what normal meant, in light of our marital troubles, but as long as that didn't involve my son and the police, I would be okay with that.

I walked into the living room. "Sorry to keep you waiting."

"It's no problem," Collins said, turning her gaze to my son. "You must be Noah?"

He turned sheepish, barely acknowledging her, gripping the edge of his shirt with small, trembling hands. I could see the worry etched across his face as he glanced at the two detectives standing before him.

"We just have a few questions for you, Noah," Collins said with a gentle smile, appearing to try to put him at ease.

Noah's eyes flickered between them. I could sense his eagerness to cooperate despite his unease. It was impressive how he was trying to be brave for all of us.

"Can you tell us about your friend, Billy?" Collins jumped right in.

I watched Noah's expression shift from nervousness to contemplation as he seemed to ponder the question. He blew away a strand of his messy blond hair and knitted his brow. I held my breath, waiting for his response.

"Well," Noah began, "he's tall with curly hair and blue eyes. He likes to play hide-and-seek with me, and we build forts together."

My mouth dropped. This was the first I was hearing any of this. As far as we'd known, Billy talked to Noah through the walls, and Noah had never seen him. "Um, hey bud." I leaned down. "I didn't think you'd ever seen Billy. Just talked to him through our walls."

"Well, I guess so, but that's how I think he looks."

Collins nodded, capturing every word on her notepad. "And how long have you known Billy?"

Noah paused, as if calculating the passage of time. "I think I've known him since the workers finished our house."

"Do you remember how you met Billy?" Collins prodded.

Noah's eyes wandered around the room before settling on a family photo displayed on the mantelpiece. It was a picture of us over Christmas, smiles plastered across our faces. With a soft sigh, he turned back to Collins and spoke in a hushed voice.

"I was in my playroom upstairs, and he started talking to me."

"Look." Jacob stepped forward. "I think you get the gist of things here. Do you really need to ask him anything else?"

Collins and Dixon traded glances when Collins closed her notepad. "You know, Mr. Hale, I think you're right." She smiled at him. "Thank you so much for talking to us, Noah."

"Okay." He looked at me. "Can I go play now?"

"Sure, buddy." I patted his back and watched him scamper up the stairs. And when I turned back to the detectives, I noticed they'd gathered their things and were preparing to leave. "What do you two think?"

159

Collins turned back to me. "Noah seems like a great kid. And I think his imaginary friend is just that. Imaginary. So, I want to thank you both for taking the time to let us figure this out. I'm so sorry we bothered you."

"No, it's okay. Honestly, I feel much better knowing you didn't find anything," I replied. "I'm just sorry for the other families. What an awful thing."

"Yes, it is." Collins handed over one of her business cards. "If either of you need anything, or have any questions, please don't hesitate to contact me."

"Okay, sure thing," I replied. "Good luck with your investigation. I hope you find him."

"Me too, Mrs. Hale."

Collins stepped outside. Dixon followed. I closed the door behind them, feeling relieved they were gone. The entire ordeal was disconcerting, and I didn't want Noah to be afraid. As I returned to the living room and noticed Jacob sitting on the couch, something caught my eye. I kept various nick-nacks and magazines on our coffee table. One of the items was missing. "What happened to my candleholder?"

Jacob took his eyes off his phone. "What?"

I walked toward the coffee table, peering down at it. "My glass candleholder. I keep it right here on the table. Where is it?"

"I have no idea."

"Noah?" I called out. "Noah, can you come down here, hon?" I set my hands on my hips. And when I heard his footfalls, I turned to him. "Noah, you didn't accidentally break anything in here recently, did you?"

"No, Mommy. I promise. I didn't break anything."

"I had a glass candleholder right here on this table. Do you remember seeing it?"

"Why the hell would he remember something like that?" Jacob cut in.

"No, I don't. Am I in trouble?"

After all he'd been through already, this was my solution? "No, buddy, you're not." I squatted to meet his gaze. "I was

160

just wondering if you'd seen it. It's okay. Go on back upstairs. I'll find it somewhere."

He ran off and I stared at the table as if it would tell me what happened.

"For Pete's sake, Lauren, it's just a candleholder. Go buy another one," Jacob said.

I glanced up at the ceiling, overcome with an ominous feeling. Jacob dismissed my concern over the candleholder, but where was it? I remembered dusting it over the weekend. I looked back at him. "What if Detective Collins wasn't wrong? What if someone *was* in our house, and our son knows exactly who he is?"

CHAPTER 40: GARY

Inside the maintenance office, the mundane tasks of my job completed for the day, I sat suspended in uncertainty. Usually, this was when the ties of familial love would pull me homeward. But tonight, and likely for a few ensuing nights, that risk was too great. Not until I was certain I was in the clear.

My earlier encounter with Cheryl, her choices culminating in her current homeless situation, had not been entirely unexpected. Yet her demands exceeded my limited means. Our agreement hung precariously, though this was a problem better suited for another time. I had far greater concerns on my mind.

The oppressive emptiness began to expand within me, clawing away at my rationality. "I have to leave," I muttered to the room.

A desperate yearning for connection, for human touch, spurred me into motion. I left the office, making my way toward the rear exit. The biting winds welcomed me as I stepped outside. Snowflakes swirled around me in a frenzy, landing on my exposed skin, yet I felt no discomfort. I was numb to all else but my family.

Patience had been my touchstone through it all. Until the failings of the Tomlins, the Pitzers, and the Godfreys forced their reckoning.

All I'd sought was inclusion — becoming part of their love and warmth. Now I waited for Lauren's open arms to welcome me, and for young Noah to take my hand. But I could no longer bear this alienation.

Inside my car, I keyed the ignition, my gaze fixed onto the flurries that dotted the windshield. This was the only path toward fulfilling my destiny with Lauren and Noah. The only thing that would keep me sane until that happened.

The old car chugged through the quiet neighboring streets, heading deeper into suburbia. I'd chosen this vehicle poorly, praying it would see me through the night. My destination remained a mystery, even to me, yet a certain instinct assured me I'd recognize it when I arrived.

Soon, I found myself navigating a serene neighborhood. The houses were silent witnesses to my arrival. A particular home caught my eye. Light spilled from its windows onto the snow-covered lawn, painting a picture of comfort and family. "They're awake," I mumbled to myself, the longing aching in my chest as I drove by.

A sense of urgency began to consume me as I traversed the shadowy streets. And I almost missed it. A small, squalid house tucked away in a cul-de-sac. Despite its neglected exterior, something about this place summoned me. A car was parked in the driveway — a sign that a family lived here. My objective had arrived.

Parking blocks away, I retraced my steps back to the house. My fingers curled around the cold handle of the switchblade in my coat pocket as I approached.

Their names were irrelevant to me, their identities meaningless. They were a family — they possessed what had been denied to me. And tonight, they would unwittingly offer what I urgently sought — a way back to Lauren and Noah.

As I entered through a rear sliding glass door, a simple lock, easily disengaged, an icy draft welcomed me. This house was cold and carried the faint scent of charred wood from an extinguished fire in the fireplace. This was not a regal home. Nothing like Lauren's. The furnishings appeared dated. The kitchen, even in the dark, looked ancient.

Creeping through the shadowy hallway, my footsteps were muffled by thick-piled carpet. I glimpsed a family photograph hanging on the wall. Three of them. Their smiling faces radiated happiness, even while it was evident they had little else to offer.

I peeked in on what appeared to be an older child, cozy in his room. An easy target. The parents must've been in the other bedroom. I walked toward their door, my grip tightening around my weapon. The father first. Then the mother. Then the child. This wasn't personal.

My chest tightened as anticipation took hold, and I opened the door. An amber glow shone from a clock on the bedside table. Faint outlines of their figures came into focus as they lay on the bed.

Killing at random felt foreign to me. They had done nothing to bring about this misfortune. They hadn't disappointed me. Overlooked me. But I would use them to serve a purpose. I would do what needed to be done.

CHAPTER 41: DETECTIVE COLLINS

A ringing phone invaded my sleep, forcing me to open my eyes to a still-darkened bedroom. I raised onto my elbow, reaching for the bright screen that lay on the nightstand. The time showed 4 a.m. I answered the call. "Collins here."

"Detective, we got what appears to be a triple homicide at 7538 Grace Street. Captain said to call you down. Thinks it could be related to your current investigation."

I sat up, the cold wood floor chilling my bare feet as I set them down. "Got it. I'm on my way." Ending the call, I stood in a long stretch. The officer's words began to sink in. *Could be related . . .*

No time for a shower. I walked into my closet and grabbed whatever I could find to throw on. A quick splash of water on my face, a brush of my teeth, and I was ready to leave. As I entered my kitchen, ready to grab a bottle of water on my way out the door, I stopped. "Dixon." Should I drag his ass out of bed and have him meet me there? I considered how this would play out. He would know what I now suspected — that the killer had chosen his next family, and it wasn't the Hales.

On my way out the front door, I made the call. "Dixon, it's me. Meet me at 7538 Grace Street. I'm on my way now."

"What? Why?" His voice was groggy.

"Triple homicide. Could be our guy." I closed the door behind me.

"I'll meet you there," he added.

I dropped my phone into my pants pocket and hurried to my car. Stepping inside, I pressed the ignition and backed out of my driveway. I knew that street. A quiet, suburban area, older, working-class family homes. The opposite of those the killer had already targeted. So why the change?

As I drove on, I considered each of the families, including the Tomlins, who I'd been most familiar with. If this was connected too, then my suspect had now murdered thirteen people. "Christ. Thirteen."

Within twenty minutes, I'd arrived. The home was hard to miss. Swirling lights of three patrol units that lined the driveway. Neighbors milled around, even in the cold weather. The sun hadn't even come up yet. Who called this in?

CHAPTER 42: GARY

Forty-eight excruciating hours. That was how long it had been since I'd seen Lauren. I'd been careful to avoid her at the office, fearing my expression would betray me and reveal what I'd done. I didn't dare return to the Hale home. But now that the police were focused elsewhere, I was free to be with my family once again.

Hiding in plain sight took skill, patience, and an understanding of human nature. I blended seamlessly into the background, no one taking notice of me. And the wealthy, especially, were among the most complacent. They believed themselves untouchable. Who would dare breach their perfect worlds? But I had, and on multiple occasions. This time was different. Lauren was different. I must not let her go.

I shook away the emotion she stirred within me, preparing my supplies from inside the maintenance office. The day's end approached, and it was time to see her. It had to be now.

My actions had been plastered all over the news. I took caution, ensuring I'd left nothing to chance. Left nothing behind. I was certain Lauren would feel safer knowing the police believed their killer had moved on. Now was my chance to reassure her.

I proceeded down the corridor. Each step brought me closer to her. Light emanated from her office. She was still here, and my heart soared.

I stopped in front of her office, glancing inside. There she was, at her desk, appearing ready to leave. "Evening, Lauren."

"Gary, hi there," she replied. "I haven't seen you around the past few days and was beginning to wonder if it was my food. How are you?"

I adored her sense of humor. "Are you kidding? I've missed your delicious leftovers. And I'm doing just fine. You?"

"All right, thanks for asking. I was just about to leave, actually. And you know what?" She raised her index finger. "I do have a little something in the fridge. Hope you're hungry."

I patted my empty stomach. "You're too kind, Miss Lauren. I appreciate all the effort you go through to bring me some of your wonderful home-cooked meals."

"Well, I'm not so sure they're all that wonderful, but you're more than welcome. It's nice to see someone appreciate my cooking."

"Oh, I see. The family not so keen on your choice of meals?" I asked, trying to keep the conversation light.

"Well, my son only wants chicken nuggets." She paused a moment, glancing away. "And then my husband, he works long hours and isn't home for dinner very often. So, I'm afraid I don't have many takers for my meals. I'm happy to see you enjoy them."

"Yes, ma'am. I thank you very much. You have yourself a good evening and hopefully, I'll see you tomorrow. I've been getting in a little late recently. Car troubles and all that. But it's all fixed now." I started away, but stopped on a dime, tilting my head at her. "Can I ask, what's your boy's name?"

"Noah."

The smile on her face at the mere mention of her son warmed my heart. "Noah. That's a good strong name."

"I think so too. Good night, Gary."

I nodded, pushing my cleaning cart through the halls, feeling lighter for having seen her. Of course, I knew what her good-for-nothing husband had done, so I knew she was holding back her true emotions. That was fine because I was going to take care of all that for her.

CHAPTER 43: LAUREN

After leaving Gary to his duties, I continued into the hall-way. Within moments, I stopped, a text having arrived on my phone. Glancing at it, I saw that it was from the detective. She wanted to meet. More concerning was that she wanted to meet me alone, away from the office, and right now. "Why?"

Could I again ask Nancy to stay with Noah past her usual time? I'd begun to feel as though I'd been taking advantage of her. Counting on Jacob to relieve her was, of course, out of the question. We'd hardly said two words to each other since the other night when Collins and her partner came to our house. Things had gone from bad to worse and we'd become stuck in this period of uncertainty. Now, I had a detective who I thought was finished with us, but I was wrong.

I typed my reply. *I can meet you at Ronaldo's, 2 blocks from my office in 5 min, but can't stay long.* I waited for her reply that quickly came. *See you in 10.*

Something wasn't right. Something must've happened, but I would have to wait to find out. I walked straight for the elevators, my mind spinning as to why this meeting was about to take place.

The elevator doors parted, and I stepped inside. Riding down, I reached the lobby and walked toward the exit. The front desk had already been abandoned. It was later than I thought.

I pushed through the exit, but rather than head for the parking lot, I walked along the sidewalk, toward the restaurant. Tammy and I often ate lunch at Ronaldo's. But this time, I had a feeling the light-hearted banter she and I shared wasn't on tonight's menu with the detective.

As I approached the restaurant, the weight of this meeting rested on my shoulders. The glow of traffic lights, streetlamps, and cars passing by reminded me of a city oblivious to its own problems. Down a few more blocks lay an encampment. I noticed the faint flames that burned, offering warmth to those who huddled around it when my foot caught on something. I looked down. "Oh, excuse me. I'm so sorry. I didn't see you."

A lump of a woman was bent over, her large coat cocooning her body. I'd run right into her, paying no attention to what was in front of me.

She returned upright. "That's all right, miss." Her face was smudged, hair ratted and unclean. "Aren't you pretty?"

"You're very kind." I raised my hand. "My fault completely. I should watch where I'm going." I walked on when she called out to me.

"Take care now."

I didn't turn back, feeling embarrassed and a little unsettled. But as the breeze rustled through the air, the chill sent my hands inside my coat pockets and I went on my way.

I'd arrived. A small Italian restaurant and café. Two sets of iron tables and chairs sat out front, empty on this wintry day. The illuminated sign above, written in script. I lingered for a moment, peering through the foggy windows, questioning if it was best to remain in the dark about certain things. It seemed I'd begun to live my life that way, closing my eyes to the problems that surrounded me, as I'd just demonstrated by nearly mowing down a homeless woman.

Taking in a deep breath of cold air, I pushed open the heavy wooden door and stepped inside. I was immediately taken in by the aroma of oregano, garlic, and freshly baked bread. It took a moment for my eyes to adjust to the dim lighting, and then I surveyed the room in search of the detective. The soft murmur of conversation mingled with the clinking of glasses and cutlery. Gentle music played in the background. And then I saw her.

Detective Collins sat alone at a table for two near the back, her eyes fixed on the phone she held. As I approached, she didn't look up, instead motioned for me to sit across from her.

"Detective Collins. Can I ask what this is about?" I pulled out a chair.

She looked up. "I appreciate you coming, Mrs. Hale. And I'm sorry to take you away from your family."

Taking a seat, I continued, "Did I do something wrong? Why am I here?"

Collins set down her phone and gave me her full attention. "The more I work on this case, the more I think that I've been played."

I reeled back. "Sorry?"

She raised her hand. "Not by you — by the person I'm after."

"I don't understand."

We were interrupted by the server. I wasn't hungry but agreed to a glass of wine. I assumed I was going to need it sooner rather than later. When he left, Collins went on.

"Would you agree to take your son to a child psychologist to get a better understanding of his new friend?"

"What?" I rubbed the back of my neck as tension suddenly struck. "Why? I thought we were in the clear. Look, I haven't heard anything or seen anything. Whatever happened at my home, it was clearly not some crazed killer waiting to strike."

The server set down our drinks. Detective Collins had ordered a whiskey and Coke, tossing back nearly half of it in one go. She set it down and captured my gaze. "A family of three was murdered in their sleep a couple of nights ago."

"Oh my God." I clutched my chest. "I'm so sorry. That's terrible."

"Yes, it is," she replied. "But the thing is, we're supposed to believe this is connected to my other investigations. I don't think so, Mrs. Hale. Not anymore." She threw back the rest of her drink. "What I saw at that crime scene was nothing like the others. The victims were murdered with what appeared to be reckless abandon. Like the killer had no concern for them at all."

"Isn't that kind of — I don't know — what they do?" I asked, feeling wrong for posing the morbid question.

"Not if I'm supposed to believe there's a connection. The other killings . . . they were done with care. Each victim, with one or two exceptions, had their throats slit. Their bodies were placed lying flat in their beds. Feet at the bottom. Hands under the covers . . ."

"Like they were still asleep," I cut in.

"Yes, ma'am. So, I thought back to you and your family. And the more I think about you, the more I think there's a possibility that what happened to that other family was meant to distract me. Redirect my investigation."

I took a long drink from my glass of white wine. "I have to ask . . . what's it got to do with Noah?"

"Billy, Mrs. Hale. I think this has everything to do with Billy. The idea that your son happened to make up this friend around the time your renovations were completed. Only months after the murder of the previous family. Given the timespan of all the murders in question, it strikes me as too coincidental. Your home fits his M.O. Your family. It all fits."

"And so now you want to have Noah talk to a psychologist?" I continued. "To what end?"

"I've already broached the subject with a doctor I've worked with in the past. It took her a little bit to get back to me — and of course, I'm still working my other investigations.

So, I apologize for not reaching out sooner. That said, I was wondering if you'd be open to letting your son talk to her. To learn more about Billy."

The mention of a child psychologist only deepened my concern surrounding Noah's make-believe friend. Detective Collins seemed convinced he could be real. And if he was, where was he, and would he come back?

"Did your husband seal that dormer vent yet?" she asked.

"He did, yes. What good will a psychologist do, anyway?" I asked. "Noah told you everything. There's nothing else to say on the matter."

At this, she fixed her gaze on me again. "Yes, ma'am, he did. However, I think with the doctor's expertise, she can draw out more information. More details."

"But you said no one was in our house," I pleaded. "Are you saying you were wrong?"

Collins closed her eyes. I knew she felt like she was beating her head against a wall, but I was the one who was going to have to answer for this when Jacob became aware.

"I'm saying I'd like to give this one last shot, just to see if I'm on the right track." She raised her hands. "If nothing comes of it, well, then I can keep working another angle, but if your boy knows more . . ."

I wanted to tell her about what happened last week when Noah said to Jacob that Billy knew what he'd done. At the time, it made no sense to me, except to say that Noah must've seen something and claimed it was Billy. But now, in light of this, maybe I was wrong. "Okay."

I saw the relief in her face. "Thank you," Collins said. "I know this hasn't been easy, and I appreciate your cooperation."

"When?" I shrugged. "When do you want him to meet this psychologist?"

"The sooner the better." She raised her hand to garner the server's attention. "The bill, please?" Collins turned back to me. "I was thinking tomorrow morning, 7 a.m., before you need to be at work and before his school."

"I can do that." I stood, preparing to leave when Collins called out.

"Mrs. Hale?"

I turned back to her, and for the first time, I saw concern in her eyes. Worry, more like. "Yes?"

"I hope I'm wrong about all this."

"So do I, Detective. I'll see you in the morning."

* * *

I walked inside our home that had once felt so comforting, but somehow seemed different to me now. As though it was no longer mine. My husband wasn't the man I knew anymore either. In fact, if I looked in the mirror right now, I wasn't sure I'd recognize myself.

"Mommy!" Noah ran over to me, wrapping his little arms around my waist.

"Hi, sweetheart. Did you have a nice day?" I looked up to see Nancy. "Thanks for sticking around. Things should be getting back to normal soon."

"That's perfectly fine." She reached for her coat that hung near the front door. "What else would I do with my time if not look after this lovely little boy of yours?"

Gratitude for this woman swelled in my chest. "I appreciate that. Good night."

She stepped out into the cold night air, closing the door behind her.

I squatted low to look Noah in the eyes. "So, what should we have for dinner?"

"Spaghetti!" he shouted.

"Sounds good to me. Then why don't you bring down a coloring book and some crayons? You can sit with me while I cook." I wanted my son near me. I was feeling more alone than ever.

CHAPTER 44: JACOB

Something had to give. I checked the time on my phone and noticed everyone had left the office. Everyone except Maddy. I couldn't risk her coming out with the fact that I'd been skimming from the partners, from the clients. How could I have been so stupid to have revealed those things to her? This woman, who I thought I cared about. Now, I couldn't stand the sight of her. I'd made the worst mistake of my life, and it was about to cost me everything. My job, my family.

I was to blame, of course. Now, I didn't know how to break free. Maddy wanted to keep me, and I wanted to go. Then there was the whole situation with the cops. For God's sake, what the hell was I still doing here? "Waiting for her," I said to my empty office.

Lauren would either call or text soon enough if she didn't hear from me. What excuse could I possibly make to her now? She'd know who I was with — what I was doing.

"Hey, there." Maddy walked into my office in bare feet, holding her glossy black high heels with the crook of her fingers, dressed like a temptress in a slim black skirt and low-cut blouse. I would've easily indulged, had her threats not brought me to my senses. "Looks like everyone's gone home."

"Looks that way," I replied. "Maddy, I should really get home, too. All this stuff with Noah, I mean . . ."

Her expression hardened in an instant. "You know I don't like it when you talk about your family, so why do you keep doing it?"

"I'm sorry," I muttered, feeling heat rise to my cheeks. "It's just . . . I don't know, everything is so complicated right now. I feel like I'm in over my head."

"You always have been," she countered. "It's why I fell for you in the first place. You were the underdog, the one everyone overlooked. But not me."

"I know," I whispered, trying to keep my emotions in check. "But I think we both realize this isn't healthy anymore. And it's not fair to either of us."

Maddy tilted her head, a small frown creasing her brow. "Is that so?"

"Yes, it is." I took a deep breath and rose from my chair. "I need to go home. Jesus, Maddy, I told you what the cops said."

"Yeah, you did. You said they don't think whoever they're looking for was even at your house. So, I don't get it. Why are you still worried about it?" She dropped her shoes and began to unbutton her blouse. "Come on. Let's start over, okay?" Maddy walked toward my desk, sliding her finger down her blouse, revealing her lacy lilac bra.

I hesitated; my gaze locked onto her beautiful form. The lust and desire in her eyes were undeniable. "Why can't you let this go? You're so beautiful. I can only imagine how many men would want to be me right now."

"And don't you forget it," she shot back. "You're mine, Jacob. And you know what will happen if you choose her over me."

I did know. I knew I'd end up dead or in prison. Maddy's words hung in the air, a looming threat I couldn't break free from. I glanced around the room, the walls closing in on me, suffocating me. Could I really continue living like this?

Summoning every ounce of courage in me, I stepped away from her, my voice resolute. "No more, Maddy. I won't let you hold me hostage with your threats."

Her eyes darkened, bitterness rising to the surface. "You don't mean that." She moved closer to me, touching my chest with the tips of her fingers.

I pushed her away. "I do mean it. If you want to tell the partners, then so be it. But remember that you knew, and you said nothing when you'd had plenty of chances. What do you think that'll do to you and your career?"

"Well, I don't know. How about I grab my phone and make the call to Victor right now, and tell him what you've been up to?" She reached for her phone.

I swiped it from my desk, knocking it to the floor. "Don't."

She smiled. "Then I suggest you rethink your plans for this evening, Jake. Because tonight, it's just you and me."

CHAPTER 45: GARY

The news had made me out to be a monster. Murdering an innocent family of three was hardly the worst thing I'd done. The upside was that I'd accomplished my goal. The police had focused their energy on this new investigation, moving on from the Hales, leaving them to me.

In the early morning hours, I returned to the neighborhood for the first time in days, changing my vehicle location again for safe measure. I snaked through the streets, sticking to the shadows and keeping an eye out for police. The homes here lay far back and were surrounded by fences, shrubs, and trees, rendering home security cameras useless for anything beyond their front yards. Police and passersby were my immediate concern. But right now, neither were in my view. Was I in theirs? Time would tell.

I arrived at the Hale home. The sight of it warmed my heart. Still, I had to remain vigilant as I cast my gaze in all directions. I shoved my hands into the pockets of my coat. A hooded fleece covering my head kept my identity obscured.

When I reached the side gate, I tugged on it, but it wouldn't open. I peered between the slats of the white paneled gate and spotted a padlock on the inside. *Shit.* Clearly, they'd taken some precautions while I was away. Now I would be forced to scale the fence.

Using every ounce of strength in my arms, I hoisted myself up and over the fence in one fluid motion. Landing with a soft thud on the other side, I straightened my coat and surveyed the backyard. Moonlight spilled across the dormant lawn, highlighting the bare tree branches and lifeless rose bushes.

I pressed forward, skirting along the edges of the house. My footsteps crunched lightly on the icy ground as I approached the trellis that would lead me back home.

My foot was positioned on the bottom rail as I paused to listen for any signs of movement within the house. Confident its occupants remained fast asleep, I began to climb, using each ivy-covered lattice as my foothold.

Nearing the top, an unexpected creak echoed through the stillness. A loose section broke on one end, dangling precariously. My heart stopped, and I froze mid-climb, my body pressed against the icy facade of the house. It remained suspended, swinging gently until finally coming to a stop. Confident it would not detach and fall to the ground, I continued my ascent, reaching the top without further incident.

I balanced myself on the narrow ledge, eyeing the oval-shaped dormer vent before me. The *secured* vent. In a moment of panic, I clenched my fist, my breath coming in shallow gasps. But then I contemplated a solution. I had come too far to turn back now.

Taking my chances, I reached out and pushed against the dormer frame, hoping to dislodge whatever was used to keep it shut. My boot slipped, forcing me to clutch the metal frame for dear life. The dangling piece below me broke free, falling to the ground with a mild thud. Was I next?

I searched for another foothold, realizing that a fall from this height would not go unnoticed. I might not even survive it. In the bitter cold, I gathered my wits, and tried again. Securing my step, I attempted to dislodge the dormer frame, freeing the door enough to allow me to enter. Every move I made seemed acutely loud. With my elbow, I thumped on the door. Over and over, I tried, until it budged. A small gap appeared between the door and the frame.

One final effort and the vent gave way with a metallic screech that cut through the silence. For a moment, I feared the noise would draw attention from either inside or outside the house, alerting someone to my presence, but nothing happened. The house remained silent, as if holding its breath in anticipation of my arrival. I hoisted myself through, stepping lightly onto the plywood floor. A smile tugged at my lips. I was home.

CHAPTER 46: LAUREN

My eyes snapped open when I heard the noise. Surrounded by darkness in our bedroom, I lay still in our bed, waiting for it again, but after several moments — nothing. Had I dreamed it? It wouldn't have been the first time. But, considering all that happened, I would not discount it so easily.

I looked at the other side of our bed, but Jacob wasn't there. Then I remembered I'd insisted he sleep in the guest room. I'd gone to bed early and hadn't heard him until he entered our room. When he'd walked in, my stomach turned at the idea of what he'd been doing, so I demanded he leave. He did so without argument.

When I checked the time, it showed 3 a.m. If the sound wasn't a figment of my imagination, then surely, Jacob would've heard it, too. I tossed the covers away and sat up, pressing my bare feet on the thin rug beneath our bed. It did little to absorb the cold.

With a moment to gather my thoughts, I stood, reaching for my robe that lay on the bench at the end of our bed. Tying it around my waist, I put on my slippers and shuffled to the door. Were my son not on the other side of this door, just down the hall, I might have reconsidered this investigation.

But if the worst came to pass, I had to protect him. And I would — at any cost.

I turned the doorknob and eased the door open, peering into the hallway that let in the moonlight from downstairs. The soles of my slippers scuffed the floor, forcing me to take each step with caution to silence the sound.

As I approached Noah's room, I hesitated, listening for any signs of movement. His rhythmic breaths were barely audible. I gently opened the door, revealing a sliver of light that spilled into the hallway. His nightlight.

A sense of relief swept through me when I saw Noah asleep. His tousled blond hair lay across his forehead as his sprawling body was outlined under the covers. He was safe.

Leaving his room, I continued into the hallway toward the landing. The house was void of sound. Not even the ticking of a clock, or the hum of the heating. Every step felt like a muted thud in this stillness. I'd begun to think this was all in my head.

The stairs were before me now. Stepping down, the living room came into view. Moonlight and streetlamps filtered through the lightweight curtains, casting a blueish-gray tinge over the room. I walked through to the other side, onward to the guest room next to the den. Opening the door, my eyes were drawn to the solitary figure stretched out on the queen-sized bed, wrapped in a blanket. Jacob. The lines in his forehead had softened. His brow relaxed, as if he lay under the sun on a warm beach without a care in the world. A pang of sadness overcame me, even as anger simmered beneath the surface.

I approached him, reaching out to shake his shoulder. "Jacob. Jacob, wake up."

He stirred, his eyes flickering open before registering my presence. Confusion clouded his gaze for a moment, and when it seemed recognition had dawned, he sat up with a start.

"Lauren?" He rubbed his eyes as if trying to clear away the remnants of a deep sleep. "What are you doing up?"

"I heard something." My curt reply came out harsher than I'd intended.

He cleared his throat. "It's just your imagination getting the best of you, Lauren. The cops searched this place inside and out. No one's here. You're safe. Go back to bed."

I turned around, discounting his demand, and walked upstairs again. Only this time, I stopped at the attic scuttle and looked up. An instinctive fear consumed me. My skin tingled over what might be up there, no matter that the police had been here and searched twice now. It was Detective Collins' words that haunted me. *The murdered family of three was a distraction.* I had a son to protect. And if Jacob wasn't going to do something, then I would.

I pulled down the scuttle door and lowered the wooden ladder. The steps creaked under my weight, but I pressed on, knowing I wouldn't sleep unless I saw for myself that we were safe — and alone.

As I entered the attic, the air grew colder. A thick fog seemed to hover inches from my face, obscuring my vision. The attic was nearly bare now since the remodel. If someone was here, they couldn't easily hide.

It was all I could do to stop the rising panic within me. The weight of the last few weeks, the stress, the suspicion, the fear, it all lodged in a ball in my chest. But as I continued on, I saw nothing. I heard nothing. And when I set my gaze on the dormer vent — the one Jacob had finally secured — I noticed it was still closed. The knot in my chest loosened. I could breathe again. Now, I could go back to sleep, knowing we were safe.

* * *

Getting out of the house this morning while Jacob readied for work had taken some doing. But I'd had to get Noah to this psychologist by 7 a.m. Jacob hadn't seemed interested in the least in what we'd been doing up that early.

We were here now. After losing a fair amount of sleep last night, thanks to my irrational fears, I felt ready to get this over with. The detective was wrong. She had to be.

The lobby of the doctor's office was small, but uncluttered. Decorated in neutral tones and comfortable seating. A door on the far wall seemed to be the entrance to the psychologist's private office. Through the frosted glass, I could see the warm glow of a lamp and what appeared to be bookshelves on the back wall. The door was adorned with a small sign that read, *Dr. Elizabeth Kearney, Psychologist*, in block letters.

I squatted low to meet Noah's gaze. "Okay, like we talked about. The doctor is going to ask you about Billy. Answer as honestly as you can, and everything will be fine."

"I already talked to the police, Mommy," he whined. "Why are we here?"

The lobby door opened, and Detective Collins walked inside. "Noah? Good morning. How are you?"

My son immediately eyed the bag she held. "What's that?"

Collins raised it. "This? I figured when you were finished, if your mom didn't mind, you might like a donut. So I picked up a few."

Noah's eyes lit up. He was given donuts only on special occasions, but if I denied him this, then I truly was the worst mother in the world.

"Can I have one, Mommy?"

I rubbed his shoulder. "Of course. Just as soon as we're finished here. We'll head back to school, and I'll even let you eat it in the car." My attention was drawn to the doctor, who emerged from her office.

Collins introduced us. "This is Mrs. Lauren Hale, and her son, Noah."

The doctor approached with an outstretched hand. "Noah, it's very nice to meet you. I'm Dr. Kearney."

"Go on." I gently nudged my son. "Shake the doctor's hand."

"Hi," he whispered.

The doctor then set her sights on me. She was younger than I'd expected. Short, dark, hair worn in a bob. A casual sweater over top of dress pants. "Mrs. Hale, thank you for allowing me to speak to Noah. I assume you would like to sit in on the conversation?"

"Yes, please." I looked at Collins. "Will you be in there, too?"

Dr. Kearney raised her hand. "We agreed it would be best if our talk involved just you and Noah. Notes, however, with your permission, will be shared with Detective Collins when we're through."

I nodded. "Okay. Can we get started? I don't have a lot of time."

"Yes, of course." Kearney gestured toward her office. "Right through here."

Collins reached out for my shoulder. "I'll be out here."

"Thank you." I turned to Noah. "Come on, bud, let's go inside."

We settled into large comfortable armchairs while Dr. Kearney sat across from us in a rolling desk chair. She held a notepad and wore a pleasant smile. The bookcases I'd seen from the lobby lined the back wall and were filled with various books on mental health. A few house plants were dotted around, and a lamp illuminated the top of her desk.

"I want to thank you for agreeing to see me, Mrs. Hale, and you, Noah. So for the sake of time, let's get started." She flipped through a file folder before continuing. "Noah, can you tell me exactly when you met your friend, Billy?"

My first thought was that he'd already answered this question. I had no idea what new information Detective Collins hoped to garner, but now that we were here, I guess I'd find out.

Noah answered the doctor, calmly, matter-of-factly, as if nothing seemed out of the ordinary at all. "I heard him in our walls after all the workers left."

"We just had our home remodeled," I cut in.

"Ah." The doctor nodded, jotting down something in her notepad. "So was it Billy who talked to you first?"

"Yeah," Noah said.

She wrote down more notes before pressing on. "Have you ever seen Billy?"

"No, he only talks to me. I don't see him."

I creased my brow, because when Collins asked him this question, he'd offered a description of Billy. Why had he made it up then, but not now? Then again, he was four.

"All right," the doctor added. "And has he asked you anything about your family?"

"Uh-huh," Noah replied. "He's asked me about Mommy, and he told me to tell my daddy something." Noah looked down. "But when I did, Daddy got kinda mad at me."

"Oh, honey, he wasn't mad at you," I jumped in, offering him a comforting hand.

"Mrs. Hale, it's okay. It's important we understand what it was Noah felt at the time, or how he perceived things."

"Sorry, of course." I leaned back, clasping my hands in my lap.

"Noah, you said you thought your dad got mad at you. Why?" Kearney asked.

He raised a shoulder. "I don't know. Billy said to tell my dad that he knew about something, but I didn't know what, or why I had to say anything."

The questions continued, each one seeming to probe a little deeper. But now that it was out, that Noah told Kearney about what happened with Jacob, I wondered what Collins would do.

I'd intentionally left all that out, thinking it didn't matter. But maybe it did. And now, despite my best efforts to keep it under wraps, the truth about our marital troubles had begun to bleed through the cracks.

"Well," the doctor closed her notebook. "I think that's enough for now, Noah, don't you?"

He nodded with enthusiasm.

Kearney smiled. "All right. Why don't you head back into the lobby? There are a few coloring books in the corner. I'd just like a minute or two with your mom, okay?"

Noah looked at me. "It's okay. I won't be long."

Dr. Kearney showed him out and waved Collins in. Before I'd asked a single question, the doctor went straight for the throat. "I firmly believe Noah is certain Billy is real."

Defeated, I glanced at Detective Collins. "So whoever this guy is, was actually in our home?"

"What I mean to say, Mrs. Hale, is that Noah isn't lying," the doctor clarified. "Whatever he is telling you about this Billy, that person is very real to him. Now, I don't know what this means to your investigation, Detective, but it could also point to high levels of stress Noah might be dealing with. It's not uncommon for kids to create imaginary worlds to help them cope."

"Where does that leave us?" I looked at Detective Collins for an answer. "I came here. Did as you asked. Now what? We don't know any more than when we came in here."

"What kind of stress is Noah under?" Collins asked.

Now, I was going to have to come clean. "His father and I have been dealing with things. I suppose Noah's probably picked up on some of it."

"Such as?"

She wasn't going to let this go. I pressed my lips, considering how best to phrase this in front of the doctor. She would read about it soon enough in the doctor's notes anyway, so I might as well clarify the issue. "Jacob and I are dealing with infidelity issues."

Collins placed her hands on her hips. "And you didn't believe this was relevant?"

"No, actually, I didn't," I shot back.

Collins glanced at the file in the doctor's hand. "I'd like to review your notes, Dr. Kearney, before making a final determination." She turned to me again. "You should take Noah to school and go to work. I'll get back with you later today when I know more."

"Fine." I glanced between them. "But you need to tell me, Detective, whether my family is safe in our home. I don't know if we are."

CHAPTER 47: DETECTIVE COLLINS

When I returned to the station, uniformed officers hustled to and fro with papers and folders in hand. People sat on benches in the waiting area, looking either worried or angry.

As I headed through the lobby to the detective's bullpen, the faint scent of coffee lingered in the air. An occasional whiff of cigarette smoke hung on the clothes of the other detectives as I passed them by. Soon, I found Dixon standing at my desk. "Hey."

"Hey, yourself." He shifted his weight with an air of expectation. "What happened this morning?"

As I walked around to my chair, Dixon perched on the edge of my desk, folding his arms, waiting for an answer. "I took copies of the doctor's notes and now I need to review them. After that, I can figure out our next steps."

"You really think this kid is the key?" Dixon asked.

"Hard to say." I laid the file folder onto my desk. "I don't think he's seen this guy, but I gotta tell you, this kid knows something. This Billy? Even if he's not at the Hale home anymore, I think he *was* there. And I'm certain he talked to the boy."

Dixon grunted. "But why leave without finishing the job? Thirteen other people weren't so lucky. Thirteen. What makes this family different?"

I dropped onto my chair. "The last three, we can't connect to our suspect yet."

"Oh, come on," he scoffed. "You know as well as I do it's the same guy."

"Could be a copycat. The M.O. didn't match." I considered my words. "Sounds like I'm trying to convince myself they're not connected, doesn't it?" I raised my index finger. "I did learn something else pretty interesting."

"Oh yeah? What's that?"

"Looks like there's trouble in paradise. Mr. and Mrs. Hale are in the middle of some marital strife."

"That could affect how their son is perceiving the world around him," Dixon added.

"That's what I'm afraid of." I pulled up to my desk. "I'll tell you what, let me get through these notes. See what stands out. I have a feeling these marital issues might be worth digging into."

"Why would that make any difference?" Dixon returned to his feet.

"Check it out." I got up and approached the murder board. Examining the images of families, and locations, I turned to Dixon. "What do you see on this board?"

He seemed to examine it for a moment, then continued, "Families who live in nice homes. Not unlike the Hales."

"Families, yeah. And to our knowledge, none of these families had serious issues. None that their relatives have made us aware of."

"Okay, what's your point?" Dixon pressed, still studying the board.

"What if — assuming Billy is a very real grown man, and he was, at some point, hiding out in the Hale home — what if he picked up on the troubles between Mr. and Mrs. Hale?"

Dixon raised a brow. "And if he did? You think that's how he's been choosing his victims? He thinks they're happy families and wants to destroy that. The Hales, maybe not so much."

"Why else target them? Happy, wealthy families? Could be the guy's an orphan. Abandoned by his own family. So if he's out for revenge, he figures these other families have what he never did." I considered how this applied to the Hales. "Maybe that was why he left the Hale home. Somehow, he figured out they weren't so happy after all."

"No, I don't buy it." Dixon raised his chin. "First of all, that doesn't track with the latest victims. They didn't have a pot to piss in. Maybe they were happy, but we don't know enough about them yet. If we're assuming these latest murders were committed by the same man, then, he doesn't discriminate. He'll go after any family. So, if he had targeted the Hales, then something else set them apart. Something else kept them alive." He aimed his finger at me. "That's what we need to find out."

"Fair point," I replied. "We can't even prove the killer was at their home at all. Only the Tomlins had proof of an unwelcome guest. I'm just running on the assumption, that's what happened in all cases."

"Don't go second-guessing yourself now, Collins," Dixon shot back. "You'll find yourself running around in circles pretty damn quick, you start thinking like that. No, we're on the right track. We're just missing a piece of crucial evidence that ties all these murders together in no uncertain terms."

I considered his words, trying to fit together these puzzle pieces that, so far, had little to do with one another.

"Listen." Dixon headed back to his desk. "Give me a heads-up when you're ready to go over your findings."

"Will do." As I began to read the doctor's notes, I could see she'd asked many of the same questions I had, but when she'd asked about what Billy had told Noah, that was where things appeared to get interesting. I also found it interesting that Mrs. Hale conveniently left this part out the first time around.

Noah's response indicated that Billy had seen something his father had done — not Noah, himself. Was Billy created as a way to shield Noah from his own confusion? Possibly, but I was no psychiatrist. Nevertheless, given what I knew about the kid, he didn't strike me as withdrawn, or fearful, or any manner of emotions that get tangled up in the shit our parents do.

So, Dixon was right. No going back. No second-guessing. If I was going to do this, then I had to decide if Billy was really my suspect. Otherwise, I needed to let this lead go, and pray the blanket and pillow in the hands of Forensics turned up something worthwhile.

"Hey, Dixon?" I asked.

He turned around, setting down his cup of coffee. "Yeah?"

"You feel like making a trip?" I got up and snatched my coat from the back of my chair.

"Where to?"

"I'm right about this. I can feel it. Billy is real. And I think he could be someone who knows the Hales."

"Okay."

"We're going to Lauren Hale's office. Then her husband's. I want to find out who they know and who had access to their home."

Dixon took a quick sip of his coffee before reaching for his coat. "After you."

We carried on through the station. The hustle of the early morning invigorated me. The night shift was leaving. The day shift, coming onboard. Nothing but uniforms passing by us as we headed out toward the parking lot.

I unlocked my car and turned to Dixon. "Hop in."

When he did, he turned to me. "If the killer knows the Hales, then how does it tie to the other victims?"

"I don't know yet. Proximity? Our guy has been stalking the Alexandria suburbs for a year and a half. We ain't that big a city. The Hales survived, assuming I'm correct. So, why was that?"

"A personal connection," Dixon said, nodding. "Maybe."

I jumped onto Duke Street, hoping to avoid the morning traffic on the Capital Beltway Loop, eventually heading toward Old Town North. Dixon and I were quiet as I navigated the rush hour.

I made the turn onto Montgomery Street and continued down until I spotted the building. Ackerman & James was on the right, and I pulled into the entrance, parking near the front. I turned off the engine. "I have no legit reason for believing any of this, but I ask that you trust me. I'm going with my gut, here."

"That's what any good detective would do."

We stepped out of the car, and I adjusted my coat as we made our way toward the doors. I walked in to see the receptionist looking up at us from her desk, mild recognition on her face.

"Good morning." I flashed my badge. "Detective Collins and Detective Dixon. We're here to speak with Lauren Hale again."

"Yes, ma'am." The young woman typed something into her computer. "I'll let her know you're here. Go ahead and take a seat."

"Thanks." I waved Dixon back and we settled into the plush chairs arranged neatly in the waiting area. I was glad not to be waiting for Lauren outside again. The temperature had taken a nose-dive overnight, and now hovered well below freezing. I tapped the arm of my chair and looked over at Dixon. "So, I figured we'd ask her about her coworkers first. Maybe talk to one or two of them . . ."

"You're risking a lot of water-cooler talk about Mrs. Hale," he cut in. "She might not be willing to allow that."

"You could be right, but if we make her understand that there's a distinct possibility Billy is real, and he's someone she and her husband might know, I think she'll be open to suggestion."

I saw the wheels spinning in Dixon's mind. I hadn't convinced him of my plan. To be honest, I wasn't sure either, but to me, it was the best way to figure out how Billy knew something important about Mr. Hale, insisting Noah relay a message. No way a four-year-old could comprehend something that meaningful. "It wouldn't be the first time a vicious murderer blended in with his surroundings. Look, I struck out thinking the killer was a transient, moving from place to place, maybe living in encampments. This is the next logical move."

"I get where you're going," he replied. "It'll be tricky. She'll be reluctant to shed light on this situation."

"But if it means keeping her son safe, she'll go along with it." I heard high-heeled shoes echoing behind me and looked toward the elevator. Lauren Hale approached. I smacked Dixon on the arm to draw his attention before standing. "Mrs. Hale. I'm so sorry to bother you."

I could see she wasn't happy about our arrival.

"What are you doing here?" Her gaze searched for onlookers.

"Can we talk in your office?" I asked. "It's about Billy and how he came to know information about your husband. Information, I assume, that wouldn't be readily available to your son."

"Fine, okay. Follow me." She turned on her heel, walking back to the elevators.

Dixon and I trailed her inside and rode to the second floor. Mrs. Hale carried on into the hall and eventually arrived at her office.

"Can I get either of you anything to drink?" she asked.

"No, I'm good." I walked toward the chairs and took a seat.

"Me, too, but thank you," Dixon added, following me to a chair.

And when Mrs. Hale sat down, I began. "I had an opportunity to review Dr. Kearney's notes. To be honest, my biggest concern was why you left out the part that Billy had asked Noah to relay a message to your husband."

"I didn't think it was relevant," Mrs. Hale replied.

"Your son is four," I reminded her. "Let's be honest here, he wouldn't have understood the implications of relaying such a message. What child that age knows to make up a person to say he knew what his father had done?"

Mrs. Hale regarded both of us. "What are you saying?"

"At this point, ma'am, I don't know where else to turn. I'm saying I do believe Billy is real, and that he could be someone you and your husband know."

"A friend of the family, coworker," Dixon cut in. "Someone who'd come into your home a few times. And this person might've said something to Noah."

The look in Mrs. Hale's eyes revealed her incredulity. As if we were out of our minds. "Then why didn't Noah just say that?" she shot back. "Just say that it was a friend of ours who said these things to him?"

"Noah's scared, confused." I leaned over, resting my elbows on my thighs. "Here's what we know. Four different families inside the Alexandria metro area have been murdered over the past eighteen months. We are certain the killer had been hiding out inside at least one of the homes. You believed you'd had an intruder." I held up my fingers as if counting off. "Your son essentially relayed a threat to your husband about something he couldn't have known about. You said yourself you haven't been feeling safe in your home. Noises, and bumps in the night. Am I reaching for a connection? Maybe. But don't you want to know if someone in your circle could be a killer?"

CHAPTER 48: JACOB

She didn't bother saying goodbye this morning. Not even allowing Noah to say goodbye to me either. Here I'd been, sleeping in our guest room, having to get ready for work in the guest bathroom. All the while, Lauren pretended I wasn't there.

Except when she woke me up in the middle of the night. I'd tried to convince her it was all in her head, but it didn't help my cause. Although, I wasn't sure what my cause was. What I did know was that if I didn't continue seeing Maddy, she would blow the whistle on me.

Threatening to take Noah from Lauren, in hindsight, wasn't the smart move. I'd been angry and lashed out at her as if she was the guilty one.

We couldn't continue on this way, that much was clear to me now. But until this whole Billy situation could be resolved, what could I do? How was I supposed to alleviate Lauren's fear that someone had been, or still was, hiding in our home? It seemed insane. Even the cops ruled it out, and yet she wasn't convinced.

Noah's imaginary friend wasn't helping the situation either. It occurred to me that Noah must have overheard a conversation I'd had, and that subconsciously, his friend,

Billy, needed to confront me about it. Jesus, what four-year-old had to deal with shit like that?

I was pulled from my troubling thoughts when my desk phone rang. I answered the call. "Yeah?"

"Mr. Mullen would like to see you in his office as soon as you're available."

"Okay, thanks."

What the hell did he want? I stared off into the distance, my mind spinning with reasons why Vic wanted to see me. He was the senior partner, and only called on us when there was a problem. Could Maddy have actually gone through with her threat? But if she had, surely, she would realize it would be over between us. That wasn't her goal.

I pushed back in my chair and slowly got to my feet. My tie suddenly felt too tight, so I wriggled my index finger in the knot to loosen it. I pulled on my suit jacket, fastening the single button.

I'd been careful to bury my calculations deep enough that it would take a forensics team to uncover them. Or for Maddy to have spilled her guts. But that couldn't be it. This had to be about something else, and I needed to calm the fuck down.

I made my way through the hallway, my polished black Dior shoes echoing on the travertine floors. All the partners were on the top floor, but Vic's office was the enormous one in the far back corner, overlooking the downtown skyline. As I reached the door, I took a moment to compose myself, smoothing out any wrinkles in my suit before knocking.

"Come in," a low voice called from the other side of the door.

I stepped into Victor Mullen's office. His presence dominated the room. His large mahogany desk stood in the center, pristine, not even so much as a sheet of paper out of place. He wore a suit that cost more than my car, and his salt and pepper hair was worn short and smoothed back. But it was his eyes I noticed in this particular moment. Penetrating blue, beady eyes that evaluated my every step.

"You wanted to see me, Vic?" I asked, coming off breezy and unconcerned.

He leaned back in his leather chair, his hands steepled in front of him. An air of authority that made me uneasy. But at the same time, I respected the hell out of him.

His gaze never wavered as he observed me, his expression unreadable. After a moment, he spoke in a calm voice. "Jacob. Please, have a seat," he gestured toward the gray barrel chair opposite his desk. I obliged, lowering myself onto the seat with controlled poise.

The room fell into silence for a brief moment before Vic spoke again, "Jake, I called you in here today because an issue needs to be addressed. A very serious one. It has come to my attention that certain discrepancies have been found in our financial records. Documents have gone missing, transactions unaccounted for."

My heart quickened at his words, and I could feel a bead of perspiration developing on my forehead. Could they have discovered what I'd done? Had my carefully crafted veneer finally crumbled? More importantly, I realized this was Maddy's doing.

"I'm sure this is all just a misunderstanding," Vic continued. "One I'm certain you'll be able to clear up immediately, if not sooner."

I forced a calm smile, masking the fear that threatened to consume me. "Of course, Vic. I'm not sure what exactly is going on, but I'll do everything in my power to get to the bottom of this and rectify any discrepancies." My voice came out steady, though I wondered if he could smell the fear coming off me.

He was a shrewd man who could detect a lie from a mile away. A good trait for a lawyer. "Good," Vic said, the corners of his lips turning upward. "I knew I could count on you, Jake. You have always been meticulous in your work."

Was that relief I felt? Too soon to know, but I couldn't let my guard down just yet. If Vic suspected even an inkling of the truth, it would be disastrous for both Maddy and me. I had to tread carefully.

As the seconds ticked by, Vic's penetrating gaze bore down on me, searching for any sign of guilt or hesitation. But I fancied myself a master of deception, capable of maintaining an unwavering facade even in the face of adversity. Yet another good trait for any lawyer.

With every ounce of my willpower, I projected confidence and innocence. "Thank you for your trust in me, Vic. I take great pride in my work. I'll find out what's going on and get it straightened out."

He nodded, his already narrow eyes becoming mere slits now. "Glad to hear it." His fingers drummed on the polished surface of his desk. "But let me make one thing clear, Jake. These discrepancies cannot afford to go unresolved for long."

I stood. "Consider it settled, Vic. I'll have answers for you by the end of the day." With my hands clasped in front of me, I waited for his dismissal, wondering if I'd stood too soon, and he wasn't finished with me yet.

"See that you do." Vic returned his attention to his laptop.

"Thank you." I carried on with my shoulders back and my head held high. Any sign of weakness now would all but assure him of my lies.

When I exited his office, there was only one place for me to go. And down two floors below me, I had arrived. There she was, sitting at her desk, busily typing away, so I walked in, and it took a moment for her to notice me.

"Jake, what are you doing down here?" Maddy asked.

I moved in closer, standing directly in front of her desk. I pressed my palms on its surface and stared into her eyes. "What the hell have you done?"

CHAPTER 49: DETECTIVE COLLINS

Could I blame Mrs. Hale for her reluctance? I'd already dragged her son into this, and now I was asking to talk to her coworkers and friends. All of this because I'd had a hunch that, so far, hadn't panned out. So was I forcing the issue? Yeah, absolutely. But the only way to rule out a theory was to test it. I had no choice and nowhere else to go.

"Mrs. Hale, I know I've already put you through a lot—"

"No," she shot back. "You're wrong about this. None of what's happened to my family has anything to do with the people I work with. My friends . . ." She leaned over her desk. "Do you have any idea what will happen to me if word gets out about all this?"

"No, frankly," I interjected. "My main concern has been that your family could well be in danger, and my partner and I want to cover all our bases. But tell me, Mrs. Hale, how would this change your work environment?"

She rubbed her forehead, and I could see her wanting to speak, but holding something back. "I don't want everyone to know about the affair."

I glanced at Dixon. "The infidelity you mentioned earlier. Your husband's?"

"Well, it wasn't mine." Her eyes reddened as she fought back tears. "Look, I get you're working a serious investigation, and I absolutely do not want my family to be part of it. But here we are. Even though you've cleared our house, whoever this Billy is . . . yeah, I get it could be bad, dangerous even."

She took a deep breath, appearing to try to settle her nerves. "The thing is, what I believe happened was that Noah must've overheard Jacob talking to the woman he's cheating on me with. The two of them work together. And my son . . . I don't know . . . he must've realized it was wrong or that it would hurt me, and this was how he chose to deal with it."

I raised my index finger. "Sorry, but have you talked to Noah about this affair? Are you certain he knows about it?"

"Well, no, I'm not," Mrs. Hale replied. "But what else could explain why he confronted Jacob, claiming it was his imaginary friend telling him to say those things?"

"Exactly. That's what I'm trying to get at," I reiterated. "Mrs. Hale, please. Someone could be after you and your family. And like I said, there's a very real possibility it's someone you know."

Mrs. Hale nodded, my words appearing to sink in. She bit her lower lip, and her fingers trembled as she clutched the edge of her desk.

"You think it's someone we know?" she whispered, an eye out toward the hall.

I raised my shoulder. "It's a possibility we have to rule out. More likely? I think it could be someone you know who is connected to the killer."

Her emotions bubbled to the surface. A tear glistened as it rolled down her cheek. "But who could it be? Who would want to hurt us like this?"

"That's what we have to find out." I had to offer some sort of reassurance, but the only thing I could think of was the one thing cops were never supposed to say: "I promise you, Mrs. Hale, we will get answers."

CHAPTER 50: GARY

The long-awaited moment had finally arrived, the homecoming of young Noah from school. I was lucky to still be here, after narrowly avoiding Lauren last night in the attic. I'd been prepared with knife in hand, ready to do what needed to be done if she had discovered me. But something had stopped her from continuing her search. For me, it reinforced what I was certain was my destiny — to live as part of this family. Nevertheless, the encounter stirred a sense of urgency within me.

I'd already begun to pull at the thread of Jacob's existence, unraveling the picture-perfect life he'd risked for a woman like Madison Price. Soon, it would be time.

The echo of the front door opening reached my ears. I crept toward the dormer, cautiously peeking through the wooden slats. I observed the young boy's return, alongside his caregiver.

A proud smile tugged at my lips as they entered the house. I dropped back, hurrying to listen in on his arrival. I heard the old woman asking if he'd like a snack. What child didn't want a snack? In fact, I could've used one myself.

It would be several more minutes before Noah would be allowed to play in his playroom upstairs. I had time to plan out our conversation. To convince him of what he must confront his father with. Yes, I knew what the end result would be.

As Noah's footsteps reverberated through the house, excitement and some trepidation swirled in me. I had only just begun to imprint myself upon Lauren's heart. Would it be enough?

Noah ventured upstairs, as evidenced by the sound of the television in the playroom. I hovered near the vent where voices around the house traveled. And when I was certain he was in that room alone, I steadied myself.

"Hi, Noah, it's Billy." I waited, my ear practically glued to the vent. "Are you there, Noah?" He was there. I'd heard the television broadcasting his cartoons. "Why are you not answering me? I thought we were friends."

Silence pervaded for a moment longer, and then I heard the sound of shuffling, as if Noah was adjusting himself on the floor in his little beanbag chair.

"I'm sorry, Billy." Noah's voice finally came through. "I didn't know you were there. I didn't mean to hurt your feelings."

This was it. The moment to plant the seed of doubt in Noah's mind, to open his eyes to the truth. "It's okay, Noah," I replied, my voice gentle yet purposeful. "I wanted to talk to you about something important. Something about your daddy." I could feel his hesitation. The child wasn't ready for this, but I didn't have much choice. I had run out the clock.

"What about my daddy?" he asked.

Taking a moment to collect my thoughts, I continued in a measured tone, careful to choose my words wisely. "Noah, your daddy . . . he's not who you think he is. He's been keeping secrets from you."

I could sense his unease growing amid the quiet, until finally . . . "What do you mean?"

The weight of responsibility settled heavy on my shoulders as I prepared to turn a boy against his father. "Your daddy — he doesn't love your mommy anymore. He has a girlfriend now. He wants to be with her now." I held my breath. "Noah?"

"He doesn't love Mommy?" His voice was tiny and full of fear.

"No, and he doesn't love you either, Noah."

CHAPTER 51: DETECTIVE COLLINS

The notion that someone from Mrs. Hale's workplace could be the person we were after was a hell of a stretch. Dixon knew it, too. If anything, it was more likely to be someone in their circle of friends. Regardless, I still believed a tenuous connection existed. Or it was simply my last-ditch, desperate attempt in a case that had baffled me at every turn. Dixon would probably have gone with that.

"Mrs. Hale, can you tell me if anyone new has entered you and your husband's lives? A new acquaintance, a neighbor, friend, coworker? Someone who reached out to you, not the other way around."

She narrowed her gaze, appearing to sift through her memories. "As I mentioned before, for the past six months or so, we'd been renovating our home. Several contractors had access to the house, came and went virtually as they pleased." She raised a shoulder. "I have to say, it seems much more realistic to assume it was one of them than a friend or coworker, even if the thought terrifies me."

Dixon grunted. "That does make sense. Contractors often hire people who lay low, blending in with their surroundings. We know our guy has been lurking in the general area for longer than six months, so the timing tracks."

"It could be how he's able to gain access into the homes — all of them," I added, regarding Mrs. Hale once again. "Can you give me the names of the companies you hired? We'll start making some calls."

"Yeah, of course," she replied. "Does that mean you won't question the people here?"

"This is a stronger angle," I conceded. "So, we'll hit this first, but I'd still like you to compile a list of your friends or coworkers who've been around Noah recently. We can't afford to overlook anyone."

Mrs. Hale appeared to hold her tongue for a moment before adding, "Detective, please be straight with me. Are we safe in our home?"

She had every right to be afraid. "I'll set up a patrol in your neighborhood. Keep eyes out for people and cars coming and going. If anyone appears out of place, our officers will question them."

"We'll run background checks on everyone who's been inside your home, Mrs. Hale," Dixon cut in, his tone matter of fact. "If a name floats to the top, we'll bring him in without delay."

CHAPTER 52: JACOB

Walking out of Maddy's office and into the elevators, my heart thumped in my chest. I gripped the brass bar mounted on the wall behind me. Anger seethed in my gut. Every moment of intimacy I'd shared with her replayed in my mind. How could I have let this happen?

She'd had no response, only raising her chin in defiance. She'd wanted to see my reaction, knowing that she would come through on her threat to destroy everything I had.

Now, I had to find the so-called accounting discrepancies and fix them — fast. Was it going to cost me? Hell, yes. Enough that I'd have to insist on arrangements with the people to whom I owed a sizable debt. No guarantees they'd go along, but I had to tackle one problem at a time.

The elevator doors parted, and I released the bar I hadn't realized I'd still clutched. I stepped out, forcing a pleasant smile on my face as I passed by colleagues and junior partners. Meeting their eyes, I wondered if they knew about Maddy and me.

My office was at the end of the hall. As I returned to my desk, dropping onto my elegant leather chair, I stared at my laptop. I opened the program that tracked hours and contracts. Addendums, and phone call logs. Everything pertaining to each of our clients.

Maddy had found my forged documents, at least some of them. And now I had to figure out how to correct things without making them seem like anything more than simple mistakes. But I knew they weren't simple mistakes. They were complex efforts to skim from the firm and its clients.

I scrolled through the extensive list. Each name represented a potential nail in my coffin. I couldn't afford any slip-ups now. The consequences of my actions loomed over me like a dark cloud, threatening to shatter the life I had built.

I focused on the first client on the list: Harrison & Company. Their account held a substantial amount of money that I had siphoned off over the few years I'd been a partner here. I zeroed in on their financial statements, desperate to find the inconsistencies that could be attributed to innocent errors.

As I combed through the numbers, I understood what she'd done. Maddy had left breadcrumbs for them to follow. Little entries that would lead the accountants and IT guys straight to me. All this time, I'd believed I held the cards in our relationship, when in reality, she did. Maddy had protected herself. I'd misjudged her. She'd assured her position in the firm, while working to jeopardize mine, should the need arise. Which it now had.

Regret left a bitter taste on my tongue as I worked frantically to cover my tracks. What would she do next to keep me at her side? I feared the worst — that she would find Lauren, possibly go to my home — and reveal all of it. Not just the affair, but the malfeasance.

A knock on my door drew my attention. I glanced at it, rubbed my face in an attempt to clear away the guilt I was sure had masked it, and said, "Come in."

When the door opened, mild relief swept over me at the sight of my friend, Dennis Gossett, one of the partners.

"Is this a bad time?" he asked.

"No, no, not at all." I closed my laptop and plastered a grin on my face. "Come in. What's up?"

Dennis had been at the firm two years longer than I had. He was older than me, too, by about five years. A middle-aged family man with a wife and two college-aged kids, I'd always admired him.

He continued inside, hands in the pockets of his suit pants, a slight swagger in his approach. The recessed lighting above reflected off his bald head. He was one of those men who could pull off the look with ease, his appearance defying his age.

"Listen, uh, I heard you were called into Vic's office earlier."

Guess word had already gotten around. "He had a few questions, and in fact, I'm working on getting him some answers now."

Dennis sat down across from me, resting his hands in his lap. He sat there a moment, quiet and still. And when he scratched his smooth chin, he looked at me. The kind of look that suggested he knew more than he let on. "I wanted to let you know there are ways to handle these things."

I narrowed my gaze, as if I didn't know what he was talking about. "Sorry? I don't take your meaning."

A tight-lipped grin stretched across his face. "I think you do. Let's just say I've been where you're at and, uh . . . well, sometimes things happen, you know?"

His words spun in my mind. Surely, he wasn't suggesting what it sounded like he was suggesting. This man I believed was a loving husband and father. What could he possibly know about my situation?

"Transactions that don't make sense." Dennis shrugged. "A few transposed numbers. These are things that can be fixed. And as for the rest of it . . . I'm just saying, if you need help, I can help."

"Yeah, okay. Thanks. I appreciate it, but I think I got this handled."

He nodded with downturned lips before standing again. When he began to leave, I stopped him. "Dennis?"

He turned around. "Yeah?"

"I appreciate the offer, but I got this."

"I hope you do, man." He revealed that grin again before leaving my office.

I sat there, stunned, disillusioned even. It suddenly felt like I wasn't the only one who'd, let's just say, taken advantage of a situation. But did he know about Maddy, too? And if he did, did the help he offered extend to that situation as well? Because I was beginning to think that maybe there were avenues I hadn't considered. And maybe it was time I did.

CHAPTER 53: LAUREN

Trying to concentrate enough to get my work done had proven impossible. When the detectives left, I did nothing but stare at the photo of my family that rested on my desk. I felt like I was living a nightmare. None of this seemed real. Only weeks ago, I was just a wife and mother, getting by the best I could, not realizing the secrets that simmered below the surface. But I knew them now.

The affair wasn't even the worst of it. I felt violated. Frightened at the idea someone had been in my home, lurking in the night. Had he watched us sleep? Was he gone, and would he come back?

The more I considered the idea it had been one of our contractors, the more sense it made. Terrifying, but logical. I couldn't believe, not for a minute, that any of my coworkers or friends could have done this to us. And it simply didn't jibe with the other investigations. Unless I had a friend who turned out to be a serial killer. Stranger things had happened, I guess. Just looking at news stories about them. The ones who lived among the rest of us. Regular Joes who had jobs and families. I shuddered at the thought.

But what concerned me more now was that I truly didn't think we would be safe in our own home. Not anymore. No matter what Detective Collins said about having a patrolman driving through our neighborhood.

What could I do about it? My marriage was on the verge of collapse, with my husband sleeping in the guest room. I was at the end of my rope, yet my son relied on me. Keeping him safe was my priority.

Tammy appeared at my door. I offered a genuine smile, knowing she was the one person I could confide in. And so far, she knew very little of what I'd been going through. "Hi, come in."

The look on her face suggested she'd been as patient as possible. "You didn't come see me after those detectives left, so I figured you needed some time on your own. Is it okay to talk now?"

"Yeah, sure. Please." I gestured to the chair.

She took a seat, crossing her legs and tilting her head, her gaze compassionate. "What's all this about, Lauren? You know you can talk to me."

I glanced at the time, realizing the day was nearly over. "How much time you got?" I chuckled.

"As much as you need."

I closed my eyes a moment, grateful to have her in my life. "Where to start," I began, with a sigh. "I guess I should start by saying that I don't want to go home tonight."

"Why?" she asked.

As I prepared to speak, my attention was drawn to the hallway. "Gary, hi. My gosh, is it that time already?"

"It is. Good evening, Miss Lauren." He looked at Tammy. "Hi, Ms. Foster. How are you?"

"I'm doing okay, Gary. And you?"

Gary turned back to me. He was smiling, his eyes seeming to capture mine in a way they hadn't before. It almost looked like attraction. And then I wondered, had I given him mixed signals? I never even thought . . .

"I'm doing pretty good, actually. Thank you for asking. It's been so great working here with such kind people." He gestured toward me. "Did you know that Miss Lauren brings me dinner on most nights?" He nodded, as if swelling with pride. "Yep. Now, how kind is that?"

Tammy glanced at me with a smile. "Very kind. But that's the type of person Lauren is."

"Yes, ma'am."

He looked at me again, and I swear it was a look of almost — desire. I'd had no idea I'd led him on in this way, and suddenly felt guilty over it. "Just some leftovers. It's no big deal. Really. I'm just happy you enjoy them."

"Oh, yes. I most certainly do." He kept his sights on me for too long. "Well, I should let you two get back to chatting. You both have a wonderful evening. See you tomorrow." He walked on, disappearing around the corner.

Tammy raised her brow as she peered at me. "Sorry, but that was weird."

"What do you mean?" I, of course, figured she must've sensed the same thing I did.

"Really? You didn't pick up on the way he looked at you?" she asked. "Lauren, maybe you should be careful with him."

CHAPTER 54: DETECTIVE COLLINS

The briefing for second shift had finished and all the guys in Patrol meandered back to their bullpen, taking their sweet-ass time, talking and laughing. Meanwhile, I sat here at my desk making calls to the contractors who'd recently worked on the Hale home.

When the latest call went to voicemail, I glanced at the time. Damn, it was after five. They must've already closed. "Uh, yeah, this is Detective Sarah Collins, Alexandria PD. I'd like to speak with someone regarding a contract you had with Mr. & Mrs. Hale, 2489 Winchester Street in Alexandria. I can be reached at seven-o-three . . ."

Another call interrupted the line. I didn't recognize the number, so I ended my voicemail and answered. "Detective Collins. How can I help you?"

"Hi, this is Tammy Foster. Are you the detective who came into A&J Law Firm today to meet with Lauren Hale?"

I snapped a finger at Dixon until I drew his attention, then waved at him to come over. "Yeah, that's me. You said your name was Foster?" I jotted it down.

"Yes, Tammy Foster. I work with Lauren. In fact, she's a very close friend."

Dixon arrived and perched on my desk while I continued the conversation. "What can I do for you, Ms. Foster?" I set down the phone and placed the call on speaker.

"I'm probably being paranoid, but I'm aware of what's been going on with Lauren and, well, I was wondering if there is someone you might be interested in talking to."

I glanced at Dixon, the corner of my lips lifting into a smile. "Any information can help, Ms. Foster." I held my pen. "What's the name?"

"Gary Stokes. He started working here about a month or so ago."

I nodded, writing down the name. "What do you know about him?"

"Not much," she replied. "In fact, I had to ask HR for his last name. He's our night janitor. I guess he and Lauren have become friends and . . ."

"Friends?" I cut in.

"Yes, I believe so. I asked her about him just this evening before she left work. I don't know, Detective, but there was just something off about him."

"Does Lauren agree with you?" I pressed.

"She didn't say. I guess she's been bringing him leftovers from her house on most nights. It sounds like they're friends."

"Then why are you concerned? You said something felt off. Can you be more specific?"

She hesitated on the line, and I regarded Dixon. He gestured with his hand to prompt me to keep the conversation going. "Is this concern recent?"

"Yes, just tonight, if I'm honest. But the way he looked at Lauren. The way he talked to her. I mean, look, I'm a middle-aged divorced mom who hasn't had a date since Gangnam Style was popular, so maybe I'm no expert here. But he looked at her like he wanted her, you take my meaning?"

"I do." I shot another glance at Dixon. "Did Lauren express concern or fear?"

"No, not at all. Like I said, this is probably just my paranoia getting the better of me."

"I'm sure you're very concerned about Lauren, as you have every right to be. She and her family have been through a lot lately." I set down my pen and leaned back in my chair. "I'll look into him, okay? See if I pick up on anything unusual."

"Thank you." Relief sounded in her tone. "And please don't say anything to Lauren. I don't want her to be upset with me."

"I'll only say something if it's warranted. Thank you for reaching out, Ms. Foster. I'll be in touch." I ended the call and, raised a brow at Dixon. "What do you think?"

Dixon let out a slow exhale, his eyes narrowing in thought. He leaned back, considering it. "I think there might be something here. Clearly, Ms. Foster is a close friend of Lauren's, and her concerns for her safety are warranted."

"Agreed." I tapped my pen against the desk, pondering the situation. There was something about her words, something in the tone of her voice that resonated. "I don't want to jump the gun, but we can't afford to overlook anyone, including those who work with the Hales. I think it's wise to dig a little deeper into Gary Stokes. See what turns up."

Dixon glanced at his watch. "It's getting late. Why don't you head home and get some rest? We can hit the ground running in the morning."

"You go on. I'll run a background on him now. I can do at least that much. Then, in the morning, we can start gathering more details."

"You sure?" Dixon asked.

"Yeah. I got this. Go home. And say hi to Kim."

Dixon pushed off the edge of my desk. "All right. I'll see you tomorrow. Don't stick around here for too long. You'll get roped into the night shift's cases."

"I can hold my own around those guys." I snickered. "Night."

I went straight to work, entering Gary Stokes into the database. I hunched in my chair, chewing my lip, biting back my anticipation.

Gary Stokes, a seemingly ordinary name, but sometimes it was those ordinary ones who hid the darkest secrets. The loading icon spun on my screen, signaling the database was processing my request. This was taking too long.

The night shift had moved in, and I nodded to my coworkers, who had the daunting task of investigating this city's crimes under the cover of darkness. Minutes stretched out until, finally, the screen populated.

Several findings appeared — a birth certificate, social security number, employment history — but nothing that stood out as particularly alarming. No criminal record. It seemed he had led a relatively unremarkable life, at least up until this point.

"Hang on." I scrolled through to find that he hadn't had a permanent address in three years. "Last known — Baltimore." All other addresses were to several P.O. boxes here in the city. "Where the hell do you live right now, Gary?"

He'd recently joined A&J after a short stretch at a company called Apex Windows. Another night janitor position. And as I glanced at the address of the company, a wave of recognition surged in me. Did I know that place? How?

I pulled up the address from my files. "Oh my God." The words tumbled from my lips as I jumped up and marched toward the file cabinet near the back wall. I yanked open the second drawer and thumbed through the files, knowing exactly what I was hunting down.

When it appeared, I opened the file and scanned through the documents until I saw it. "The Tomlins lived less than two miles from that office. I've driven by there."

I could write that off as coincidence, but confirming another location would make me feel a whole lot better. So that was what I set out to do. I pulled up every file. All the victims over the course of the past year and a half. Each family had lived practically a stone's throw from where the man had worked. We'd worked every angle, talked to every friend, relative, and coworker of each of the victims. Looked into their workplaces. But this? My God, could this be the answer?

I had to take a breath. See reason. Maybe I had discovered a break in the case, but I needed to be sure. The memory of past disappointments hovered over me. I'd been down this road already and ended up hitting brick wall after brick wall, leaving concussions as reminders of my failure.

I walked to the board and the maps that were already pinned showing where each of the families lived. Not one of them had any overlapping friends or relatives. Completely unrelated. So that was strike one.

But now, I traced Apex Windows' location to the Tomlins, a family of four. The distance was under two miles, or one and a half as the crow flies. "Now what?" I stood there, hands gripping my hips, eyes locked onto the intricate web of lines and dots that represented victims' homes on my makeshift map. "Dig deeper."

I returned to my desk, taking a deep dive into Gary Stokes' life — his past becoming my present — most importantly, his employment history. And when I looked again at the results churned out by the database that pulled from every state resource available, I noticed how he'd jumped around from job to job. Mostly doing the same thing, working on a cleaning staff. A hint of satisfaction curled my lips upward as I read on. "Every job you've had over the past two years has been a night job," I murmured to myself.

It started to make sense. He worked nights, then sneaked into the homes during the day when they would be empty. Then, when it was time, he was there, in their home when they slept, having learned everything about their lives and the home they lived in.

I leaned back in my chair, my hand pressed against my forehead as if trying to physically hold back my frustration. "How in God's name did I miss this?"

Of course, there was no way to know when I didn't have a name. But could this just be a coincidence?

"No." I got up again, my chair rolling backward, and marched back to the murder board. I checked the distances from each of my victims' homes to the places Gary Stokes had worked. "Less than ten miles. Each one is less than ten miles away."

Still a good chunk of distance. I needed more. I needed to find the connection, but damn if this wasn't a hell of a good place to start.

CHAPTER 55: LAUREN

It was time to confront Jacob. About all of it. The affair, the cops, the possible connection to one of our contractors. I had to tell him, because I didn't know where else to turn. I had to know if he planned on sticking it out until all this was over. Even if I wasn't sure I'd wanted him to.

I'd arrived home before Jacob, as usual. Noah was upstairs. He'd been quiet since I got home. Nancy had said he'd been quiet for most of the day, saying nothing as they walked to his favorite place, the park, earlier. I shouldn't have been surprised. He'd been through so much, talking to cops. Talking to doctors. Noah must've been feeling terrified and alone.

Unfortunately, in this moment, I needed space to collect my thoughts. To ultimately decide on the future my son and I would have, and whether his father would be a part of that future. Yes, Noah was my primary concern, but if I didn't know what the hell to do, how could I possibly comfort him?

I'd thrown together a quick and easy meal. Not for me, not even for Jacob, but for Noah. Chicken nuggets and oven fries. It wasn't McDonald's, but he would be happy enough with it. I couldn't stand the thought of eating right now, my stomach twisted in knots. My head swam in uncertainty and fear.

I walked toward the staircase and peered up. "Noah, honey, it's time to eat." I didn't hear anything for a moment. "I made you nuggets and fries. Your favorite." Again, I waited, but there was nothing.

Now, my pulse quickened, and I climbed the stairs. On reaching the playroom, I peered inside, placing my hand over my heart in relief. "Hi, honey. There you are." Noah sat in the dark, only the light of the television on his face. "Noah? Are you okay, sweetheart?"

I approached him, squatting low to meet him where he sat. With my hand on his back, I looked him in the eyes. "Don't you want dinner? I made your favorite."

"I'm not hungry," he whispered.

"Are you feeling okay?" I pressed the back of my hand against his forehead. "You don't feel warm. Does your tummy hurt?" And then I saw it. A tear trickling down his cheek. "Hey, hey, what's wrong? Did something happen at school today?"

He still refused to speak.

"Was it talking to that doctor this morning? Did she upset you? Baby, come on, talk to me."

I watched as Noah's eyes filled with even more tears, his small frame shaking with suppressed sobs. It broke my heart to see him like this, so vulnerable and scared. I knew then that I needed to be strong for the both of us, to provide him with the comfort and reassurance he needed.

Taking a deep breath, I gently pulled him into my arms. "Hey, it's okay. Whatever it is, we'll figure it out together." I stroked his hair. "You can tell me anything, Noah. I'm right here."

He sniffled and wiped his nose on his sleeve, still unwilling to meet my gaze. Finally, in a barely audible voice, he said, "Billy says Daddy doesn't love you. He doesn't love me either."

His words echoed in my ears. "What?" I felt my chest rise and fall faster and faster as the implications sank in. "Billy told you this?" I looked around, fear gripping me. "Noah, is Billy here right now?"

* * *

The last time I'd been this thorough in searching my home was when Noah had lost his favorite stuffed animal. It had been nearly an hour, but I found no indication anyone had been inside. Noah said Billy had talked to him shortly after he got home from school, but then that was it. He went to the park with Nancy, and when they came back — nothing.

My son had been sitting in his playroom, believing his father didn't love him. This was no imaginary friend. It couldn't be.

I'd finally gotten him to sit down and eat something. Now, I sat across from him at the kitchen table, watching him pick at the last of his French fries. And then, the sound of the garage door raising captured my attention. Jacob was home.

I steeled myself, preparing to bare all to the man I thought I knew. Yet, I was afraid to let Noah out of my sight. Would someone come to hurt him? Would he overhear what I knew I had to say?

Jacob walked into the kitchen. I glanced over my shoulder to see a broken man. Maybe he'd finally begun to regret his actions. Not that it mattered to me now, because either Noah had heard Jacob on the phone again, or there really had been someone here telling him awful things. At this point, I had no idea what was real and what was make-believe.

"You two already had dinner?" Jacob walked toward us. He reached Noah, kissing the top of his head. "Hey, buddy." But Noah remained quiet and Jacob looked at me with a furrowed brow.

"He's feeling a little sad right now." I raised my hand, suggesting Jacob leave it be. "Do you have a minute?" This was going to take a hell of a lot more than a minute, but what else could I say?

"Uh, yeah, of course. You mind if I change first?" He loosened his tie.

"Fine." When Jacob headed up the stairs, I set my sights on Noah. "Are you all finished?"

He nodded, pushing away his plate.

"Do you want me to run you a bath?" I asked.

He shook his head, keeping his gaze down.

"Okay. You want to watch some more TV?"

Again, he shook his head.

"All right, buddy. What do you want to do, then?"

"I'm scared, and I don't want to stay here anymore," he replied softly.

My chin quivered. Of course he was scared. He must've been terrified. He truly believed a voice in the walls talked to him. I couldn't be sure he was wrong, no matter how hard I searched. "I'll tell you what. Would you like to stay with Grandma and Grandpa tonight? I'll even let you skip out on school tomorrow. Would you like that?"

A hint of a smile played on his lips as he nodded. "Yeah."

"Perfect. I'll have Grandpa come and pick you up in just a little bit. They'll be so happy to see you. Why don't you go and put some pajamas in your backpack okay?"

"Can I bring toys?"

"Of course you can."

He pushed back his chair, running toward the stairs and then up. I waited a moment, hearing Jacob pass him on the steps. When Jacob returned to the kitchen, he jerked a thumb back. "He says he's going to Grandma and Grandpa's."

"Would you mind calling your parents and asking your dad to come get him?"

"Why?" Jacob approached, taking a seat at the table. "What happened?"

I raised my hands with growing impatience. "Please, Jacob. Just ask them to keep him tonight, would you?"

"Yeah, okay." He grabbed his phone from his pocket and made the call.

I looked on while he talked to my in-laws. I'd been close to them. Loved them as though they were my own mother and father. Especially since I didn't have a relationship with mine. I would miss them both if we divorced.

"Okay. Dad will be here in twenty minutes." Jacob set his phone on the table. "I guess we need to clear the air, don't we?"

CHAPTER 56: GARY

As I went about my nightly duties, cleaning the offices, vacuuming the halls, my thoughts turned to young Noah. What, if anything, had he told his mother and father? It would ignite a spark that could bring about my end, but I was playing this game in hopes of convincing Lauren her boy was in desperate need of help. And that Jacob had been careless with his affair, allowing his son to overhear his interactions with his office harlot.

It was the only way to keep Jacob and Lauren apart. The only way I could isolate the man in order to accomplish my goal. I noticed, before she left earlier, that the weight of the world seemed to rest on Lauren's shoulders. It made me love her all the more as I looked in her eyes.

With Jacob gone, which would be soon, I could protect her. Both her and Noah. I'd hated saying those things to the boy, but what choice did I have? My harsh words were the only way I could ensure he would tell his mother. Eventually, confronting the father. For all I knew, that could well be underway at this very moment.

I walked into Lauren's office and felt a warm, calming sensation wash over me. The scent of her candle lingered. A light, airy lavender that pleased my senses.

I emptied her trash, wiped down her desk, and stared at the family photo that rested on top of it. Lauren appeared happy. So did Noah. *What a shame.*

Wrapping up my duties, I checked the time. It was still a little early. Maybe a visit to another diner would fill the time. I returned my supplies to the maintenance closet and carried on through the rear exit. The heavy door closed hard behind me, the automatic lock engaging.

I walked into the blackened parking lot, toward my car.

"Hey." A voice called out behind me.

My heart jumped into my throat as I spun around. "Christ, you scared me. What are you doing here?"

Cheryl advanced toward me, a noticeable limp in her gait. She wore a heavy coat, a hat pulled down over her graying hair and gloves that had seen better days.

"Still no room in the shelter?" I asked. "It's cold out." I watched her draw near, reaching around to my back pocket for the switchblade.

"You were supposed to pay me, Gary," she said, halting less than a foot away.

"I did. You got what was fair," I shot back.

"I told you what it would cost you. You still owe me."

I looked into her haggard eyes. "I don't owe you shit. Now get out of my way before something bad happens." I started to walk around her.

"Oh, you gonna kill me like you killed all them others?"

The question hung in the air, chilling me to my core. Cheryl knew about the others, about my past. I had killed people, taken their lives to survive. I was a monster, and she knew it.

"What are you talking about?" I tried to play the role.

"Don't screw with me. I know it was you. It was why you wanted to know where she was." Cheryl took a step closer, her face twisted into a sneer. "You think I don't know who you really are? That I don't know what you're capable of? Come on, Gary. What I know about you would make for a

226

very interesting conversation with the cops. And if you don't give me what we agreed on, that's exactly where I'll be going."

I tried to stay calm, but the anger lodged in my chest. "Listen, Cheryl, you're mistaken. You don't know what you're talking about."

"Oh, I know exactly what I'm talking about. You think you can keep all your secrets hidden, but unless you pay up, that isn't going to happen."

Before I could react, Cheryl lunged at me. Her jagged fingernails scraped against my cheek. "I'm warning you. Get the fuck back." As she stepped back, I reached around for my knife. "You think I won't kill you too?"

"Just give me the money and you'll never see me again," she demanded. "You gotta hold up your end of the bargain."

"I don't have to do anything." I moved in, pressing the knife against her cheek. "You really think anyone in this world is going to miss you? That you won't be just another dead homeless person?"

She held up her hands. "Listen, I just want what's rightfully mine."

"Then that's what I'll give you." I plunged the knife into her throat. Blood gushed from the wound, staining her dirty, tattered clothes, spattering onto my face. Her gaze fixed on me, eyes widening in shock as she tried to speak, but no words escaped her lips. She clutched at her throat, blood now spilling over her hands. I saw her regret. For telling me. For knowing me.

The metallic scent of blood and the sharp tang of adrenaline filled my senses. A tingle of excitement coursed through me, and I felt a sense of relief. A loose end, now tied. Cheryl's eyes closed. Her body grew limp as the life drained from her.

"All you had to do was keep your mouth shut." I wiped the knife onto her coat and used the back of my hand to clear her blood from my face. I could hear her final gasps, gurgling through the blood that still poured from her throat, her life slipping away. "Things didn't have to turn out like this."

I looked around for witnesses. There would be no one at this time of night. The parking lot was deserted. The streetlamps burned overhead, casting down rings of amber light on the asphalt. Cheryl was a hefty woman, and her dead weight would be difficult to carry.

Beyond the building lay a small patch of woods, a buffer between the commercial and residential areas. With some effort, I dragged her lifeless body toward it, tucking her away where the animals could feast. No one would miss her. No one knew she existed. She and I were more alike than she knew.

CHAPTER 57: LAUREN

When I watched Noah walk away, holding his grandfather's hand, I felt like I might not see him again. All this talk of Billy had terrified me. At this point, even though I'd searched the place high and low and found nothing, I didn't want to stay in my home either.

The beautiful home I'd spent the last six months renovating. Making mine. Believing I would grow old here, play with my grandchildren here. Somehow, that now seemed like a dream too far out of reach.

I sat on the couch while Jacob walked his father and son out to the car. I steadied myself, sipping a glass of red wine to calm my nerves. And when I heard the front door close, I knew the time had arrived.

Jacob appeared in the arched opening from the foyer to the family room. He stood there, tall and strong. Like the man I married. Only I knew better now.

"So, where should we start?" he asked.

"The police came to talk to me again today." I realized I should've started with the fact that I'd taken Noah to see a psychologist at the detective's insistence.

Jacob took a seat on the two-seater sofa parallel to me. "At work?"

"Yes, at work. Jacob, Detective Collins believes Billy is real. Even if he's not here anymore. She's certain he'll come back. And I believe her now."

"You do?" He cocked his head. "Why?"

At this, my eyes stung again. "Because Noah said Billy talked to him again today, this afternoon. And the reason why he's staying with your parents tonight is because he's afraid to be here now."

"For God's sake. Why didn't you tell me this? I could've talked sense into him. I mean, you got these cops trying to convince us someone's been in our house."

"Because there's a killer on the loose, Jacob," I shot back. "Can you blame them?"

"They have zero proof anyone's been here, Lauren. What, because our son has an imaginary friend . . ."

"No." I wagged my finger at him. "No, you don't get to do that. Dismiss me, your son, all of this. You know as well as I do what Noah said, what he thinks his friend said. So either Noah overheard something, or Billy is real. And he was here." I looked around. "Maybe he still is."

He scoffed. "Do you have any idea how insane you sound right now?" Jacob stared through the front window for a moment. "What did the cops tell you today, huh?"

"Just that they're taking this seriously. They want to look into the contractors who had access to our house. Maybe even talk to our friends. They want to make sure our family is safe, and they're not wrong." I surveyed the room, recalling my missing candleholder, the inexplicable noises in the night. All of it started to make sense. "We've had more than a few strange occurrences lately, haven't we?"

Jacob's eyes met mine, and it appeared that he was coming around. "Yeah, I guess we have. But come on, are you really gonna believe that there's an actual human being living in our house without us knowing? That's nuts."

"I don't know what to believe anymore. But I do know that Noah's the one who's been seeing and hearing things."

Desperation tightened my chest. "Whatever's happening, it's affecting him in a way that suggests it is very real. They're working on the contractors first. Then they'll want to move onto the people in our lives. Friends, coworkers."

"What, so everyone will know what's going on in our home? What's going on with our son?"

I couldn't believe his attitude. "Yes, because it's the most logical assumption. That someone we know, who knows our house inside and out . . . maybe one of them is the killer they're after."

For whatever reason, that seemed to click. The idea appeared to have taken root in his mind. "But you'd know all this if you gave a shit about what was happening to us around here. To your son. Instead, you're off fucking your girlfriend."

"All right. That's enough," he shot back.

"That's enough?" Rage brought me to my feet. "I saw you with her at that hotel last week. I didn't want to believe it, but there you were, arm around her shoulders, walking with her out of the lobby. Yeah, I saw it. All of it. The hotel where we celebrated our goddamn anniversary."

"I didn't want this." Jacob's voice softened. "I didn't want to hurt you or anyone else. I just needed a break from everything, you know?"

I had to laugh at his audacity. "Yeah, I would've liked a break too, but I would never cheat on you."

"I know you wouldn't. Not you. Not perfect Lauren," he replied.

I sat back down again, knowing this was going nowhere. "Look, right now, I just want to get through this. For Noah's sake, all right?"

"How are we supposed to do that?"

"We cooperate with the cops. I don't know if they're on the right track or not, but in the off-chance they are, I'm not sure it's safe for us here anymore. Any of us."

Jacob raised his hands. "Let's just take a step back, okay? Think about this like reasonable adults. The best explanation is that Noah did overhear a conversation. I'm damn sorry about that, truly. In fact, I'm sorry about all of it. I regret every single moment and every decision I've made after that first moment."

I looked in his eyes. They held sincerity. But this seemed too convenient. I knew this man well. He was driven by ego. I stood from the sofa and walked over to him. "Today, when I got home, Noah said Billy told him you didn't love him anymore. That you didn't love me either."

"For God's sake." He turned away.

"After that, I spent an hour searching up and down this place. I hammered more nails into that damn dormer vent, just to be sure," I continued. "But I didn't find anything. No sign anyone had been in the house. So, I honestly don't know where to go from here. But I do know this . . . I won't put Noah at risk. Maybe there's nothing to this. Maybe there is. And if there is, I gotta know that you'll stick this out with me. Because, in all honesty, I don't know if I can face this alone. After that, you can do what you want."

CHAPTER 58: GARY

Hiding a woman of Cheryl's size took longer than I'd thought. Although, to be honest, I'd rarely had to worry about such things. I'd been careful with my families, leaving them in their warm beds, as though they merely rested. That was how I'd wanted to remember them. There were, of course, exceptions. But I'd wanted to look down on their peaceful faces and recall the love I'd felt. Until they disappointed me. I supposed that was to be expected with family. Would Lauren disappoint me, too?

Hours had passed, and I'd returned to the Hale home. Now, I stood on top of the trellis in the dead of night, examining the dormer vent. I stifled a chuckle when I noticed the access had been well-secured. Nails, by the look of it. *Now you make sure it's closed?*

The wind howled, pushing icy air through me as I balanced precariously on the trellis. Only one solution remained. I would have to climb down and walk back to my car. My risk of being seen increased by the moment. If not for the bitter winter and the late-night hour, I would surely have been discovered. I still might be.

In the trunk of my car, I kept tools for times like these. Within minutes, I'd made it back, unlocking the trunk and

233

peering inside. A car's engine sounded in the distance. I pulled back, surveying the street. All was quiet, but the faint glow of headlights appeared.

Closing the trunk again, I squatted on the other side, away from the approaching vehicle. Was it a cop car? I didn't dare look up to find out. The headlights grew brighter as it neared. I shivered under my coat, not from the cold, but from fear of being captured. I closed my eyes, as if that would make me invisible. I didn't want this to be over. I wasn't finished yet. Lauren must come to know how much I love her.

The car came slowly. Painfully so. It had to be the police, and they were on the hunt. Moments went by. Tick tock. Tick tock. The lights passed, and now, only a red glow faded in the distance until it disappeared altogether. They were gone. But I knew they were here now, and I would take every precaution. This would end soon, but it would end on my terms.

I rose again, taking care to scan the immediate area. All was dark. All was quiet. Opening the trunk, I saw the knife I'd used on Cheryl. It lay in the trunk near the spare tire, wrapped in a newspaper. She and I could've been allies, had greed not gotten the better of her.

My duffel bag sat in the center, half-unzipped. I rummaged through it and found my pry bar. Small, lightweight. I'd hoped it would be enough to pry the nails from the old wood frame that secured the vent to the house.

Once again, I made my way to the Hale home, taking extreme caution to steer clear of any vehicles. Shadows concealed my movement. Walls barricaded around the luxury homes kept those inside from observing the world around them — the dangers that lurked. Cloaked in black, and carrying my pry bar, I imagined the nightmares the sight of me might conjure.

Ahead, the Hale home appeared. I trudged up the long driveway, sticking to the shadows. My cheeks were red from the cold and my nose dripped. A thin layer of ice had formed on the ground. It crunched under my shoes with each step. Could anyone hear me?

Again I scaled the trellis, trusted pry bar in hand. And with careful precision, I gently loosened the nails. The frame suffered from mild rot, making it softer and easier to dislodge the fasteners.

Time remained a constant worry, knowing that each minute I spent out here was a minute in which I might be discovered. Or perhaps a bad dream might awaken Lauren, forcing her to search her home out of fear. Noah wanting a glass of water, hearing a strange noise on the side of the house. Any number of things could derail my plans, until . . . "There we go," I whispered.

The vent teetered on its hinges. I slipped inside. With the chilly air blocked out, I regained feeling in my face. My mouth moved freely and the numbness in my cheeks subsided.

I settled into my little corner, wrapped in the blanket I'd kept hidden, and prepared myself for what lay ahead. Silence enveloped me, yet I could almost hear her soft breaths. Lauren lay just feet below me. Warm in her bed. I had to save her. And it had to be now.

I walked softly to one of the storage boxes around the corner. Inside was where I'd stashed the knife from the butcher block in the kitchen. I held it in my hands, letting the cold steel press against my palms, thinking about how it would feel to penetrate Jacob's chest. The resistance as I pushed it deeper into his flesh, until reaching his beating heart. The blood as it poured out. The muscle would spasm around the knife, refusing to let go. And then I would gaze into Jacob's eyes as he wondered who I was and why I'd done this to him. "Don't worry, Jacob. I'll take care of your family. They're mine now."

Armed with my knife, I proceeded with cautious steps toward the attic scuttle. This was how it always ended. I had thought things would be different this time, but Jacob destroyed what he had helped build. So now I had to destroy him, hoping no one else got in the way. Yet also knowing that it wouldn't stop me.

The attic door groaned lightly as I pushed it open. Lauren was already on heightened alert. No telling if this might awaken her. It was too late now, there was no turning back. For the moment, the house remained at peace. It wouldn't last.

Looking down, I saw only darkness at the bottom. I descended, carefully stepping onto the newly laid wood floor that held firm under my boots. The familiarity of the home comforted me. I knew where to go without the aid of lights. I was a specter, the object of nightmares, the prickling on the back of the neck. But they made me this way.

I gripped the stair rail, quieting my footfalls as I descended to the first floor. My target awaited me in the guest room, asleep. It was the least that he'd deserved for his transgressions. I admired Lauren for kicking him out of their marital bed and was happy to take care of the rest.

As I reached the room next to the den, I pushed open the door that was already ajar. Inside, Jacob lay sound asleep, as though without a care in the world. He was lying on his stomach, his head resting on the pillow. A thick cover pulled up to his waist, leaving his back exposed. The perfect canvas for the gruesome display to come.

Anger at what he'd done heated my face. I began to close in on him, tightening my grip on the knife. My gaze shifted to the door, and I briefly ran through my plan of escape, having mere seconds to flee. But when the floor above me creaked, I halted. Was it Lauren or Noah?

I looked again at my target. Jacob remained motionless. Probably due to that empty fifth of Jack sitting on the nightstand. If I made my move now, whoever was awake upstairs would find me, leaving me with no choice but to end this the way I always had before. But something in me proved reluctant.

I strained to hear the sound again, even while praying it wouldn't repeat. I took another step toward my goal, and there it was. The sound of the floor creaking. As I clutched the knife, ready to give that man what he deserved, I wondered what she would do. Lauren would look at me like the monster I knew I was. She wouldn't understand why.

Movement caught my attention. Jacob shifted his arm. If I stood here much longer, he would awaken. I couldn't take him on. He was far stronger than me. Now, I'd run out of time. I was trapped between my desire for revenge and my desire for my family.

Weakness took over, and I retreated into the shadow of the hall, squeezing into the coat closet. Here I would stay, biding my time until I could escape back into my private alcove. Among the heavy coats, I heard no sound. Had Lauren come down? Was she here? Was it Noah?

I couldn't be sure how long I'd waited, but a hint of light seeped in at the bottom of the door. Dawn must've been near.

I cracked it open, craning my neck just enough to see. The house was silent. I stepped out again, noticing the stillness. But the day was set to begin soon. My window of opportunity had closed. For now.

I slipped out through the kitchen, not daring to risk going upstairs again. I made my way to the garage side door and outside, back to my car. Under the soft gray hue of morning, I hurried through the still-quiet streets. The memory of looming patrol cars still haunting me. Minutes later, I was safe. I sat behind the wheel, hammering my fist against my temple. Why couldn't I go through with it this time?

But I knew why. I loved them. I loved Lauren and Noah unlike any other family I'd known. I had to find a way to keep them.

CHAPTER 59: DETECTIVE COLLINS

Dixon and I got an early start this morning. I'd hardly given him a chance to get his coffee before nudging him out the door. After I filled him in on my theory, I could see the spark in his eyes. He knew I'd stumbled onto something real. Something that could bring this case to a head.

I drove away from the station, Dixon in the passenger seat, flipping through the reports. "We hit up Apex Windows first, talk to Gary Stokes' boss and go from there."

He grunted, still reviewing what I'd discovered. "Then we've got United Properties, and First Colonial Financial."

"Right." I headed west toward the 395. "All three were in fairly close proximity to the victims' homes."

"But let's not overlook the fact that none of the victims were employed at these companies," he pressed. "We still don't have a direct link between the killer and his targets."

"I get that. But if we start hearing the same stories from these employers — his work schedule — when he clocked in and out — when he quit . . ."

"It'll reinforce the possibility of a connection. If that coincides with each murder, it's enough to hunt down Gary

Stokes and bring him in for questioning." He pointed ahead. "This is it. Apex Windows. Make a right up here."

It was 8 a.m. on the dot, and I figured the place would be open. I made the turn and parked near the front of the building. "What's the manager's name again?"

Dixon scanned the information. "Luis Gutierrez. Night manager for security and housekeeping."

"He might've already gone home," I said, cutting the engine.

"Then we talk to the day manager and have him pull the file. Either way, we aren't leaving here without some answers." Dixon opened the passenger door and stepped out.

I met him on the sidewalk leading to the entrance. We walked inside to a small lobby with wood-look tiled floors, and light gray walls with a few pieces of bland artwork. Scattered around the area were various product displays — window styles and colors. A few chairs were pressed against the wall for customers. I spotted a long reception desk near the back, where two people were stationed.

With a smile on my face, I approached. "Good morning. I'm Detective Collins and this is Detective Dixon. Alexandria PD." I displayed my badge as confirmation. "Is Mr. Gutierrez available?"

The older woman behind the desk examined my credentials and eyed me as though she worked in passport control. "Yes, ma'am. He's still here. I'll call him."

"Appreciate it." I nodded to Dixon, and we stepped back, meandering through the windows on display.

"He'll be out in a moment," the woman called out.

I acknowledged her with a brief nod. Dixon and I didn't speak as we waited. Both of us seemed to understand the importance of this meeting. Only a moment later, a man appeared from around the corner. A little bleary-eyed, he ambled toward us. "Mr. Gutierrez?" I extended my hand.

"That's me." He regarded us with some apprehension. "What can I help you with, detectives?"

"We're interested in a former employee of yours," Dixon said. "A Gary Stokes."

I opened the file and retrieved a photo of Stokes from his Apex Windows ID badge. "What can you tell us about him?"

Gutierrez examined the photo. "He worked here for a few months. Sometime last year, I want to say. Didn't particularly stand out. Showed up, did his job. Didn't make any trouble for anyone." He narrowed his gaze. "Why are you asking? If you're looking for him—"

"We know where he currently works," I interjected. "We're just trying to get some background information."

Gutierrez sighed and rubbed his face. "I guess I can spare a few minutes. Come on back to my office. I'll pull his file and tell you what I know."

We followed him through a long, unadorned corridor painted stark white. It was lined with commercial-grade beige carpet that appeared worn. He walked inside his office and sat at an old oak desk surrounded by metal shelves that were crammed with miscellaneous equipment. Extension cords, batteries, fire extinguishers.

He cleared his throat and pulled up to his desk, turning on his computer. "It'll take a minute for this to boot up. I just shut it down, thinking I was leaving. Anyway, I'll get Gary's records and print them off for you."

"We're particularly interested in when he started working here and when he quit. Did he give notice, or a reason for leaving?"

"Notice?" He shrugged. "This isn't the kind of job that requires notice. But I guess he did leave pretty unexpectedly. Just didn't show up one night. No calls. No texts. It happens like that sometimes. I cut his final check and mailed it to the address we had on file."

"Which was?" Dixon asked with anticipation in his voice.

Gutierrez peered at his computer, typing in a few commands. "Looks like a P.O. Box. And I can tell you, the check was cashed. Here, let me print all this up for you." He pressed a button and turned around to the printer on his credenza. "Gary worked here from October last year to late December." He grabbed the papers and handed them over.

I studied the information for a moment. "Do you have copies of his timesheets? What days he worked, the hours."

He aimed his finger at the bottom of the paper I held. "Should be down there, or on the next page."

I flipped it over. "Oh, here it is."

Dixon leaned over to view the report. "It tracks," he whispered.

I looked back at Gutierrez. "This is great. Exactly what we needed. Thank you for your time, sir."

"That's it? That's all you wanted to know?"

"For now, yes. We have other places to check out today, but if we have further questions . . ." I reached for one of my business cards and handed it to him. "I'll be in touch, or feel free to reach out if you think of anything we should know."

Dixon was already on his feet as I stood. We headed toward the door when Gutierrez called out.

"Why are you looking for him? What did he do?"

I shot a glance at Dixon before returning my attention to the man. "We're interested in talking to him, that's all."

Gutierrez crossed his arms. "Uh-huh. Well, let me just say that Gary Stokes was a strange dude. Kept to himself. Didn't talk to his coworkers. Sometimes disappeared without clocking in or out. Took me a while to figure out that one. Reminded me of the kind of guy you didn't want to get on the wrong side of, you know?"

I pinched my lips and nodded. "You might be onto something, sir. Thank you again for your time."

We walked back to the car in silence. I considered what we'd just learned and how it might tie to Lauren Hale. We reached my car, and I pressed the remote to unlock it. It took me a minute before I felt Dixon's gaze on me. "What is it?"

"If we hear the same thing from the other two employers, and then cross-reference his final days with when the murders occurred, then we might actually have something."

"I think so, too," I replied. "This has to happen today, though, because if Stokes is our guy, he's gotta be getting spooked by our visits to Lauren Hale."

"If she and her family are his next targets," Dixon continued. "Then it'll happen sooner than we think."

His words rang truer than ever. For the first time, I believed the Hales could be in real danger.

I unlocked the door and slipped behind the wheel. Dixon entered, and when he closed his door, my phone buzzed in my pocket. I answered, "Yeah, Collins here."

"Detective, we had a call that just came in. The body of a woman was discovered outside the downtown area, near an office complex."

"Okay," I replied, returning a curious gaze at Dixon. "Who's on shift right now?"

"Well, we figured you'd be interested in it because the body's near the Ackerman and James Law Offices. We know you've been working—"

A jolt of energy surged in me. "Send me the location. We're on our way." After ending the call, I turned to Dixon. "A body's been found near Lauren Hale's office."

He scoffed. "Tell me that's a goddamn coincidence, and I'll tell you about some swampland I got for sale in Florida."

Despite this disturbing find, I cracked a smile at Dixon's comment. Our age difference became glaringly apparent. "We're gonna have to put this other shit on hold until we figure out what's going on."

When I merged onto the highway, I checked my speed. For a moment, I considered turning on my siren and lights, but thought better of it. Still, my mind spun with how all of this connected to Lauren Hale and her family.

Dixon seemed to pick up on my impatience. "Hey, Collins."

I glanced at him.

"Take a breath. We don't know anything yet. We don't even know if Stokes is our guy. But whoever killed this woman . . ." He stared through the windshield. "It doesn't fit the M.O."

He was right, but that didn't stop me from racing toward Ackerman and James.

Along the street that fronted the office were several patrol units. Lights flashed, but no sirens sounded. People from the nearby offices and restaurants stood on the sidewalk, dressed in overcoats and hats, looking on. Down the block was a homeless encampment with several tents that lined the street.

I pulled into the parking lot. "They're around back."

"I see them," Dixon replied. "Park here and let's see what we've got."

We got out and headed back to a wooded buffer area, where police tape had been wrapped around trees.

I glanced up at the building, wondering if Lauren was there. "We need a patrolman to go in there and keep folks inside."

"Too late." Dixon pointed to several people standing yards away, toward the back exit. "I don't see Mrs. Hale, though."

We made our way toward the cordoned-off area. I fastened my coat as I scanned the surroundings. A dumpster was near the back of the building. An adjacent parking lot lay along the rear property line, and another building butted up against it.

The responding officer guarding the area caught sight of our approach. "Detective Collins, thanks for coming down." He nodded at Dixon. "Detective."

"You want to show us what you got?" Dixon asked.

"Back here." He waved us back and on reaching the body, he pulled down the tarp that covered her. "Coroner's on the way."

"The sooner we get this body out of here, the better," I said, studying the victim. "She looks homeless."

"Yeah, we figure she came from that nearby encampment." The officer aimed his index finger down the street.

"Older woman, possibly late forties, early fifties. Stab wound in the neck, but no one's touched her, so we don't know if she's sustained other injuries."

"Who found her?" Dixon asked.

"Sanitation. The dumpster was emptied this morning. The driver went out to close the lid, noticed a blood trail. Called us to come check it out."

"Yeah, she didn't die here." I retrieved my phone, taking a snapshot of the victim.

"Very little blood for a hit to the neck," Dixon replied. "Looks like she was dragged. Let's see this trail." He turned around, retracing steps toward the dumpster bin. "I see it. A faint trail. Last night's light flurry probably turned to ice, washing away some of it, but that worker has a good eye."

I followed the trail and turned back to the officer. "Any sign of the murder weapon?"

"Not yet, Detective. Forensics will be here soon, and we'll be on the hunt for it in the meantime."

I nodded, keeping my gaze on the woman. "What about ID?"

"That's a big negatory, ma'am."

I glanced at Dixon. "Should we?"

He nodded, picking up on my meaning. "Let's go talk to those guys and see if we can figure out who she is."

We started away, but I called out to the officer. "We're going to have a chat with the people in the encampment. Make sure you keep the public and the folks who work in that building away from here."

"Copy that, Detective."

We headed over to the collection of tents, cardboard boxes, and makeshift shelters. A bleak scene. "Let's talk to that guy over there." I nodded to a middle-aged man perched on a crate, wrapped in a parka.

"I'll follow your lead," Dixon replied.

On our approach, the man kept his gaze aimed down. "Excuse me, sir. Mind if we ask you some questions?" I asked.

He slowly raised his head, casting a wary eye at us. "About what?"

I swiped open my phone to display the image of the woman. "I apologize for doing this to you, sir, but have you ever seen this woman?"

He studied the screen, squinting hard, and scratching his bristly chin. "Christ. Looks like Cheryl to me, but I seen her look better than that." He raised his brow. "She's dead."

"Yes, sir, she is. Don't suppose you have a last name?"

"Nah. I can tell you she's been hanging around here a few months. Me? I'm going on a year at this spot. But Cheryl . . ." He shook his head. "I'd say probably three, four months maybe. Don't know where she came from."

I surveyed the grounds. "Anyone else around here you know who might've talked to Cheryl recently?"

He turned right and aimed a finger. "You might have better luck with Nicky, over there. I seen them two talking before."

A spark of hope ignited in me. "Thank you, sir, we appreciate the help." I nudged Dixon and we started toward the woman.

The encampment spanned half a city block, having spilled out of the nearby park grounds. The worsening crisis now had its own team of officers assigned, who did nothing but patrol this area.

Chances were good that if Nicky couldn't help, one of our own still might. But I crossed my fingers for a quick answer, because I had no idea how long Gary Stokes would stick around.

What we needed now was confirmation of who this dead woman was, and if she mattered to our investigation. "Excuse me," I asked, my voice elevated above the crowd. "Nicky?"

The young woman looked to be eighteen, maybe nineteen. Her long black hair appeared greasy. She wore a heavy puffer coat with several rips in the black fabric. As we drew near, I realized she was an addict. Her glossed-over eyes, rotting teeth, and sores on her face were clear signs of a meth addiction.

Nicky turned to us, seeming to wonder if she'd done something wrong.

I sensed her wanting to run, so I raised my hands in a non-threatening gesture. "It's okay, Nicky. We just wanted to talk to you. You're not in any trouble."

She appeared to relax a bit. "Why?"

We stopped in front of her. I showed her my badge. "Do you know a woman, maybe in her forties, named Cheryl?"

"Why do you want to know?" Nicky pressed, darting her gaze between Dixon and me.

"I'm afraid she's dead." I turned around, aiming my finger back toward the crime scene. "She was found just over there, behind that building in the woods." When I turned back, I could see the pain in her eyes. "I'm sorry. I was told you talked to her sometimes. Were you two friends?"

Her features hardened, as if acknowledging pain might somehow weaken her. In the streets, weakness was something to be taken advantage of. "We talked sometimes." She wiped a tear from her cheek. "She's really dead?"

"Yes," I replied. "My partner and I are trying to get some information. The man over there mentioned her name was Cheryl. Of course, she didn't have any ID on her. Do you know her last name?"

"No. She never said and I never asked. That's not how it works out here, you know?"

"Yeah, sure." I sighed, trying to figure out what to say next. "Did Cheryl tell you about any family she had? We'd like to do our best to track them down."

"Won't you get, like, DNA or something, to identify her for sure?" Nicky asked.

"That'll take a long time," Dixon cut in. "We're looking to do what we can now to find out who did this to her."

Nicky hesitated for a moment, then took a step back, shielding herself in her coat. "Yeah . . . uh, I haven't been here that long. Cheryl's been here longer. But yeah, she said something about having family. A daughter. Mentioned her daughter lived around here, or something. Worked for a law firm or something. I don't remember. Cheryl didn't like talking about who she was before."

I nodded, not wanting to press too hard. "Did she ever mention her daughter's name?"

Nicky looked up as if thinking about the question. "Um, I think she said her name was Laurie, or Lauren. Something like that."

I stopped cold, the name ringing in my ears. "Lauren?"

"Yeah, maybe that's what it was."

"Who lived or worked around here somewhere? For a law firm?" I asked.

"That's what I said."

Dixon and I traded a knowing glance when I turned back to Nicky. "Thank you, I appreciate you talking to us. I'm sorry for your loss." I spun around, marching back toward the scene. It was all I could do not to sprint.

Dixon jogged to catch up to me. "Hey, wait up. What's the plan?"

I stopped and squared up to him. "We both heard what she said. Are you shitting me right now? Lauren? Lauren Hale works less than two blocks away. You think that's a coincidence?"

He raised his hands. "Yeah, okay. I picked up on it. But think about this a moment. Have you ever asked Mrs. Hale about her parents? Her mom? Look . . . I'll admit this does feel like it's connected. The location of the body . . . I get it. But tread carefully, Collins, all right? First of all, we don't have confirmation of the victim's identity." He thumbed back. "You got a guy who thought it could be a woman named Cheryl. And that girl we just talked to . . . hardly a reliable witness."

I glanced away, shaking my head. "Don't give me that shit, Dixon. We both know what's going on here. If Cheryl is

Lauren's mother, and now she's dead? And Gary Stokes works in that building over there with Lauren? Jesus, come on." I hesitated, working to make sense of it all. "Look, I think we need to at least talk to Lauren Hale. Ask her about her mother. Then, we'll have a better idea."

CHAPTER 60: LAUREN

The detectives appeared at my door. I'd only just arrived at the office, barely having set down my cup of coffee. The traffic heading in was backed up because of whatever happened in the woods behind our office. Cop cars all over the place. But when Collins appeared, panic shot through me. "What's going on? Is my son okay?"

She entered with Dixon beside her. "This isn't about Noah. Mrs. Hale, are you aware of what's going on out back?"

"No. I was late because of whatever it is, but I assumed it had something to do with the encampment down the street. It's not that unusual around here. Why? What's going on?"

I didn't like that they exchanged glances as if deciding who should be the one to tell me the apparent bad news. "Please, Detective, what's happened? Why are you both here?"

"A homeless woman was murdered," Collins began. "Her body found in the wooded area next to your parking lot."

"Oh, no." I closed my eyes a moment. "Can't say I'm surprised, unfortunately. But what does it have to do with me?" I caught sight of Tammy as she approached behind the detectives.

"Excuse me." Tammy squeezed between them, walking toward my desk. "You okay, Lauren?"

"I don't know. I'm waiting for them to tell me why they're here." My best friend stood next to me, taking a defensive stance.

Collins rubbed her forehead. "Mrs. Hale, this may seem like a question out of left field, but what is your mother's name?"

"My mother? Why on earth are you asking me about her?"

"Please . . . her name?" Collins asked again.

Tammy grabbed my hand. I looked at her. She seemed to already know what had yet to dawn on me. "Cheryl Wilcox. Now will you tell me why you're asking?"

"When was the last time you saw her? Does she live nearby?"

This was beginning to get on my nerves. "Look, Detective, I haven't seen my mom since I was seventeen. I have no idea where she lives. Do you mind letting me in on whatever this is about?"

Collins glanced down, clearing her throat. "We think the homeless woman, whose name we believe is Cheryl, could be your mother. And we'd like to ask if you'd be willing to come down to the scene now to confirm."

Tammy's hand rested on my shoulder, offering comfort, but I couldn't process any of it. Numbness settled over me, blocking out any emotions I should have been feeling. Part of me wanted to go see for myself, to finally have closure about the woman who used me to further her own gains. But I remained skeptical. "You don't know for sure if it's Cheryl?"

"No, we don't," Dixon replied. "We were told her name was Cheryl and that she had a daughter, Lauren, who lived or worked for a law firm in the area."

"And given where this all happened," Collins added, "it's too much of a coincidence, Mrs. Hale. It would only take you a moment to confirm."

"Do you want me to come with you?" Tammy asked.

"No. It's fine." I couldn't look her in the eye. "Maybe it's not her. I don't know why Cheryl would be here, of all places."

Tammy stepped in front of me, acting as a shield. "You're really asking Lauren to view a dead body at a crime scene to tell you whether it's her mom she hasn't seen in years?"

I saw a look of sympathy in Collins' eyes. She said, "If it is her, then it's probably connected to our investigation. And the longer we wait—"

"We should go now." I walked around my desk, pulling my coat off the back of my chair. "I'm ready."

The detectives nodded and I followed them toward the elevators, not looking back at Tammy.

We stepped inside when the doors parted. No one spoke a word. I stood in the back, staring at the detectives in front of me. Finally, I broke the silence. "What if it is her? What then?"

Collins peered over her shoulder. "Then there's someone else we need to talk to right away."

"No one you talked to offered a last name?" I pressed.

"No."

"Lots of people are named Cheryl." I waited for Collins to respond. She only looked at her partner. That same silent look that was starting to set me off.

I followed them into the lobby. Several staff members stood around, hands in pockets, peering through the window. They noticed our arrival. It wouldn't take them much to figure out I was being escorted outside by the police. Collins and Dixon just had that look about them, and they'd been here a few times already. My coworkers could put two and two together.

Collins opened the door, holding it for me. I still felt a strange numbness to all of it, unsure of what I was about to see or how I should react to it. So many things had come to pass over the course of a few weeks, this almost didn't faze me.

"Right over here, Mrs. Hale," Collins said, gesturing toward the wooded area next to our parking lot.

Two officers appeared to stand guard. Collins approached them, speaking at a whisper, and then they parted. I walked between them, following the detectives until I stood before it. The body of a dead woman, in the wooded area several yards from my office.

Right away, I noticed that her neck had been punctured. A knife, probably, but I didn't ask. Dried blood left a red stain down her neck, and onto her dirty coat and clothes beneath.

"The coat," I said. "I've seen her before."

"You have?" Dixon asked. "When?"

"I don't know exactly. I think it was when I met you, Detective Collins, inside the restaurant the other night. I'd run into her. My God, I didn't even . . ."

"Mrs. Hale," Collins began. "Do you recognize this woman as Cheryl Wilcox, your mother?"

I hadn't seen her in so long, her face was so different, especially in this current state. But her lips . . . I remembered them. Mostly because she used to wear a scowl that sent shivers down my spine as a child. She looked old, so much older than when I saw her last. The sad part was that she must only be in her mid-forties, but to see her now — geez, she looked sixty. Then again, I couldn't recall her exact age. I just knew that she was young when she had me.

Was I supposed to cry? I didn't feel like crying. I felt sad for her and the life she chose to lead. I felt lucky to have escaped when I did. But for her to have been murdered . . .

"That's her," I finally said.

Collins moved toward me. "We believe she's been living in that encampment over there for a few months. Three or more. That was according to a couple of people we talked to." She studied me a moment. "You didn't know she was here?"

"I had no idea. I haven't looked for her in a long time, not since before I got married. Did she know that I was here? That I worked here?"

"I'm going to assume so," Collins replied. "But what I'm most interested in learning right now is who did this to her."

I pondered how my mother knew I was here. Had she tracked me down, and if so, why? It was a strange sort of coincidence that she would be found so close to my office, otherwise. My current life had taken me away from the shadows of my past, and into a world of responsibility and stability. A world that I didn't want to be pulled away from, though it seemed to be happening, nonetheless.

I shook off the thought, returning my focus to the detectives. "I've tried to cut ties with my past. I haven't communicated with her in years."

Detective Collins sighed, her eyes scanning the area around my mother's body. "It's not uncommon for people in her sort of situation to seek out their children, especially if they think there's a chance of getting money, or help. In my experience, they'll do whatever it takes to survive, even if that means reaching out to their estranged families."

My mother's life was a series of hardships and struggles, and I couldn't help but feel some pity for her. "Why is this happening now? With everything going on . . . why now?"

Collins glanced at Dixon and I was sure they'd asked themselves that very question.

"This is about the killings, isn't it?" I pressed. "Somehow, you think this is tied to my home and my family — to Billy."

Collins raised her shoulder, and I could see the hesitation in her eyes. "There are a lot of moving pieces here, Mrs. Hale. And we are working our way through this maze."

CHAPTER 61: JACOB

Every set of eyes I passed in the halls this morning seemed to bore into me, their gazes filled with curiosity, suspicion, and undoubtedly, a touch of judgment. Word had clearly spread like a disease that the senior partner had summoned me, questioning me about suspected wrongdoing. But what they didn't know was that last night, I had painstakingly rectified every mistake, carefully correcting the errors that had threatened to tarnish my reputation. It had cost me dearly, but I had legitimized my transactions, leaving no room for doubt or accusation.

Yet, despite my efforts to salvage my integrity, a lingering unease gnawed at the pit of my stomach. Maddy, who always seemed to have her finger on the pulse of office gossip, could still make things infinitely worse for me. If she chose to do so, I swore to myself that I would not go down without a fight. If my world was crumbling around me, then damn it, I wouldn't go down alone.

I stepped inside my office and flicked on the lights. The morning rays shone through my windows, bathing my desk in their glow. I dropped into the comfort of my leather chair, wondering whether Vic had reviewed the information I had provided last night. Would the consequences of my actions be severe enough to strip me of everything? My position? My clients? My livelihood? Or had I done a sufficient job of covering up my misdeeds that I would survive this mistake? And the ensuing fallout with the people to whom I owed a great deal of money.

Maddy knew too much. I had let myself believe that she was on my side, that she would defend me. But Maddy was always on her own side, driven by self-interest. Maybe we were meant for each other.

In the heart of this maelstrom, I found myself revisiting memories of my past mistakes, realizing that they had finally caught up with me. Not to mention the rest of the chaos in my life, which had been consumed by killers and ghosts living in my house.

My desk phone rang, jolting me out of my self-indulgence. I recognized the caller, and my pulse quickened as I reached for the receiver.

"Jake," Vic's voice boomed on the line. "I've had a chance to review what you sent over. I have to say that it looks suspicious as hell. You understand what I'm saying to you?"

I licked my lips, preparing to spin an intricate web of lies. "I understand, Vic. It is not easy for me to admit to my mistakes, but I am prepared to face the consequences and take full responsibility for my actions. I hope that you will consider the effort I put into making a course correction. I must reiterate that my intentions were pure. My execution, poor."

He was silent for several moments, filling me with dread. "Jacob, I appreciate your candor, but the consequences of your actions reverberate far beyond just you. Our clients must be told of these errors as well, which will put the firm in a very troubling light. And I must tell you that this is a situation I will need to discuss with the other partners."

I leaned back in my chair and rubbed my forehead. "Of course, Vic. I'll be here, ready and willing to address any questions or concerns they may have."

As the call ended, I slumped back in my chair, the reality of my situation crashing down on me. Vic hadn't bought it, and I doubted the other partners would either. Dennis had warned me, even offering me what seemed an unthinkable solution. I was a dead man walking.

A text arrived on my phone. "Jesus, what now?" I picked it up and swiped open the screen.

Look outside.

I spun around to my window, standing up to see into the parking lot. There he was, Bushnell's crony standing next to my car. "What the . . . ?" He smiled, then proceeded to run something sharp along the side of it, etching a deep line all the way. I pressed my hands against the window. "No. Stop!"

Another message arrived.

Next time, don't be late, or the damage to your car will be the least of your worries.

The man drove away. I inhaled a deep breath, rage and fear playing tug-of-war in me. Walking out of my office, head held high, I searched for Maddy.

I arrived at her office, walking inside without knocking. She glanced up at me from behind her desk. Her beautiful green eyes didn't seem so beautiful to me now. I'd begun to hate her. And I had a feeling I wasn't the only one.

"What do you want, Jake?" she asked.

Her tone was cold. Matter of fact. As though I was a pariah, and we'd never known each other on an intimate level. "I've cleaned it up. All of it. So unless you want to go down with me, I suggest you do what you can to quash the rumors."

Maddy leaned back, tilting her head. "Why would I be in any trouble at all?"

I grabbed the arms of her chair and spun her to face me. "Because you knew about all of it. You said nothing until it suited you. Don't fuck with me, Maddy. You have no idea what I'm capable of."

CHAPTER 62: LAUREN

My mother's body was being loaded into the coroner's van.
I watched, not really feeling anything, yet I knew something
had changed in me. Was that much of a surprise, all things
considered?

I walked over to Detective Collins, who stood with her
partner and another officer. "Am I free to go back to work
now?"

Her look suggested I was in denial. "You want to go back
to work after all this?"

I shrugged. "I have a busy day ahead. Detective, Cheryl
meant very little to me. I'm sad she suffered. That part is hor-
rible, but there's nothing for me here."

Collins ushered me away from the others. "Look, Mrs.
Hale, I gotta tell you, this whole situation isn't sitting right
with me, you know?"

"I assumed that much. You have another murder investigation. But my priority is, and will remain, my family. What
are you doing to find the man you think could still be after
us?"

"Look, I think it's fairly clear these situations are connected. But I will say that we're following up on a few leads,"

she added. "In fact, we were on one when we got the call about this."

"Anything I should know?" I looked closely at her, sensing there was much more to this than she wanted to say. "Detective?"

"I don't have anything concrete yet, but I hope to before the end of today. Lauren, I'd feel a whole lot better if you and your family stayed with a relative for the time being. I just don't know what we're up against."

"Forgive me for saying this, Detective, but you've done a pretty good job scaring the shit out of me and my son. Every noise, every whistle of the wind that blows through my house, I think someone's inside. Do you have any idea what that feels like?"

"No, I don't—"

"No, you don't," I shot back. "I'm dealing with a troubled marriage and my son who doesn't know truth from fairy tale right now. How long do we stay away? Forever? Do you have someone in mind you believe will come for us? Do you have a shred of evidence to suggest we're in real danger? Because I will tell you, Detective, right now, I feel like I'm losing my mind. I don't know what to believe, because I have nothing from you. No shred of proof."

"Well, your mother was just murdered. I think that's pretty significant."

Her biting tone wasn't lost on me. "Then tell me who you think is responsible, Detective." I raised my hands. "I'm all ears."

"Believe me, we're working our asses off to figure out what the hell is going on, and whether you and your family are in the crosshairs of some crazed killer." She inhaled deeply, gazing up at the gray sky. "Look, you want to go back to work, fine. It's probably the best place for you right now. Your son's at school. You should arrange for him to stay with his babysitter."

"He's with his grandparents, actually," I said.

"Even better. Give me the rest of today, all right? I promise to have answers for you."

"Then I'm going back to work." I turned on my heel, passing the coroner's van on my way to the office, nodding curtly to Detective Dixon.

Inside, Tammy stopped me at the lobby door. "What the hell's going on, Lauren? Was it her?"

I looked at my closest friend, a mother figure I'd come to love so much. Then I looked at the faces of all the people lingering in the lobby. Their morbid curiosity getting the better of them. "It was her. But it doesn't involve me at all."

* * *

Hours stretched long into the afternoon. I stayed at my desk, working, pretending I hadn't just seen my mother's lifeless body, after she'd been brutally murdered. I didn't call Jacob. What could I say?

Jacob knew so little about Cheryl. Whenever he'd asked, I'd given him a vague description of her before slyly changing the topic. And he was self-centered, so he didn't push, instead preferring to talk about what interested him.

Tammy observed me occasionally, curious and slightly worried, but she didn't press for more details. The ticking of the clock was the only sound in my otherwise quiet office. But I couldn't escape the nagging thoughts that haunted me, the images of Cheryl's body etched in my mind.

Detective Collins' promise of answers seemed another attempt to keep me in the dark. She knew more than she'd wanted to say. Why keep it from me?

A knock on my door drew my attention. I looked up from my computer screen to see Jacob's mother with Noah beside her. "Hey. What's going on?" I immediately stood. "Is everything okay? What are you doing here, Ann?"

She smoothed the wrinkles from her sweater and patted at her short, perfectly coiffed hair. "Noah and I were having a

259

good time. This afternoon, after lunch . . ." Her lips pressed together, the fine lines around them turning white. She was afraid.

"It's okay. Just tell me what happened."

"Noah drew something. You should see this, Lauren." Ann held out a folded piece of paper.

I narrowed my gaze, taking a step back. "You came here to show me a drawing?"

She let go of Noah's hand and moved closer to me. This woman, who I'd loved like a mother, suddenly seemed terrified. Her dark brown eyes, creased by heavy crow's feet, bore into me. In a low tone, she continued, "Lauren, you need to see this."

Before this went any farther, I squatted down to Noah. "Hey, buddy? Would you like to say hello to Tammy? I'll bet she'd love to see you."

He nodded. "Okay."

"Great. Let's go."

Tammy was delighted to see Noah, and he was already chatting up a storm when I returned to my office.

"Have you talked to Jacob?" I asked Ann.

"No, I knew he'd be busy. I thought it best to come straight here."

I wanted to roll my eyes, knowing Jacob's parents always gave him a pass. He was always so *busy*, doing so *well* for his family. "Sure. What is it you wanted me to see?"

She handed over the drawing and I examined it. "What am I looking at? A stick figure? Someone lying down?"

"Lauren, when I asked Noah who he was drawing, he said this person was his friend, Billy. He said Billy lives in your walls, and that he'd seen him. Well, of course, I assumed it was his imagination, but I asked him a few more questions." She hesitated. "Honey, I think this person might have been an intruder. Jacob told us about what's been going on, about you thinking someone's been inside your house."

"He did?"

"Well, yes, but he sort of shrugged it off. Now, I'm not sure that was the way to go."

My heart dropped into my stomach. "Noah said he saw him *in* our house? Not just the walls?"

"Yes. He said he got out of bed the other night. He'd heard something. Went downstairs and saw this Billy walking into the living room."

I began to tremble. It was only last night that I'd insisted Noah stay with Ann and Jack. So this had to have happened only a day or two ago. "Why didn't he tell me when it happened?" The question was more to myself than Ann. "Did he say anything else?"

"Just that he went back upstairs and went to sleep." Ann appeared almost as panicked as I was. "Now, I don't want to frighten you, Lauren, but my God, what if you were right, and there has been an intruder in your home? Could you imagine?"

As a matter of fact, I could — all too well. I clutched the drawing in my hand, my mind racing with the implications. In that instant, I realized just how vulnerable my family was. I let out a shaky breath and tried to keep my emotions in check. "What did Noah say about Billy after that?"

"He didn't say anything else."

"Thank you, Ann, for bringing him here. You did the right thing. I'll call Jacob and we'll call the police, just as a precaution."

"Of course. I just feel awful about this, Lauren. I mean, I suppose it could be the boy's imagination, but he spoke as if it were absolute fact."

"I'm sure. Thank you, I'll handle it from here."

"Please do let me know if there's anything happening, would you? I can't bear the thought of you three in that house without knowing what's going on."

"I understand. I'll absolutely keep you posted."

"Should I bring Noah back home with me while you sort all this out?"

"Please, yes. If you don't mind. Thank you, Ann. Noah's lucky to have you for a grandmother."

We collected Noah from Tammy's office, and then I showed them to the elevators. Stepping inside, Ann looked at me with fear in her eyes.

"It's okay," I said. "I'll be by later this evening."

When the doors closed, I returned to Tammy's office. "Thanks for that."

"Anytime," she replied.

That was when I noticed the clock. "It's four thirty?"

"Yeah. Why?"

"Detective Collins promised me answers. Today. Where the hell are they?"

CHAPTER 63: DETECTIVE COLLINS

The sun had fallen behind the distant trees, its fading light casting a golden glow across the horizon. I realized time was running out. This was our last stop, the final place we needed to search before making a crucial decision. "If I'm wrong . . ."

"One step at a time," Dixon jumped in. "We need to cover all our bases on this lead. Given what we have right now, I firmly believe we're on the right track. We'll still bring in Stokes today. I'm sure of it."

"Yeah, you're right." I stepped out of the car, securing my coat around me. Dixon caught up to me as we headed toward the entrance. The financial firm appeared to still be open as I reached for the door. "In the nick of time."

"Yep," he replied. "We'll stick to the plan — find out if his history lines up with our murders."

Standing outside the double door entrance, I checked the time. "We know where Stokes will be. His shift at Ackerman & James is set to start."

"We have the upper hand, Collins. Don't forget that."

We entered the financial firm where Stokes worked just before the murders of the Godfreys. A couple with a baby on the way. That case was particularly disturbing. They were murdered in their bed, the unborn baby dying inside the mother. She was eight months pregnant, and her stomach had been sliced apart.

Out of all of the cases, this one had hit me hardest. Still, if we were close, and I believed we were, this could be over in a matter of hours. And we'd have saved the lives of another family — the Hales. Dixon was right. We did have the upper hand. Stokes had no idea we'd made the connection between the homeless woman and Lauren Hale. If he was still after the Hales, he'd show up at work tonight, if nothing else, just to see Lauren. How long he would stick around after that remained to be seen. But I wasn't going to take any more chances.

The office was clearing out as the day came to a close. As with the other employers, Gary had worked here as a night janitor. So far, this whole thing was fitting together, piece by piece.

This time, Dixon took the lead, asking the front desk to speak with the manager about Stokes. He walked back to me. "He'll be down in a second. You all right? Cause you don't look it."

"I'm just thinking back to this case."

"Harding was on it," Dixon replied.

"Yep. Until he got transferred. We didn't pick up on a connection then. If we had . . ."

"You can't think like that, Collins. Trust me, I know," Dixon added.

"Yeah. Sure." A moment later, I spotted the man who appeared to be the guy we needed.

With an outstretched hand, he approached. "Hello. I'm Ron Vought. You're here about Gary Stokes?"

"Yes, sir," I replied. "We'd like to ask you a few questions."

"Shoot." The unassuming man, who appeared to be in his fifties, thrust his hands into the pockets of his khaki pants.

I went into the usual: the where, the when, and the why.

"Well, I can tell you, he did his job just fine," Vought began. "Came in on time. But there was something strange."

I raised my brow. "What's that?"

"Well, after he quit, I don't know why I felt like I needed to look, but I checked out our security cameras. Strangest damn thing, but it was like Gary took off in the middle of his shift on several of the nights he worked." He raised his hands. "Not all the time, mind you, but then he'd come back. I don't know what he was doing, or whatever, but I thought it was strange."

"Sounds like it." I figured I knew exactly what he'd been up to, but this also gave me a reason to check A&J's security cameras. A possible nail in the coffin. "And when he left, what day was that?"

"I'd have to check the files again, but it was around last summer, I guess."

So far, that tracked, but I needed something more concrete. We were also pressed for time if we wanted to make it back to Ackerman and James. That was certainly now our next stop. "Hey, would you mind firming up that date for me and sending me a text message as soon as you can?"

"Yeah, of course. I'll go do it now, if you want to stick around." He thumbed back.

"We should get going, but just as soon as you can, yeah?" I asked.

"Sure thing, Detective. So, uh, what's the deal, anyway?" Vought shrugged. "Gary get into some kind of trouble? I always thought he seemed a little off."

"Get back to me as soon as you can with that date, would you?" I said, glossing over his question.

"I'll get on it now."

"Appreciate it." I hurried toward the lobby, noticing Dixon rushing to catch up. "We have to get to A&J right now. That's three for three."

"Yep." Dixon checked the time before following me out into the parking lot. "We'll hit traffic. Do we want to call Lauren Hale and have her collect her family so they can hole up with a relative?"

I hesitated, considering Dixon's suggestion. Calling Lauren Hale would be the responsible thing to do, ensuring her safety. But there was also a part of me that didn't want to give Gary Stokes any hint that we were closing in on him. If she wasn't there, he might know something was up. "Who do we have nearby who can keep eyes on Mrs. Hale?"

"Forensics might still be out there in the woods, but we're losing light, so I'm not sure," Dixon replied. "I can make a call and find out. Why?"

"If Stokes is watching her, and she's not there, it could raise his alarm bells," I replied. "We can't risk tipping him off."

Dixon nodded. "And you don't think PD's eyes on her will do the same thing? What if we ask one of our people to bring him in now?"

"Yeah, all right. Make the call. See who's in the area."

We jumped into my car, hitting the city streets, stymied by heavy traffic. Darkness had fallen and the city's lights illuminated around us as I merged onto the highway, back toward Ackerman & James. Traffic snarled our efforts and I'd begun to lose my patience. "Come on, goddamn it." I felt Dixon's eyes on me as he spoke on the phone.

"No one?" he asked. "Look, just have a unit head over, will you? We're not far." He nodded. "We'll be there in twenty."

"Fingers crossed," I replied, slamming my hand down on my horn. "Move it!"

Dixon ended the call and gripped the handle of his door. "They're sending someone. Forensics already cleared out."

After a few more miles, we'd gotten through the worst of it, reaching the downtown area. Lauren's office was on the outskirts, just west of it.

It was almost five-thirty when we pulled into A&J's parking lot for the second time today. Dixon and I exited the vehicle. The lot had virtually emptied. The police tape wrapped around the trees in the nearby woods had been taken down. It was if someone hadn't just died there at all.

"She's still here." I nodded toward her Lincoln Navigator. "That's her car over there. Where the hell is the patrol officer?"

"Don't know. Let's just get inside. If it makes you feel any better, we know Stokes waits until his victims are asleep. Defenseless. He's a coward who won't dare try anything here."

"I hope you're right." We reached the entrance, and I pushed open the still unlocked door. "They haven't closed for the night yet. Chalk one up for the good guys." Inside, the woman at the front desk was collecting her things.

She noticed our arrival. "Hi, there, I'm so sorry, but we're closing for the night." It was then that she seemed to recall Dixon and me. Her expression shifted. "Oh, you're the detectives. What can I do for you?"

"Is Mrs. Hale still here?" I asked.

"Yes, ma'am. She's in her office." The woman reached for the phone. "Should I call—"

I raised my hands. "No, we'll go up. We know where it's at. Have a good night, miss."

CHAPTER 64: GARY

I'd walked into the maintenance office, passing by Lauren's on the way. She wasn't there, but her light was still on, and I'd seen her car in the parking lot.

With Cheryl's death, I knew it was only a matter of time before they figured out the connection. So, with my options running thin, there was no choice but to finish what I'd set out to do. It had to be tonight — or not at all. I couldn't bear to think about that scenario.

I'd let too many obstacles derail me and had risked too much. I wanted Lauren and Noah in my life. It was still possible we could be one big happy family.

For now, I clocked in, ready to begin my duties as always. Placing fresh cleaning supplies on the cart, I prepared to head back into the hall, and hopefully, find Lauren before she left.

I reached into my pocket to grab my ID badge. But as I felt around for it, I realized it wasn't there. "What did I do with it?" I scoped out the desk, moving papers and objects in search of it. I needed the badge to get access to the elevators once they locked the front doors.

And in a moment of swift recognition, I recalled leaving it downstairs at the security desk. It had to be scanned in by staff before I entered. I would have to go down to retrieve it.

Opening the door, I stepped back into the hallway. Most of the offices were already empty. I continued on, heading toward the elevators when, from the corner of my eye, I saw two people emerge from beyond the corner. If I was a betting man, I'd bet they were cops. And as the female walked down the hall, her suit jacket opened. Strapped to her waist was a gun. Yeah, they were cops.

I quickly rounded the corner to stay out of their view, pressing myself against the wall. Why were the police here? Had they found Cheryl already? Did they know Lauren was her daughter? I couldn't risk being caught now, not when I was so close.

With caution, I peered around the corner to get a better look at the officers. They seemed focused, talking in hushed tones as they headed into the hall. Unnerved by this unexpected development, I urged myself to stay calm. There had to be another way out of this situation. Glancing around, my sights landed on a door marked 'Stairwell.' That was how I'd make it out of here.

I hurried toward the stairwell entrance. As I pushed open the door, a gust of cold, stale air greeted me. Taking one last glance over my shoulder, I stepped inside and closed the door behind me. The clatter of my footsteps echoed off the concrete walls as I descended the steps, skipping every other one to hasten my exit.

Arriving on the ground floor, I crept toward the exit, listening for any signs of activity outside. This door led to a short hallway and then into the lobby, where I would find my badge sitting on the security desk. I pushed it open, craning my neck to see. I couldn't see much, but the good news was that I didn't hear much either. I stepped out, swallowing my fear, slowly walking toward the lobby. The front desk was empty. Everything seemed to be business as usual.

I made my approach. There was my badge, right there on the counter. I reached for it.

"Hey, Gary," the security guard appeared out of nowhere.

I felt a jolt of fear shoot through me as I tried to maintain a calm demeanor. "Evening, Phil. Looks like I left my badge down here when I came in." I grabbed it. "You getting ready to head home?"

"Yes, sir."

"See you tomorrow, then." I carried on, casually walking back toward the elevators. But what would I do when the police saw me? Were they there for me, or for Lauren?

No, I had to go back . . . back to my office to wait them out. If they'd been after me, they would've already realized I wasn't in the maintenance room and all hell would've broken loose. They had nothing. I was being paranoid. I'd been cautious for so long, and I knew I hadn't screwed up.

CHAPTER 65: DETECTIVE COLLINS

"Mrs. Hale," I said, standing in her doorway with Dixon next to me. "We promised you answers. And we have them." Before we got into what we'd learned, she marched over to us, holding a piece of paper.

"You need to see this."

She handed me a drawing. I took it and glanced up at her. "Is this your son's?"

"Yes." Mrs. Hale folded her arms as if a chill took hold. "My mother-in-law drove down here a little while ago. She said Noah drew this and told her it was Billy."

I wasn't sure how to take this news. I glanced at Dixon, who seemed just as perplexed. On the one hand, I was looking at a child's drawing of what could only be described as a stick figure with short hair scribbled onto the head. On the other, did that mean Noah had actually seen Billy?

"Noah said he saw Billy in our living room. I assumed it happened the other night, but Noah doesn't have much concept of time," Mrs. Hale added.

I sensed the rising panic in her tone. She still didn't know why we were here. We were wasting precious time mulling over a child's drawing. We knew Stokes was real, and that he could be here in this building right now. The rest no longer mattered. If he'd already fled, then I'd call for backup to meet us at the Hale home. "Dixon and I have been running on a lead we think will bring this to a head. That's why we're here."

"What is it?" Mrs. Hale darted her gaze between us. "Do you know who he is? Is there someone in my home?"

Mrs. Hale looked at her friend, who'd entered the office. Ms. Foster stood beside her once again. Lauren Hale no longer had a mother, but this woman here, she seemed to be the next best thing. "We're here to find Gary Stokes. What can you tell me about him?"

Her face contorted and she glanced at Ms. Foster. I wasn't going to reveal what Foster told us.

"Gary?" Mrs. Hale appeared bemused. "You think Gary has something do to with this?"

"What do you know about him?" I pressed.

"Well, Gary has been working here for, I guess, a month or so now." She looked at Ms. Foster, who nodded. "He works in Maintenance on the night shift."

Ms. Foster regarded me. "I did think he was acting strangely yesterday."

"No, I didn't pick up on that at all," Mrs. Hale cut in. "Gary's been so nice. Always says hello, asks how my day went. I even bring him leftovers sometimes." She looked at her friend. "No way it could be Gary."

"The lead we've been running down has everything to do with Stokes," I said. "The places he's worked and where they were in relation to all the victims' homes. Mrs. Hale, it all tracks. We're here to talk to Gary Stokes, and it needs to be now."

"Oh my God." She looked down, almost as if searching for an answer. "You think he's Billy."

CHAPTER 66: JACOB

Desperation clawed at my chest as I realized the consequences of my actions. I had threatened Maddy, leaving her ammunition that could damn me in court.

No, this couldn't be happening. I needed to speak to Vic again. Find a way to fix this mess before it was too late.

I stormed back toward his office. His assistant tried to stop me, but I brushed past her, feeling at my wit's end. "Don't even try it. I need to talk to Vic now." I pushed inside, and there he was, surprise masking his face. "Vic, come on. You know that was all just a misunderstanding. Accounting errors. You know me."

He seemed to realize this confrontation was unavoidable. "I thought I did, Jake. But I've talked to the partners. We agreed the best way to move forward was to buy you out of the firm. Now, if you disagree, we can go ahead with criminal charges." He leaned back, steepling his fingers. "The choice is yours."

"I can't believe you're doing this." I tugged on my suit jacket in defiance. "You can't just kick me out of the firm. We have an agreement."

"You might want to take another look at it, Jake. You breached that agreement."

I turned on my heel and started to leave when Vic called out to me.

"Jake?"

I spun around. "Yes?"

"We'll do our best to keep quiet about your inappropriate relationship with a member of your staff. She could, of course, come forward with charges of her own, but that'll be up to you to deal with."

I sneered, my gaze burning into him. "As if you haven't done the same thing." I turned my back to him, certain he'd heard what I'd said, even if he didn't acknowledge me.

The walk to my office felt humiliating. Everyone knew. Maybe they hadn't known about the affair, but they knew about the money. I hadn't called Lauren yet. God knows what I was supposed to say to her. We'd just added a hundred grand to our mortgage. I owed another two hundred grand for bets I'd placed with people I should've known better than to tangle with. And now I had no job. No pension. I supposed it was better than jail time, but in light of my looming debts, I was about to face far worse.

No law firm in Alexandria would touch me now. Word would spread. The partners would make sure of that. And all this because of her. Because Maddy couldn't be happy with the way things were. So now my life was over.

I entered my office and began to throw my things in boxes. My law books would have to be put on a dolly and wheeled out. The only saving grace was that it was after five and most of the staff had gone home.

The pang of betrayal and humiliation nauseated me. That was when an epiphany struck. I suddenly understood how Lauren must've felt, learning about the affair.

My thoughts turned to my wife. What was I going to tell her? That I'd lost everything for a fleeting moment of desire with someone else? That my career, my reputation, and even my own beliefs had dissolved into a tangled mess of lust and regret? Dear God, how would I tell her about the gambling debt?

I felt an unshakeable sadness as I looked around my office. This was my life, my identity, and in one fell swoop, I had lost it all.

When I emerged into the corridor, box in hand, the few remaining staff members looked at me with revulsion. I carried on, nonetheless. As I reached my car, I got an up-close view of the damage that bastard had done. I set down the box in the backseat, then closed the door and ran my finger along the gouge. The entire length of the driver's side, now marred with a white jagged line. "You son of a bitch." And he'd tacked on ten grand to my next payment — a penalty for being late.

I tamped down my rising anger, knowing I had a more pressing concern. Slipping behind the wheel, I stared at the building that bore my name. Mullen, Gossett & Hale. *Not anymore.*

She was still inside — Maddy. Probably waiting for me to clear out so she wouldn't have to face me. "Spineless bitch."

I sat there for several minutes, until finally, the rear lobby doors opened. A wry smile pulled at my lips. "She emerges," I whispered. I wondered if she would look for my car, or simply walk over to hers, not thinking twice about me.

Within moments, she'd climbed into her Mercedes, taking no notice of me or anything else around her. I waited for her to pull away, and I followed. "You think you can destroy my life without consequences?"

As I trailed behind Maddy's car, revenge consumed me. I couldn't let her get away with what she had done. She had seduced me, manipulated my emotions, ultimately leading to the downfall of everything I had worked so hard to build.

The city lights streaked by as I continued to tail her along the streets. My anger fueled my determination, and a plan began to form in my mind. She needed to pay, to feel the same pain that she had caused me.

As Maddy drove on, oblivious to my presence, I wondered how far she would go to protect herself. Would she have the guts to confront me head-on?

Finally, she turned off Belle View Boulevard, entering the parking lot of her condominium complex near the Potomac. I parked several yards away and waited. She soon stepped out of her car, locking it behind her.

I stepped out into the darkness, moving swiftly but silently to catch up to her. I was only a few feet away when she turned around. Her mouth opened and her eyes widened. She was about to scream. Before she let out a peep, I snatched her, spinning her around, and clamping my hand over her mouth. "Just calm down, Maddy. I only want to talk."

We were too exposed. I had to get back to my car. "Walk with me." She struggled under my grip, her legs tripping over each other. "I'm not going to hurt you, just come with me, goddamn it."

We arrived at my car. I struggled to contain her movement while opening the passenger door and shoving Maddy inside. I quickly locked it while I jogged around to the driver's side.

Slipping behind the wheel once again, I fixed my gaze on her. "I just want to talk to you, Maddy, okay?"

"What the hell is wrong with you?" she said, her voice raised, tinged with panic.

"Look, I just need you to go back and talk to Vic. Tell him you made it look like I was skimming from the clients, okay?"

"Why the hell would I do that?" Her eyes scoured every inch around her, searching for an opportunity to escape. I could see the wheels turning in her mind, contemplating every possible scenario that could unfold from this situation.

"Because Maddy, if you don't do as I say, things will get much worse for you. Trust me, you don't want that."

Her gaze pierced through me like a dagger. There was fire in her eyes, a fierce determination dampened only by her fear. "You think I'm scared of you? You don't know anything about me."

I leaned in closer, narrowing the distance between us. My voice dropped to a low whisper. "You should be scared, Maddy, because I promise you, I will win this."

She stared back at me, her resolve crumbling. I could see the uncertainty in her eyes, the awareness that she had underestimated me. And in that moment, I had her exactly where I wanted her.

"Fine," she whispered. "I'll do it. But you have to let me go, and you have to promise not to hurt me."

I nodded, my eyes never leaving hers. "I promise I won't touch you again. Just make sure you keep your word, and no one will get hurt."

With that, I unlocked the door. Maddy opened the passenger side and stepped out. She looked back at me. "You can go fuck yourself, Jake. I'm not helping you do shit."

Something in me snapped. The world turned red. What had been only a flame of hatred toward this woman was now a raging inferno. I threw open my door, jumping from my seat, and charged after her. Maddy ran, her legs pumping, but her shoes slowed her pace. She stumbled, falling onto the asphalt.

I caught up to her, straddling her, pinning down arms that were bloodied from the asphalt scrapes. I placed my hands around her delicate neck, the tender muscles caving beneath my grip. "You have no idea what you've done to me."

"You did this to yourself!" Her words came out deep and guttural. "Get off!"

As I squeezed, I could feel her struggle against me. I wanted her dead. Out of my life forever. Her legs kicked while I kept her arms pinned. Her tiny frame, unable to move me. I felt her weakening, fueling my desire to crush the life from her.

Her eyes bulged; her lips turned purple. Maddy looked at me, knowing death was near, and that I was the one to bring it. Her eyes fell shut, and then . . . she went limp.

I gasped, releasing her neck. The shock of my actions settled around me. I sat there a moment, feeling as if this was a dream. But this was no dream. Maddy was dead. I killed her.

The lawyer in me took over. I had to get the fuck out of here. Fast. I glanced around. No one had seen what I'd done. I could still get away. I got up, raising Maddy's limp body, dragging her along the length of the darkened lot until I reached the alley next door to her building. I tore away a part of my shirt, wiping from her body any hint of my fingerprints, my sweat. Anything that could tie me to her.

I carried on, deeper into the passageway, until spying the dumpster. I raised her slight figure and threw her inside. "Christ, Maddie. All you had to do was talk to Vic. Why didn't you just do what I said?"

CHAPTER 67: LAUREN

My mind reeled at the notion that Gary Stokes was a killer. But the prospect seemed all too real now, in light of what I'd learned about Noah. In light of what the detectives learned about Gary's history. Billy was no imaginary friend.

"He's here, or at least, he's usually here by now," I said. "But any number of people could've worked in any number of places around your victims. What sets Gary apart?"

Tammy placed her hand on my forearm. "I don't know, Lauren. All of this stuff started happening when he came to work here. You see that, right?"

"I guess so, but the idea it could've been one of the contractors who worked in our house — that makes more sense. They'd know the ins and outs. Our work schedule." I turned back to the detectives. "Right? Did you even look into those guys, like you said?"

"We did, Mrs. Hale," Collins replied. "Nothing hit."

I paced my small office. "Well, look. You're the cops. If you think Gary's the guy who's been in my house or was responsible for murdering all those people . . ." I shook my head in disbelief. "Then do what you have to do. He's here."

279

Collins glanced into the empty hall. "Mrs. Hale, you should go home now. We'll bring Gary into the station. You and your family will be safe. We've got it from here."

"Yeah, okay." I walked back to my desk as they disappeared down the hall. Tammy stood in the middle of my office, sympathy in her gaze. I asked, "You believe them?"

"I don't know what to believe, Lauren. I really don't. This whole thing is just so surreal. But what matters to me is that you and Noah are safe. You should go home, like the detective said. They'll talk to Gary. If he's the guy, then count yourself lucky. I know I will."

"Right, of course. I'd better go pick up Noah from Ann's house." I gathered my things, feeling Tammy's gaze still on me.

She said, "If you need anything, Lauren, just call. No matter what time it is."

"I will. I promise." I walked out of my office, instinctively looking down the corridor as if I would spot Gary. He wasn't there.

Outside, I noticed the dark clouds overhead, making it feel later than it was. The air was chilly, and I zipped up my coat. I wanted nothing more than to pick up my son and go home. All the stuff with Jacob? That was for another day.

Pressing the ignition, I drove out of the parking lot, careful to avoid the 495, taking surface streets to Jacob's parents' house. I passed by Loftridge Park, on my way to Rose Hill.

I wondered if I should call Jacob. What would I say to him? Tell him the guy I worked with was Billy? That he was a killer? I hadn't even mentioned my dead mother.

Minutes later, I'd arrived, ready to take my son home. I'd never wanted to be home with him more than at this moment. I made my way up the front path and stepped onto the porch. Before I could ring the doorbell, Ann opened the door. "Hi, is Noah ready?"

"Yes, of course. Come in, Lauren." She stepped aside.

I walked into their beautiful home. It was larger than ours. Jacob's father, Jack, was a lawyer too. In fact, Jacob was a lot like his father. Maybe not in every way, I hoped.

"Mommy!" Noah ran toward me.

I bent down and opened my arms, pulling him close. "Hi, sweetheart. Are you ready to go home?"

"Yeah." He turned back to Ann. "Bye, Grandma."

"Bye, sugar," she said, before turning to me. "Everything okay now, I take it?"

"Yeah, I think it is. No need to worry about anything anymore," I replied.

She placed her hand on her chest and sighed. "Well, that's a relief. You drive safely, Lauren, all right?" She kissed my cheek.

"I will. Goodnight, Ann. Thanks for looking after Noah."

"Anything for my grandson."

She closed the door as we walked outside. "Go on, bud. Hop in the backseat." When I reached the car, I secured his seatbelt and walked around to the driver's side.

Soon, we were on the road again, only about ten minutes from home. I drove in silence, my mind racing as Noah seemed absorbed in his own thoughts. I had to decide soon about how to handle this situation; we couldn't stay in limbo forever.

As I pulled into the driveway, I saw Jacob's car parked in the garage. He had made it back from work early, a surprise, and maybe a blessing.

I turned off the engine and took a deep breath, preparing myself for the conversation ahead. We walked inside, Noah's small hand gripped tightly in mine.

Jacob sat at the kitchen table, a glass of wine in front of him. That was unusual because he wasn't much of a wine drinker, preferring beer instead.

"I can get dinner started," I said.

"No, don't," he cut in. "We can order takeout." Jacob turned to Noah, a smile playing on his lips. "Hey, buddy. How you doing?" He opened his arms. "Come here and give me a hug. I missed you today."

For all of Jacob's faults, he had always been a good father. Even if he wasn't around as much as some dads. When he *was* there, he was attentive to our boy.

"What happened today?" Jacob asked him. "Did you do anything fun at Grandma and Grandpa's?"

I would have to intervene and explain all of it, so I walked over to Noah. "Why don't you go upstairs and play, so I can talk to Daddy?"

Noah looked at me, and I thought I saw fear in his eyes. "What about Billy?"

Jacob slammed down his glass of wine, splashing its contents onto the table.

"For God's sake!" I shouted at Jacob.

"I'm so sick of hearing about Billy. Now, go upstairs! Billy isn't real, all right, so get it out of your head right now!"

"What the hell is wrong with you?" Tears welled in my eyes as I watched Noah retreat up the stairs, his small figure disappearing into the darkness. My heart pounded in my chest, a rising tide of anger surging through me.

Jacob slumped back in the chair. His face contorted with frustration. "I just can't take it anymore."

"*You* can't take it?" I fumed. "What about Noah? Can you imagine how scared and confused he must be right now?"

Jacob's eyes flickered with guilt before he averted his gaze, unable to meet my accusing stare. "I didn't mean to explode like that. But this whole Billy thing . . . it's tearing us apart."

"What's tearing us apart is your goddamn affair," I lashed out. "Why did you even bother to come home, huh? If all you wanted to do was yell at our son."

"I got fired today, all right?" he shouted back at me. "I lost my job, and that's all there is to say about it."

My mouth dropped. "What? How?" This couldn't be happening. Not with everything else going on.

"It doesn't matter how. I got fired and that's it." He looked at me. "And as far as the other thing . . . you don't have to worry about that anymore. It's over." Evidently he couldn't even bring himself to say the word *affair*.

His words settled around me and my head spun. I struggled to process the weight of Jacob's confession, even if the truth had been hanging over our heads for months. The admission of his affair felt like a punch to the gut, amplifying the pain and confusion that already consumed me. I staggered backward, clutching onto the kitchen counter for support.

"Over?" I repeated, my voice barely a whisper. "How can you expect me to believe that? After everything we've been through?"

Jacob's face softened, remorse etching deep lines into his features. He reached out, attempting to bridge the divide between us with a touch. I recoiled, stepping away from his outstretched hand.

"I'm so sorry," he whispered. "It was a mistake — a terrible mistake. But it's over now, I swear it."

The room hung heavy with silence as I grappled with conflicting emotions — hurt, anger, fear, betrayal — each vying for control over my racing mind. The image of my mother's lifeless body still flashed before my eyes. The idea my friend, Gary, was a killer . . . I wanted to scream.

My breathing quickened, echoing in my ears. I sat down at the kitchen table across from him. "I have to tell you about some things that happened today."

CHAPTER 68: GARY

The moment had arrived. The knock on the maintenance office door sounded, and I knew who stood on the other side. All I had to do was remain calm. They had nothing on me. If they had, I would've been their first stop when they came in. Instead, they went to see Lauren, probably because of what happened to Cheryl. I was almost sorry she had to die.

The door opened and I smiled. "Evening. What can I do for you folks? You know, the office is closed right now, so—"

The female officer held out her badge. "Detective Collins. This is Detective Dixon. Alexandria PD. Are you Gary Stokes?"

"Yes, ma'am. What's this about?"

"We'd like to ask you some questions."

They both stepped inside.

"Sure, but I am on shift. I should probably reach out to my supervisor—"

"We've already talked to him." Collins pulled out a chair to sit down. Her partner joined her, and then she began. "We've been looking into your background, Mr. Stokes."

I tilted my head. "Why is that? Have I done something wrong?"

"Your previous employers — and you've had quite a few over the past couple years — it seems they've been in close proximity to several crime scenes I've been investigating."

"Crime scenes? I don't understand."

"Murders, Mr. Stokes," she added. "Brutal murders of thirteen people. Four innocent families."

"My God." I darted my gaze between them. "You think I killed thirteen people?"

Detective Dixon leaned forward, his expression stern. "We're not saying that, Gary. But it's our job to look into any potential connections. You seem to have been in the right place at the right time pretty frequently."

I chuckled, trying to disguise my unease. "I was just working, Detectives."

Collins crossed her arms. "We have to consider all possibilities, Mr. Stokes. We have your employment history. We've spoken to your previous employers. I'm going to give you some dates, and I'm going to need you to explain your whereabouts on those dates."

I shook my head. "How far back are we talking? My memory isn't as good as it used to be. But I can assure you, I've been working at honest jobs, just trying to make ends meet."

Dixon interjected, "Then maybe you can explain the fact that you conveniently changed jobs around the times each murder occurred?"

"I don't know what to tell you." I rubbed the back of my neck. "You'd have to give me those dates. But look, I work as a janitor. It's not the kind of job that requires a steady employment history. Should I be concerned here? Do I need a lawyer?"

"Only if you're guilty," Collins shot back. "Look, we're going to need you to tell us your home address, because it wasn't on file here. And we'd like to know your daily schedule. We will be reviewing the company's surveillance cameras."

I raised the corner of my lip. "Be my guest. I have nothing to hide. I come in, do my job, and go home. The reason there's no address on file here is that I've been living in the homeless encampment nearby. Forgive me, I realize that's unsavory, but it happens even when you work hard every night, as I do."

The detectives glanced at one another, and then Collins turned back to me. "Are you aware a woman, who also lived in that encampment, was found murdered in the early hours of this morning?"

"Of course I'm aware. Everyone in the camp was talking about it. Not sure what it has to do with me. Unfortunately, we're targeted often — the homeless. It's not the first time one of us has been murdered."

Collins appeared to grow irritated. "We'll need you to come down to the station."

"May I ask what for?"

"We'd like a DNA sample as well as fingerprints," Dixon added.

I drew back in confusion. "Why would I be okay with that?"

Collins leaned in. "The question, Mr. Stokes, is, if you're innocent, why wouldn't you be?"

"Fair point, detectives. I understand your need to gather evidence, but as I said before, I have nothing to hide. I came to work last night as usual, I did my job, and then I left."

"It's our duty to investigate every possible link, no matter how tenuous it may be," Dixon said.

"Believe me, I understand your responsibility to protect and serve. I'm just asking you to consider the facts: I'm a janitor with no fixed address, and I work in a place where people from all walks of life come and go. You're asking me to come with you, and offer you my prints and DNA, but for what?" I gauged the detectives' reactions. Both appeared exasperated. I knew I wasn't going to talk my way out of this, whether or not they had evidence. "That said, I'll go with you, just to prove my cooperativeness and innocence."

"Thank you." Collins stood and moved around toward me, offering me her hand.

"I got it." I stood on my own and trailed them into the hallway. I wondered if Lauren was still here. Would she see this? And if so, would she help me? But as we carried on toward the elevators, I noticed her office light was off. She was gone. Now I wondered how it would be possible for me to see her again.

CHAPTER 69: MADISON

My eyes popped open as I gasped for air. Where was I? My head pounded and the smell . . . Jesus, what was that smell? My throat ached as if I'd swallowed glass. The ground beneath me was damp and cold, seeping through the fabric of my clothes and chilling me to the bone. I looked down, realizing I sat on . . .

Oh my God.

The walls around me, I knew what they were. I was in a dumpster. "Help! Help!" My voice was barely above a whisper.

I stood on wobbly legs, gripping the metal wall, and sinking deeper into the trash. It began to come back to me. Soon, the memories rushed back in a torrent. I clutched my throat where phantom fingers seemed to squeeze, as if I was still struggling to breathe. As my thoughts cleared from the fog of fear and pain, I remembered how I ended up here, and who did this to me.

Looking down at my legs, I could see my pants were soiled with food and blood, and my shoes were gone. The heels of my feet were bloodied and raw, as if I'd been dragged or forced to walk barefoot over glass.

"You tried to kill me." The words came out hoarse. I pulled up, my arms weak, managing to gain enough leverage to hoist over the dumpster's edge. And then I spilled out onto the cold concrete, cringing from the sharp pain in my shoulder. I struggled to return to my feet, and when I did, I peered around. "Where's my phone?" Panic edged into my voice. "Shit. You took it, didn't you?" Frantically patting down my pants pockets yielded nothing. "My keys, too."

I realized then that I was alone — no ID on me, no phone to call for help, and I wasn't entirely sure where I was as I stared into the dark alleyway. But somewhere in the distance, faint but unmistakable, was the low hum of cars passing by. A road. A lifeline.

My first step sent pain searing up my leg, a hot knife cutting through the cold numbness. I could hardly stand on my injured feet, but I had no choice. I had to push on. I had to get to the end of this alley and to a road. Find someone, anyone who could help. I had to call the police and tell them that Jacob Hale, the man I'd once loved, tried to murder me.

As I took cautious steps to avoid broken bottles and sharp stones, I drew nearer to buildings in the distance. I recognized it now. "Home."

The parking lot would be just ahead. I had no idea of the time. How long had I been out? It was dark, but was it too late? Would anyone be in the lobby? Surely, a night staffer would be there. Without keys, I wasn't getting in the door.

More agonizing steps and then I saw it — the parking lot of my complex. I was going to be okay. I just needed to get help.

The lobby doors were just feet away. I was almost there. But when I reached for the handle, the door was locked. I tugged and tugged. "Come on. Please." A tear fell down my cheek. I cupped my hands over my eyes, peering through the glass doors. "Is anyone there? I need help."

No one was at the desk. The lobby was empty. "Help! Please!" I raised my voice as loudly as I could. The building required a key card for residents to enter, and after 8 p.m., the doors were locked to non-residents. So, it was at least after eight. "Hello!" I yelled. "Can somebody help me?"

Defeat weighed on my shoulders, but when I saw some-one inside appear from a back room, a spark of hope shot through me. "Help me. Please, I live here. Can you let me in?"

I had no idea what I looked like. Would he think I was some lunatic, or would he believe me?

The man walked back to the front desk, and I thought I'd lost him. Or maybe he was going to call the police. No, he came back with keys in his hands.

I stepped away as he unlocked the door and pushed it open. "Miss, are you okay?"

"No, someone tried to kill me. We have to call the police."

"Oh my God. Come inside, we'll get you cleaned up." He ushered me in. "What's your name, Miss?"

"Madison Price. I live here. Unit 3126."

"I'm so sorry. I didn't recognize you. Sit down. Let me get you some water." He walked me toward the sofa in the middle of the lobby, next to the gas fireplace that provided me much-needed warmth. My teeth stopped chattering after a few moments.

The man returned. "I've called the police. They're on their way." He handed me a bottle of water. "Here, drink this."

I opened the lid and poured a little down my throat, quickly coughing it up. "I'm sorry. It hurts to drink. My throat." I pressed my fingers gently on my neck, wincing at the pain.

"Holy shit." He looked at me. "Your neck. It's black and blue."

Within minutes, I heard the sirens. The assistant man-ager, a young guy, probably younger than me, walked toward the lobby doors. "Thank God. The cops are here." He opened them, waving them over. "She's here. In here."

I heard the heavy footfalls move inside, and as I glanced up, I saw two uniformed officers staring down at me. An older man, heavy-set, and a woman, who looked to be about twenty-five.

"Miss, we've called an ambulance," the female cop said. "We're going to take you to the hospital and get you checked out, all right?"

I nodded. "But you have to arrest him."

"Who, miss?" the older man asked. "Who did this to you?"

"Jacob Hale. We worked together. He tried to kill me."

The officers stepped away and I could only hear low murmurs coming from them. Then I heard the guy speak into his radio.

"Copy, we have a witness statement. Suspect is Jacob Hale."

"Madison," the assistant manager said gently, placing his hand on my shoulder. "You're going to be okay. Just focus on your breathing and let the professionals take care of the rest."

I took a deep breath, trying to really hear his words. The officers approached me once again, their faces sober.

The older one reached out to me. "We need to get you to the hospital, Madison. It's important that we assess your injuries and make sure you're okay."

"What about Jacob?" I asked. "You have to find him."

"Yes, ma'am. I've called it in. We'll find the person who did this to you."

CHAPTER 70: DETECTIVE COLLINS

Dixon and I stood at the front desk inside the station with Gary Stokes in tow. The man I was certain was responsible for a string of horrific murders. "I need an interview room."

The officer behind the desk typed on his keyboard. "Two and three are open, Detectives."

"Thanks," I nodded to Dixon. "Three?"

"You got it." He placed his hand on Stokes' shoulder. "Let's go have a chat."

I stopped a moment when I heard a call come in. I peered over my shoulder as the officer continued.

"Madison Price at Colony House Condos off Belle View Boulevard. Yes, sir." He nodded. "Got it. BOLO on one Jacob Hale . . ."

My heart caught in my throat. I spun around and returned to the desk. The officer was still writing down the details. "Hale? Did you say, Hale?"

The officer raised his hand at me, wanting me to wait. But this couldn't wait. Not a chance. "I know Hale. I know him!"

"Hang on a second, Officer Shaw," he said into the phone. Then he looked at me with noted irritation. "Sorry, Detective. You said you know him?"

Adrenaline surged through me. "Yes. What happened?"

"A Miss Madison Price claims he tried to murder her tonight. She crawled out of a dumpster inside an alley, beaten and battered. She was near her condo when it happened."

"Okay. Let me talk to Shaw."

He handed me the receiver.

"Officer Shaw, this is Detective Collins. I know Jacob Hale, and I know where he lives. I'm asking that you do not issue the BOLO. Let me bring him in."

"He attempted to murder Ms. Price, Detective," Shaw reiterated.

"I hear you. This is a whole lot bigger than you know. Please, I'm working on something, and he's tied to it. Let me track him down, and I'll bring him in."

"All right, but I'm noting in my report that I wanted to issue the BOLO."

"Fine. Thanks, Shaw. I owe you."

Turning around, I quickly jogged to Dixon, who'd just returned to the lobby after putting Stokes in the interview room. "We need to bring in Hale."

"Why? What happened?"

"I'll tell you on the way." I started ahead, toward the exit.

"What about Stokes?" Dixon called out.

I shot a look at the officer behind the desk. "Room three. Don't let him leave."

"Copy," he replied.

I turned back to Dixon. "We'll let him stew for a while." I pushed through the doors and jogged to my car. I heard Dixon behind me. "Let's go, man. Hale just tried to kill a woman. I'm guessing his mistress. We gotta get him before he runs."

Dixon jumped in the passenger seat, and I started the engine. My left hand gripped the steering wheel as I slammed the gearshift into reverse with my right.

"You mind filling me in what just went down back there?" Dixon pointed a thumb backwards.

I quickly brought him up to speed, then turned to him to ask, "Why the hell would he try to murder this woman?"

"Do we know who she is?"

"Get on the horn with Officer Shaw. Her name is Madison Price. He's getting her over to the hospital to get checked out. Find out exactly what went down," I replied.

Dixon grabbed his phone and made the call. He placed it on speaker. "Shaw, it's Detective Dixon. I'm here with Collins, and we're on our way to bring in Jacob Hale. How is he connected to your victim?"

"Madison Price says she works with him. They were romantically involved, according to her. He got fired today and blamed her. He got violent. Tried to strangle her."

"Jesus," I said. "Hey, Shaw, it's Collins. Are you planning to get a full statement from her?"

"Once she's checked out, yes. She's sustained some fairly serious injuries."

"Copy that," I replied. "Keep us posted, and we'll do the same. Collins out."

Dixon ended the call. "What the hell does all of this mean? And what about Stokes?"

CHAPTER 71: GARY

As I sat inside the interview room, a stark, dull space with only a table and four chairs, I realized I'd run out of options. But a spark of hope remained. I was so careful not to leave anything behind. I'd even disposed of the knives I'd used.

I was going to have to play this cool, and calm, as if I had nothing to hide. My only careless action was in taking Cheryl's life. It had all happened so fast, I didn't take my usual precautions, and the knife was in my car. If they found my car . . .

I couldn't think about that right now. I could only think about Lauren and Noah. My family, who was now left without me.

I sat in the room, waiting for the detectives to return. How much time had passed? When would they come back? I had no intention of staying here, and unless they pulled evidence out of their asses, they couldn't keep me. I had to get home — to my family — and take care of them. Keep them safe from Jacob.

It had been half an hour. "Son of a bitch," I muttered. I got up from the chair and opened the door, peeking into the hallway. A few officers hurried along, entering the other rooms, but no one was coming toward me. I stepped out for a better look toward the lobby. The officer behind the desk when I'd arrived was no longer there. It was someone else.

Holy shit. Could I do it? Could I simply walk out of here? They'd taken no prints, no DNA from me. Who even knew I was in here? I hadn't given them any identification. My God . . . did they just forget about me? Something had to have happened. But what did that matter to me? If I walked out of here . . .

I took a deep breath, stepping into the hall, letting the door close behind me. Distancing myself from that room was the best way to avoid questions. To my left was the lobby. To my right, a door with an exit sign above. That was my way out. The adrenaline pumped through my veins, sharpening my senses. With a final glance back into the empty hallway, I exited the building and disappeared into the darkness.

CHAPTER 72: LAUREN

Jacob and I had been sitting in silence for the past several minutes, the air heavy with a tension that seemed to thicken with each passing moment. I had shared with him the news about Cheryl. Her brutal murder and the subsequent call from the police asking me to identify her. Then about Gary. Jacob, who had never met Cheryl, looked lost, seemingly unable to process it all.

"What are we going to do about Noah? After what happened today, Jacob . . . Maybe it's best, until Detective Collins books Gary on charges, we all go somewhere else?"

I'd pushed aside the reality of his affair and what it meant to our marriage. It wasn't as difficult as I thought it would be, perhaps because deep down, I'd already known about it.

"We can send Noah to stay again with my parents," Jacob suggested, his gaze firmly planted on the floor. "But this information . . . Lauren, I honestly don't know what to do with it."

The man sitting across from me was no longer the man I thought he was. I'd always believed him to be my protector. My rock. Maybe it was unfair to place such expectations on any man, but that was how I felt. As I looked at him now, I saw someone else entirely — a man riddled with shame, regret, and a hint of fear. He feared Billy as much as I did. And until we were certain about Gary, a killer could still be coming for us.

A knock echoed through the house, startling me out of my thoughts. I shot Jacob a glance. "Are you expecting anyone?"

"No." He quickly rose from his chair and pulled back the blinds on the breakfast nook window for a better look. "Shit," he muttered under his breath. "The detectives are here."

A wave of confusion washed over me. "Why are they here? They're supposed to be questioning Gary."

Making my way into the foyer, I opened the door, but before I could even get a word out, Detective Collins pushed inside, her hand gripping the butt of her weapon like a lifeline.

"Where's your husband?" she asked, her eyes scanning the room while Dixon entered behind her.

"In the kitchen." I closed the door. "What's going on?"

Collins reached the kitchen and with Dixon at her side, she turned to face Jacob. Her voice was firm and steady: "Jacob Hale, you're under arrest for the attempted murder of Madison Price."

I lost my breath, standing in stunned silence. Jacob appeared ready to bolt, but Detective Dixon grabbed my husband by the arm and pulled him close.

My gaze shifted between the detectives and Jacob. I tried to read my husband's face, but I saw nothing. "What the hell is she talking about?"

While Collins cuffed Jacob, she asked, "You want to tell her, or should I?"

"Jacob?" I knew exactly who Madison Price was, but to hear that my husband tried to kill her? "What did you do?"

"He's coming with us, right now, Mrs. Hale," Collins said. "We still have Stokes at the station as well. We're close, just like I said."

"What am I supposed to do?" I felt my chest tighten as they pulled Jacob toward the front door. "Jacob, did you do this?"

"Call Vic, Lauren, all right? Just call him and tell him to come down to the station."

They started out toward the door, and I stood there, having no idea what was going on or how I should react. "Detective Collins, what's happening?"

"Get someone to look after your boy, then come down to the station," she replied. "I'll explain everything when you get there."

I watched them practically drag Jacob to the car and push him into the back seat. I locked eyes with him. And that was when I saw it. He was guilty.

When the taillights faded from view, I returned inside, closing the door and securing the deadbolt. And when I turned around, I saw Noah standing on the bottom step.

"Where are they taking Daddy?" he asked.

I approached him, squatting to meet his gaze. "It's okay, buddy. They just want to ask him some questions about work. It's fine. Nothing to worry about, okay?" I tried to read his face, but I couldn't tell whether he believed me.

"I tell you what — how about I call Grandpa and see if he can come get you again tonight? Would you like to stay with him and Grandma again?"

"No, I just want to be home. I want you and Daddy to stay home with me."

I felt the sting of tears threaten to reveal my true feelings to him. But I had to be strong. He needed that right now. "I know you do, sweetheart, but there's just a lot going on."

I returned upright. "Just for tonight, okay? Tomorrow things will look a whole lot better." I walked into the kitchen where I'd left my phone. Jacob had asked me to call his boss — well, former boss now — but what could he do? He wasn't a criminal attorney. Could we really be talking about attempted murder?

I closed my eyes, wanting to crumple to the floor and just wait for all of this to pass. But I couldn't. I had a son to care for.

I snatched my phone from the counter and returned into the foyer, where Noah still waited. "Go on upstairs and pack your pajamas and whatever else you want, okay?"

A tiny spark appeared in his eyes. "Okay." He ran upstairs.

I walked into the living room, eyeing the contacts on my phone. I supposed the first call should be to Vic, so I dialed his number. I wondered if he would recognize my name when it popped up. And if he did, would he bother answering? He'd just fired my husband. Now, I was calling to ask him to help get him out on bail for attempted murder.

The phone felt heavy in my hand as I waited for him to answer.

"Hello?" Vic's deep voice filled my ear.

I swallowed, trying to gather my courage before speaking. "Vic, it's Lauren Hale. I hope it's okay to call you."

He fell silent for a moment, and I could almost picture him staring at his phone, wondering why I would be calling him. "Lauren, if this is about me firing Jacob . . ."

My voice wavered, "Jacob's been arrested. He's been charged with attempted murder."

There was a long pause before Vic finally spoke, his tone subdued. "Oh, Lauren, I'm so sorry to hear that. I have to ask . . . was it Madison?"

It was all I could do to hold back my sobs. He knew about the affair. That meant everyone did. "Yes," I choked out. "Please, Vic, he asked for your help. Can you go to the police station? I don't know what else to do."

He sighed. "Lauren, you know I'm not that kind of lawyer."

"I know, but I'm guessing he asked because he thought you might know someone who could help."

"Let me see what I can do. I'll call you back."

The line clicked. He was gone. I dropped onto the sofa, feeling at the end of my rope. And I wondered if we were still in danger. Did Collins get it right about Gary? It still seemed unfathomable to me. I rubbed my face, processing all that had happened.

"Mommy?"

I sucked in a ragged breath, steadying my nerves as I got to my feet. Walking toward the stairs, I glanced up to see what Noah wanted. "Oh God." I pressed my hand against my chest as a weight dropped into my stomach. "Gary, what are you doing here?" He stood on the landing, holding my son's hand.

"Mommy, this is Billy," he said. "I told you I wasn't lying about him."

My heart thumped in my ears, nearly drowning out all other sound. That man no longer looked like the Gary I had met. Instead, he glared at me with unrecognizable eyes. I feigned composure for Noah's sake. "How did you—"

"The attic," he cut in, pragmatically. "Jacob didn't do a very good job of sealing the dormer."

"But I thought you were at the police station."

"Oh, I was." A peculiar, crooked smile arose on his lips. "Guess they forgot about me."

My denial of the outlandish notion someone had been hiding in my house now mocked me. "Noah has nothing to do with any of this. Just let him go and tell me what you want."

Gary looked down at Noah, smiling. "All I've ever wanted, Lauren, is for us to be a family."

CHAPTER 73: DETECTIVE COLLINS

We walked into the station, Dixon leading Mr. Hale inside. I approached the front desk, nodding at the officer behind it. "We're preparing to book Jacob Hale. Who do you have keeping eyes on Stokes?"

The officer donned an air of confusion. "Sorry, Detective. Who?"

"Gary Stokes. He was in interview room three." I could feel my patience waning with every passing second. "Who's been checking in on him?"

He peered at his monitor and pressed the keys, his fingers moving with a slow deliberation that plucked my last nerve. "Uh, there's no one in room three right now. I'm afraid I don't know who Gary Stokes is. Could he be in Booking?"

I turned to Dixon, feeling my pulse quicken. "The fuck?"

Dixon moved toward the desk, keeping his hand clutched on Hale's handcuffs. "You sure about this? Did someone else check him out? Look again. I told whoever was up here an hour ago that Three was occupied."

The officer keyed in more commands and shook his head. "No, sir, Detective Dixon. I don't show a Gary Stokes in the system at all. I did just come on shift. I can try to call Stone. He was the one you must've spoken to."

"Oh my God." I rocked back on my heels. The oversight was on me. I should've logged him in. And like a punch to the gut, I knew where Stokes was headed. "He's going after Lauren."

"What?" Jacob struggled to free himself from Dixon's grip, his eyes wide with terror. "Let me go! What the hell did you two do? Someone's after my family. Let me go!"

"You're not going anywhere, Mr. Hale." Dixon's powerful voice resonated.

I said, "I have to go back." Panic clawed at my insides as I charged toward the exit once again. My legs pumped harder than ever as I was certain lives were at stake. I jumped into my car and spun my tires, the screech echoing in the parking lot.

I dialed Lauren's number, praying she would pick up. Her phone rang and rang, each tone reinforcing my fear. "Goddamn it. Voicemail." I had to leave a message. "Lauren, take Noah and get the hell out of your house. Now! I'm on my way." My chest tightened as I sped down the highway, the roar of the engine drowning out everything else. There was no time to waste. Lauren and Noah's lives were in danger. And it was my fault.

CHAPTER 74: LAUREN

My feet refused to move. I was frozen in a state of disbelief, staring up at my son, who was holding hands with a man who I now knew was a brutal killer.

"I'm sorry about your mom," Gary said.

We were locked in a standoff. If I could keep him talking . . . "How did you know?"

"She thought she could keep bleeding me dry, so I had to put a stop to it. But you remember what she was like, right? A taker. Nothing but a taker."

"How do you know my mother? Did you . . . did you kill her?"

"Like I said, she didn't leave me any choice." He squeezed Noah's hand.

"Ouch. Mommy?" His little face cringed with pain.

"Stop. You're hurting him."

"I'll bet she never told you about me," Gary continued.

"What are you talking about?"

"She and I go way back," he added. "We were together for a while. Before she became who she was . . . Oh, I guess we were pretty young. Not much older than twenty." He cocked his head. "So, she never said a word about me, huh?"

"Why would she?" A sickening feeling swirled in my stomach.

Gary grinned at me. A closed-lip, knowing grin. "Well, I figured you might want to know who your father was."

A vice grip squeezed my chest. I could hardly breathe and I grew lightheaded. "No, you're not my father."

"She was the only real girlfriend I ever had, come to think of it. Course, she never told me about you. But as luck would have it, we crossed paths once again only recently. Call it kismet. I'd been on the hunt, so to speak," he snickered. "Needing a place to hole up for a while. Ran across her unexpectedly. Recognized her, and we got to talking. She wanted money, of course. That was when she told me about you. And where I could find you, if I was interested."

I wondered how Cheryl even knew where I was, where I worked. Had she been keeping tabs on me all this time? I'd never know now, because she was dead. And my father . . . dear God . . . my father now stood before me, holding his grandson hostage.

"Cheryl got greedy," he continued. "The information came at a price, but I got what I wanted. And now I'm here, ready to be part of your family."

"You think we're going to welcome you with open arms?" I felt my face heating. "After what you've done to so many innocent people? I don't want anything to do with you. You're a monster. Now step away from my son."

Gary looked down at him. "You're not scared of me, are you, Noah? We're friends, right?"

He nodded, but I sensed an underlying fear. But then Gary let go of him. I gasped, holding out my arms. "Noah, come see Mommy."

My son ran down the steps. I pulled him into a tight embrace, like I'd never get another chance to hold him.

Gary descended the stairs, standing on the bottom tread, towering over us. "I've come to make things right. To protect you from the monster your husband is. To show you the love and support that your mother couldn't give."

My gut wrenched, but if I could buy just a little more time, I might be able to get us clear of him. Noah started to whimper. I had to make my move.

"I just wanted a family of my own," Gary pleaded. "But your mom took that from me. I've been searching for it my whole life, and when I found out about you, Lauren, well, that changed everything. I came here to save you and my grandson. I've heard the things Jacob's said to his mistress. The way he talks to you. I couldn't let that stand, could I?" He pulled a knife from the waist of his pants. "Why don't we have a seat in the living room and talk this through?"

"If you want to tell me what's going on, I'm listening," I said, hoping to gain control of the situation. "But please, put down the knife. We can talk without it."

He snorted. "The only way I'm leaving here is with you and Noah. I want you both in my life. You're my daughter and he's my grandson. Don't take him from me like your mother took you."

I backed away, keeping a firm grip on Noah's hand, and never taking my eyes off the knife. "Put it down, Gary."

He tilted his head, raising the knife. "Why don't you call me Dad?"

He lunged from the step, coming right for us. I yanked Noah to the side just as Gary tried to take hold of me. Noah screamed.

"It doesn't have to be this way, Lauren. I love you," he said. "I love Noah. We can figure this out together. Please. Let's work through this."

"You're crazy. Stay away from us!" I spun around to the front door. It was locked and I fumbled with the deadbolt. I heard Gary's steps draw near.

"Lauren, stop. You'll only make things worse. Please don't make me do something we'll both regret."

I dragged Noah with me into the kitchen. A set of knives stuck out from a butcher block. I yanked one of them out, shoving Noah behind me. "Get back, Gary. Don't come any closer."

Gary froze, his eyes fixed on the knife in my hand. Noah cried as I shielded him.

"Don't come any closer!" My voice shook, but my grip was steady.

Gary's eyes narrowed. "You won't use that on me. You don't have the guts to murder your own father. Your own flesh and blood." He took a step forward.

I swept the knife in front of me. "Stay back!"

He halted, raising his hands. "Let's think about this, Lauren, all right?" But then he crept forward.

I slashed at him. Both of us stared at the deep gash in his arm that spilled blood. He looked in shock, clutching the wound and recoiling.

"You shouldn't have done that, Lauren." In one swift move, he lurched for us again.

I shoved Noah down behind the kitchen island, dodging left. My knife clanged against the stone countertop, and I almost dropped it. With a swift kick, I aimed for Gary's knee and felt a satisfying crunch as it connected. He let out a pained grunt and stumbled, giving me the perfect opportunity to send my elbow flying into his face. The impact was brutal, causing blood to spurt from his nose in a violent spray. The metallic scent filled the air as he crumpled to the ground.

I scooped up Noah with my right arm, holding the knife in my left hand. We sprinted for the front door. Gary snatched at my shirt. His fist twisted in the fabric. I spun, swiping the knife at him again. The fabric ripped and his grip broke.

The front door was still locked. Undeterred, Gary hobbled toward us. Whatever fatherly love he might have felt was long gone. Only murder remained in his eyes.

"No one takes my family!" he roared.

His knife gleamed as he charged. I braced myself, ready to protect Noah at all costs, when the front door splintered open behind me. I pulled us clear of it as it swung. There was Collins, standing with her gun aimed. "Drop the weapon! Hands in the air!"

Gary stopped, eyeing the gun, eyeing me.

"Drop it, Stokes, now!" Collins demanded.

I saw defeat in his eyes. He chucked the knife at her. Collins fired off a shot. Ringing sounded in my ears as I pulled Noah close. I turned to see Gary's body jerking back from the hit, while his knife clattered as it fell to the floor.

Then I looked at Collins, the knife at her feet, and a wisp of smoke wafting from the end of her weapon.

Gary stumbled, falling back against the bottom step. We locked eyes, and I saw that they were the same as mine. I was the daughter of a killer. He tried to smile as blood spilled from his chest. My stomach turned, sickened by him. Sickened that I'd finally seen the resemblance. Only a moment or two had passed, and he was gone.

Detective Collins grabbed my shoulder. "Are you two okay?"

She shook me out of my trance. I looked down at Noah, my knees buckling as I clung onto him. "It's over, baby. It's okay. We're safe now."

EPILOGUE

Three months had passed. Jacob still awaited trial for the attempted murder of Madison Price. Gary Stokes, my father, was dead. He'd murdered my mother, and thirteen other people over an eighteen-month span. The worst serial killer Virginia had ever seen in modern times. All the victims were families. Some had been young children. Some were expecting a child yet to be born.

Noah and I were the lucky ones.

Jacob had tried to make amends, but he'd morphed into a stranger, a shadow of the man I once loved. He told me about his gambling debts, leaving me with no choice but to sell our home, his car. Everything we had to pay them off so they wouldn't come for my son and me. Jacob no longer had the means to pay for a good defense lawyer now, but that wasn't my problem.

Our beautiful colonial home, once a symbol of our shared dreams and aspirations, had become a nightmare to me. A reminder of lies, betrayal, and death. So putting it on the market was an easy decision in any case.

And now, Noah and I sat in the car, having just arrived at the humble abode I was pretty sure we were going to call our new home. It was significantly smaller. The harsh reality was that I couldn't afford to keep my son and me living the lavish lifestyle to which we'd become accustomed. But honestly, I didn't mind. I'd carried on with my job, Tammy becoming an even closer ally and friend to me as everyone knew all that had happened.

I shoved the gearshift into park and looked at Noah in the back seat through the rearview mirror. His eyes were wide and curious as he took in our potential new home. "What do you think, buddy? It's nice, huh?"

He only shrugged in response. We'd been going to therapy for a while now. The same doctor Noah had talked to months ago to help Detective Collins solve her case. Turned out, we were a pretty significant piece of that puzzle.

I stepped out of my Lincoln, walking around to the rear passenger side to let Noah out of his seat. "Come on. Let's go have a look around, okay?" My voice held an encouraging note.

Standing outside the front door was Amanda, my realtor. She'd found this place for me. We approached her with cautious optimism. "Good morning, Amanda. Thanks for coming out."

"Of course." Her smile was warm and welcoming as she turned around and unlocked the door. "Come on in."

"Thanks." I surveyed the open floor plan. It was a newer home, smaller, but it radiated a certain charm. "I really like the kitchen."

"It's super adorable," Amanda replied, mirroring my enthusiasm. "So this is the second time you've been here. Are you thinking about putting in an offer on this one?"

"There's just one thing I wanted to check out. Would you mind keeping an eye on Noah for a few minutes?"

"Of course. Sure. Anything I can help with?"

"No. No, I got this. In fact, I need to do this myself." I began to walk throughout the house. I examined every square inch of the place, leaving no stone unturned — the attic, the crawlspace down below, the backyard, the side yards. It was a lovely spring day, perfect for such an exploration. The house was only about twenty minutes from work too, which made for a manageable commute.

Eventually, after some time, I returned to Amanda, wiping the sweat from my brow with a chuckle. "I guess it's a little warmer than I expected."

She fixed her gaze on me with bewilderment. "Everything check out? You've been gone a while. I was about to hire a search party."

I laughed at her light-hearted jest. "Oh, no need for that. Just making sure I know every little nook and cranny of this place. You never can be too careful."

"Careful?" Amanda asked, with a quizzical tilt of her head.

I swatted my hand in dismissal of my own words. "Nothing. Never mind." A moment of contemplation passed before I made up my mind and declared with conviction: "But you know what? I think I'll take it." Turning to Noah, who was playing with his toy car on the floor, I reached out my hand to him. "*We'll* take it."

THE END

THE JOFFE BOOKS STORY

We began in 2014 when Jasper agreed to publish his mum's much-rejected romance novel and it became a bestseller.

Since then we've grown into the largest independent publisher in the UK. We're extremely proud to publish some of the very best writers in the world, including Joy Ellis, Faith Martin, Caro Ramsay, Helen Forrester, Simon Brett and Robert Goddard. Everyone at Joffe Books loves reading and we never forget that it all begins with the magic of an author telling a story.

We are proud to publish talented first-time authors, as well as established writers whose books we love introducing to a new generation of readers.

We won Trade Publisher of the Year at the Independent Publishing Awards in 2023. We have been shortlisted for Independent Publisher of the Year at the British Book Awards for the last four years, and were shortlisted for the Diversity and Inclusivity Award at the 2022 Independent Publishing Awards. In 2023 we were shortlisted for Publisher of the Year at the RNA Industry Awards.

We built this company with your help, and we love to hear from you, so please email us about absolutely anything bookish at feedback@joffebooks.com

If you want to receive free books every Friday and hear about all our new releases, join our mailing list: www.joffebooks.com/contact

And when you tell your friends about us, just remember: it's pronounced Joffe as in coffee or toffee!

Printed in the USA
CPSIA information can be obtained
at www.ICGtesting.com
LVHW030732240824
789102LV00013B/164